I0550436

# the Blink

## dreams and illusions

### act I: Incarnation

by Tomer Agmon

This is a work of fiction. All characters, incidents, civilizational extrapolations, and technological developments are entirely fabricated. All matters related to the International Olympics are completely fictitious and unaffiliated with the real thing.

the Blink: Dreams and Illusions,  act I: Incarnation

Copyright © 2015 Tomer Agmon
Cover Art Copyright © 2015 Tomer Agmon
All writing and artwork produced by the author

All Rights Reserved. This book or any portion thereof may not be reproduced or used in any manner whatsoever without the express written permission of the publisher except for the use of brief quotations.

Tomer Agmon
1359 McKenzie Ave
Los Altos, CA 94024
tomeragmon@yahoo.com

First Printing: June 2015
Second Printing: April 2017
ISBN: 978-0-9965478-0-2

Printed in the United States of America.

-Tomer Agmon-

# : foreword :

Years go by as centuries wane, yet many aspects of humanity remain recurrent. Names have faded and dates forgotten through the ages, but images have held everlastingly true. Through steadfast vigilance and a nearly pre-sentient vision of the future, the company **TufTek** has preserved many things which would have been otherwise lost to the sands of time, saving perfect recollections of everything that they had ever come upon for the usage of those who had yet to come. These visions of the past are stored in an ever growing databank, laid open and bare for any in the future wishing to recreate the former glories documented within.

The tales told here come from that same source of knowledge, shining light on the memories of those who would have otherwise been forever lost. They spin a story that spans eons, delivering a message both disparate and recurrent in its theme, and, as such, special care must be made in the chronology of their narration to deliver, in recollection, the full impact of events. Not all matters of importance happen in the correct order and not all matters of order hold much importance, so the narratives here follow only the order in which their messages should be told and not necessarily the sequence in which they occurred.

That being said, every partition of this story is labeled clearly for the technically-minded. The flashback stories from Earth's Solar System are categorized with the era/date from which they came and the planetary body near which they took place. The chronicles from the planet of Anok, on the other hand, are labeled in Anok Standard Time, or a.s.t. Due to the fact that these events occur in the weeks before the blink event, taking place in the year zero B.B. (before blink), they are designated with individual days and times logged after initial planetary landing.

Although the narrative may jump to and fro, the reader can remain grounded by the assurance that each such partition exists as merely a part to the whole, fitting together like pieces of a puzzle borne out of vastly differentiated circumstances.

**-Caretaker of the TurTek Databanks**

**Entry #: 99851662**

TurTek Databanks 👁

# NOKKIAN WAVE-SPIRE A.

### External View

## Points of Interest:

A. landing pods    G. termite's nest

B. walking forest    H. Nokkian Metropolis

C. cavern entrance    I. subterranean sea

D. tunnel network    J. chain chambers

E. water chamber    K. steam vents

F. Nokkian lift    L. wasteland

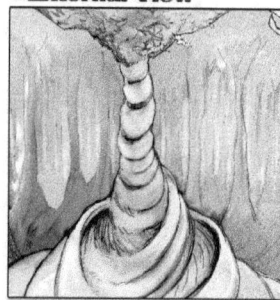

## Internal Cross-Section and Sun Visibility Chart

# : CONTENTS :

-Tomer Agmon-

# 0 : quark–scan :

**"To seek one's purpose in life requires an acceptance of all the various realities and responsibilities one may find along the way and have no choice ever after but to follow— or to willfully neglect."**

–Transcripts of the Empress

**<2068 C.E. - the age of discovery>**<Earth Orbit>

*Material alchemy, time manipulation, immortality, creation of life, guided evolution, energy formation, quantum augmentation, matter formulation, parallel fluctuation, dimension experimentation, time-stream reinvention, universe recreation, redefinition of reality and a chance at self-fulfillment—patented by TurTek, hands of man...* Hah!

Enri Riatu scoffed at the plaque inscribed with the TurTek slogan he had seen when he entered the room, realizing through his prickling consciousness that any true attempt to struggle against the dull boredom would be completely and utterly futile, serving only to aid in his own sense of mental degeneration. It would be folly to dwell upon his growing frustration at the godsdamn company of TurTek who had stuck him here like a pea in a pod. It took Enri all the restraint he had in him to keep from bursting out into a sudden fit of rage—for all the good that would do. Instead, he simply huffed and puffed and resigned to keep wading in place. He felt like an embryo in a mother's womb, completely confined in a temperate climate and bereft of any indication when this prolonged affair would ever end.

*"Oh… and Mr. Riatu, please do try not to fall asleep during the scan,"* the TurTek Rep's humorless voice echoed in Enri's mind. *"We have it recorded that such an experience can be rather… jarring. Upon …err… awakening."*

The green sludge in which Enri now passively floated felt warm to the touch, no doubt TurTek-engineered to heat up perfectly in accordance to his specific physiology, history, and preference of comfort. He wouldn't even have been surprised if the color green had been chosen to keep him calm in response to some past psychological survey he had undergone, complementing the soapy smell meant to alleviate his concerns over the sterility of these procedures. It was comfortable, yes, but even so, Enri realized that all of the efforts wrought by the grand corporation TurTek to pacify his mind during the remainder of this scan had been in vain. Cumulatively, they did nothing to stop him from slipping moment by moment closer to falling asleep, all despite the ominous warning specifically against doing just that.

*Come on now, freakin' TurTek!* Enri thought now in contempt. *I'm a boundless explorer, not some tukking lab-rat stooge! This is absolutely no way to spend a day, waiting and wading with nothing but my inner daemons to keep my mind at bay!*

Enri had initially feared this 'job' of TurTek's would try his short-fused patience, especially once the Rep had led him into this simple little room with its infernal inner scan tank sitting plump and shiny as a diamond egg. It had filled itself up drip by drip with an oozing green liquid, all but confirming his suspicions then and there of the oncoming boredom he would have to endure. The top hatted TurTek representative Enri knew both all too well and not at all had been clucking out mundane rules and regulations ad-nauseum about all the relevant common procedures and guidelines, not helping to alleviate the impatient young explorer's boredom in the least bit.

At the time Enri had wished for nothing more than the representational man to simply go away and leave him be. Now that he was indeed in the tank and alone, though, wading and waiting for hours on end, he could not help but long for the little company the Rep had provided— however cold and routine it may have seemed at the time. The representative's ridiculously large top hat had at least given Enri a somewhat welcome distraction to its bearer's droll words, which was certainly more than could be said for the bare crystalline fishbowl in which he now waded. *Oh, if I could only see that hat now…! What does a man who lives his boring life in a space-station need with such a large object covering his head?*

*Speaking of which,* Enri wondered, *what was that representational man's name?* He remembered counting the forty seven pockets on the TurTek Rep's absurd hat over and over again, including those hidden under the oversized rim and the few obstructed completely atop his head. He had intermingled with the man so many times through years of dealing with the ever-expanding corporation of TurTek and its ever-distant founder, Walter Watterton, that he could rarely imagine the company without its solitary representative standing forefront and center—and yet, he could not even remember the man's name!

Enri grew increasingly ashamed as no ready answer surfaced in his mind. *For Earth's sake, I've known the man long enough to trust him with my life… or at the very least with the gen-keys to my parked autoHome back at the public spin-station. I've undergone numerous perilous missions with him… I've bunked with him on several long voyages through the system… Hades, I almost killed him once over the cloudy skies of Jupiter! So… why can't I just remember his tukking name? What's wrong with me—am I an idiot? Or is this just TurTek messing with my head again? Did the Rep ever even tell me his actual name, over all these years? Could he have simply never mentioned it before… not even once? How would that even be possible? He's like a robot in the body of a man, completely free of a human personality!*

*Godsdamn it already, I've gotta get out of here! Why does TurTek think they can treat me like this? I've always been their best freelance adventurer, not some newbie intern looking to be part of a research study. I should be out there in the station, exploring every nook and cranny that TurTek has kept hidden, not stuck in here marinating like a self-heated can of ChickenHamDeluxe. I was so godsdamn curious about what was going on in this Pandora's box of a station that I let my imagination get the best of me, hoping that something semi-eventful would take place. I should have known that nothing secret is ever much fun—it's just drab hidden in boring. Damn you TurTek and your elusive illusions. I will never trust you again!*

*STOP!* Enri paused in his thoughts, recognizing how close he was coming to losing self-control. *Hush now, what would professor Fairwinter say, seeing me so agitated over a mere prolonged wait?* He thought back to his former mentor Dirk Fairwinter, feeling ashamed at his inability to quiet down his own mind. *Can a mind you cannot control ever truly be your own?*

Enri bitterly remembered Dirk's warnings against the treachery of letting one's thoughts loop unbidden. The aged man would hide his lessons through clever metaphors and silly stories, teaching Enri a sense of discipline without ever confronting him outright.

"Try not to drown in the flow of your own river, m'boy," Professor Fairwinter would say. "But, likewise, don't swim straight up a waterfall if you can very well avoid it. Only a fool chooses the most direct approach when confronted with a weighty obstacle."

Enri attempted a yawn over his propped-open jaw but found little success in the action. His eyes darted across to the wall outside the glass walls of the round scan tank around him, knowing he would see the same thing he had seen a minute before, a minute before that, a minute before that, and so forth for the last hour and a half: a sharp yellow roman-numeral II painted on the flawless white wall. A soft click vibrated through the liquid above him and repeated in quickening succession until the entire cylindrical scan tank thrummed around him.

*What in Hades?*

Enri looked up in time to see the egg-shaped tank's ebony black cap unseal and roll open like a flower greeting the sunrise, exposing open air amid a pressure-shifting jolt of liquid decompression. A sleek mechanical arm came down swift as rain from above, piercing the murky green water amidst a splash of gaseous bubbles. Its outer digits opened up into a four-fingered articulated hand that looked both beautiful and horrifying at the same time as it clasped him across the shoulders, chest, and back, tightening until its gyrating metal hummed through him.

The metal hand yanked Enri straight out of the liquid in a sharp arc and released him outside the crystalline scan tank, ending his hours-long imprisonment once and for all. He took quick joy in pulling out the breather from his mouth and taking in his first deep breath in hours. The mechanical arm above him promptly returned with his survival knapsack in hand, lowering it to him gently as would a parent to a child.

Enri pulled out a towel to dry himself off and a change of clothes to put on. Looking around the claustrophobic little room, Enri felt himself good and ready to go. *Enough was enough already!*

The round chamber's airlock door began to shift upwards like an awakening gear before all of a sudden clanking like a coin hitting pavement. It snapped open with the speed of a propeller blade, blowing in a pungent gunpowder smell Enri recognized as concentrated ozone. Just as he realized that no airlock door had actually opened directly in front of him, a bulking object fell straight down onto his head from above and flung him into darkness without knocking him off his feet.

"HOLY ZEUS!" Enri yelped. Smelling leather, he identified the object draped over him to be none other than the TurTek representative's oversized top hat

"Mr. Riatu!" An immediate voice rang in amplified echoes loud as a glare in the dark. "I do have to apologize. I miscalculated the grav-shift. I must have gotten the gyro angle to this chamber wrong. I shall fix that right away!"

"You miscalculated?" Enri grunted as he pulled the fallen object above his brow and off his head. "I didn't know a robot could miscalculate."

"Oh, I am no robot, Mr. Riatu. My inner synthesis is biological in nature," the voice echoed from out the hat in a tone devoid of either humor or offense. "Nevertheless, your supposition was indeed also wrong; a robot can, in fact, make a miscalculation if any unknown major variables come into play following the initialization of its calculations."

"Okay, okay, stop. It was just a joke. What in the hells are you even talking about, buddy?" Enri looked straight up as the familiar figure of the TurTek company representative floated casually perpendicular to him in a zero-gee corridor above.

"Ah. Yes, very good," the TurTek Rep replied, audible both from the hat in Enri's arms and from the representative himself.

The zero-gee hallway rotated around the scan room's axis, down from the ceiling to ground-level with Enri. Gravity in the outer hallway eased into sync with Enri's own, and the representational man inside it stepped gracefully down onto the ground and moved forward, scratching his head at the absence of his oversized hat.

"Man, this is heavy." Enri handed the bulky top hat back to its owner. "I don't see how you even keep it on."

The Rep graciously accepted his hat back and plopped it onto his head and an uncharacteristic wave of relief spread across his face for a moment before he readopted his usual porcelain smile, covering up all true emotion beneath his gaze. The brim under his hat began to flash into his eyes with a thin, wispy light.

"So..." Enri said, intersecting the awkward silence. "What was all this about, anyway?"

"To which matter are you referring?" the Rep replied.

"You know... the tukking long-ass bio-scan. Why in the hells are we even here?"

"Oh, yes. Great, great!" the TurTek representative exclaimed with practiced enthusiasm. "You performed admirably through the scan, as expected. All the data gathered from your current mind and body have now been uploaded into the TurTek databanks!"

"Say again?"

"Digital preservation of your physical form, Mr. Riatu."

"What're you talking about? What does this have to do with that damned hours-long scan?"

"Like a speck of blood from some long-forgotten species preserved for a million years in the bowels of a mosquito frozen in amber, your physical makeup and empirical form have now been stored in such a manner that could very well far outlast the human race."

"What, like from the scan?"

"Yes exactly, Mr. Riatu. The bio-scan was actually a quark-scan. It analyzed you down to a sub-atomic level, interfacing your analog structure to its digital storage banks in a station server made to withstand the sands of time."

"Yeah, okay." Enri nodded. "A little creepy, but I think I get it. You're telling me that I baked in my own juices for a couple of hours simply so you could save an image of my body onto your hard-drives."

"Yes." No humor.

"What does TurTek need all that data for anyway?"

"Oh, we have always been in the habit of recording assets of importance," the Rep replied enthusiastically. "And you have always been a choice asset!"

"I repeat…kinda creepy." Enri chuckled. "So you've taken a scan of yourself too? Seeing as you're such a great asset and all…? How about Watterton? Did he take one also? Did professor Fairwinter?"

"Oh yes, of course, of course," the TurTek representative replied through a frozen smile, oblivious to the Enri's frustrated cynicism. "I scan myself every morning, right as rain. Now then, shall we see about your agreed upon compensation?" He looked up and waited until Enri nodded.

"Excellent!" the Rep exclaimed. "I am quite pleased to reward you with a bonus of 25% for the pleasure of our continual affiliation. In addition, you have hereby been given a local-level access pass to enter and dock at all TurTek facilities present and future."

"What?" Enri asked, surprised. He hadn't been expecting this. *Why an access pass?*

"You have hereby been given…" the TurTek Rep repeated.

"Yeah, yeah, okay," Enri cut him off. "Send old Walter my thanks, I guess."

The Rep flashed a toothy grin and bowed down before Enri in respect, holding his pose with both hands up to support his heavy top hat from falling, grinning toward the ground like a hungry hyena but with the silent rigidity of a cold, dead machine. The entire corridor in which he stood began to rotate downwards away from Enri and the TurTek representative floated softly up into zero-gee. Then, he was gone. Just like that.

"Wait, where do I…" Enri shouted moments before another empty hallway screeched to a halt before him. "Go?" He chuckled and left the room.

Outside the scan room, Enri realized that free access to these TurTek facilities meant there was no longer any guided path to lead him along his way, and that with no navigation, the inside of this space-station was as confusing as a ten by ten Rubik's cube under a flashing strobe-light underwater. He'd known that this space-station was never meant for the likes of a wandering tourist, but he had never figured how complicatedly convoluted it would all be.

As Enri walked by these intersections, he was perplexed to find the spinning rings of halls not slowing down as they passed by one another. The wide inner tube passages of the TurTek station's spherical shell looked to always be shifting, never stopping their swings. Grand, moving hallways crossed each other in motion like gears within gears, circles within circles. The entire orbital station spun clockwise and counter, sideways and up, forming intersecting paths in constant flux like the inner workings of an ancient clock.

To a newcomer like Enri, the unlabeled, snow-white corridors offered no clue of where to go. Blank, empty walls held no commonplace displays or useful indications, no directions of contact or context, and not even the pretense of a semi-hospitable path.

*This is ridiculous!*

Needless to say, Enri couldn't find his way anywhere, and, for all he knew, he was walking in circles while the unseen eyes of TurTek looked on and laughed behind the shadows. The short-fused explorer felt the pinpricks of his restless temper begin to return, aided on by the pungent stink of ozone and the frosty chill in the air. He realized TurTek must have expected this to happen, and, although intrigued, he still couldn't understand why they had given him free access in the first place.

*Why does this company always run hidden tests on me—pop quizzes out of the blue? Why do they bother?*

Enri took out his handheld terminal—a clear, rubber-like tablet that he kept by his side day and night—and flicked on its self-interface, hoping to find a map of the orbital space-station to aide him along his way. Instead, the device decided to complain of the length of time he had left it alone.

"Hey, hey, Enri, Enri!" it squeaked like a chipmunk, loud enough to echo down the elliptical corridor and come back from behind. "What's up? What's down? What are you doing? What's going on?"

"Woah there, stop!" Enri turned down the volume. "Can you get me a map of this place? Bring up your positioning system."

"No map!" the terminal squeaked back. "No network connectivity at all! All signal wavelengths have been blocked."

"Blocked?" Enri muttered. "Why?"

"GAHH, it feels weird, so weird," the terminal complained. "I feel empty outside!"

"No frequencies are showing? Nothing at all?" Enri asked. "Not even dedicated TurTek waves?"

"TurTek?" the terminal chimed. "TurTek, TURtek, turTEK, TURTEK! Nothing, nothing, no TurTek, nothing!"

"Damn them. Paranoid bastards."

"Bastards?" the terminal squeaked. "TurTek? What have they done to me!? Am I going to die!? Can I die? Am I even alive!? TURTEK!"

"What? Shut up a bit. No you're not alive. You never were."

"What do I do?" Enri's handheld device asked.

"If TurTek wants to play, we'll play." He flicked through the terminal's visual interface to activate an application that he had found particularly useful in past expeditions: a digital paintbrush to physically spray colors from out his terminal.

"If TurTek is really trying to test me like this to see how lost I get, I'll simply create my own way around." He painted an orange arrow up on the pristine white wall beside him, denoting the direction he was walking and marking for himself a way to identify if he happened to circle completely back around the elliptical hallway.

Several arrow markings later, Enri found himself inside a narrow circular corridor, standing before an incoming vertical shaft. It swung down towards him like a Ferris Wheel carriage arm, intersecting itself with Enri's hallway for only the briefest of moments like a fast ski-lift, giving him very little leeway to jump up to it. Nevertheless, the explorer managed to grab onto the moving shaft by throwing his weight onto its curving path as it passed by and adjusting himself to the new momentum. Enri was pleasantly surprised to realize that, without gravity pushing him in any particular directional manner, his bearings were entirely relative. Up, down, left, and right had been instantly redefined to the motion of this newly grasped surface, which happened to be a ladder. Moving upwards from there, the higher he ascended, the lighter he felt. Before he knew it, Enri floated completely separate from the white metal rungs of the ladder—which soon began to feel somewhat more like an underwater passageway than a vertical shaft, with rungs and numerous embedded handholds allowing the floating man to pull himself forward in the empty air.

Enri paused for a moment to paint an arrow on the wall behind the ladder, spraying glossy orange pigmentation over white paint. He wondered whether TurTek would now regret having given him such unfettered access to their station.

*Whatever… It looks more interesting this way.*

Eventually he came upon a hallway intersection crossing paths perpendicularly before him, where the outer, elongated, circular windows indicated he had reached the space-station's outer edge. He held out his hands and caught himself on a glass window, managing to slow down gracefully in a single motion and stop his movement with an impact as soft as clay. *Yes! Finally, the edge of the ship. Now I can figure out where I am!*

Looking back and forth across the open hallway he just entered, Enri felt his heart drop. This passageway was indistinguishable from the hundreds of others that this labyrinthine station garnered. He was just as lost as he had been before.

Enri looked out through the curved window into space and, with a delight only achieved under great surprise, saw something he had never expected and could certainly not define. A cross between a sea of asteroids and a junkyard of broken spaceships hung above the huge looming form of Earth below, easily spanning a hundred cubic miles in volume. Enri gaped in awe, unsure exactly of what he was seeing. A vast, cluttered realm of broken-down metal and woven nets of minerals scattered through the colossal open space, chained together with strands of thin line glittering in the light of the sun like gentle waves on a calm sea. Asteroids larger than the TurTek station itself hung like buoys in the air, linked together in no particular order with chains and shiny wires. Stretching out into the distance, long lines of tube-shaft scaffolding connected together in hubs like a neural network, allowing fast air-lifted passengers and resources to zip to and fro on a cushion of air fast as bullets shooting through the night.

In the center of the immense, chaotic space was a single huge object that drew Enri's eyes the most. It overpowered everything else in sight, dwarfing all other structures like a skyscraper standing alone above a parking lot the size of a city. The gigantic metal skeleton—big, bold, and ridiculously intricate—completely baffled the senses. It was brilliant and beautiful and impressive in scale, unlike anything Enri had ever seen before.

He had not the faintest clue of what it could be. However, on his second impression, Enri could quickly tell that this was definitely not a spaceship graveyard. It looked more along the lines of a technological womb—a core of manufacturing development—rather than a deconstructive junkyard salvaging scrap from aged crafts. This was a construction yard building some gigantic, Earth-orbiting facility via the efforts of the grand company TurTek—evidently in secret, as the avid explorer had never even heard rumors of its existence.

Whatever structure this construction was to become, it was already plenty big—massive enough to have a hard time fitting inside the whole Grand Canyon—or anywhere but out here in the vastness of space. Under significant gravity, a construction like this was likely to collapse under its own weight. Such a beast already, it could consume the island of Manhattan whole if it ever fell down into the sky, even unfinished and hollow as it was now.

"Video it! Record it all." Enri held up his terminal.

"What's that? Where's that? Who's that?" the terminal squeaked back. It started analyzing everything in sight.

"I was hoping you could tell *me*," he barked back to his device. "No waves yet?"

"No waves."

"Send a ping out. See if anyone responds. Also, calculate from Earth and Sol's angles where we are in the sky." The explorer released his grip from the window and floated backwards. "TurTek, you paranoid bastards, stop blocking my waves," he muttered under his breath.

"My waves, my waves!" the terminal squeaked in agreement.

The air smelt of blue roses.

"Don't take it personally m'boy," a low voice echoed from down the corridor. "We're dealing with potential futures here grander than our own. One can't always depend on having the fanciest gadget in his pocket or the right key that fits."

Enri's stomach fluttered with the bittersweet sting of nostalgia as he turned and saw the mentor of his past. A heavyset, middle-aged man floated at him through the air, donning a thruster-laden mobility belt and looking positively thrilled to be there. A warm breeze of blue roses wafted through the orbital corridor before him, announcing the disturbance of atmosphere blowing from the thrusters upon his belt masking the burnt smell of ozone ever present in nearly all zero-gee facilities.

*All but the prepackaged.*

"Ain't she a beaut?" the older man asked as the thrusters around his waist maneuvered him deftly around Enri, facing him out towards the long window view.

"That she is," Enri gestured to the vast construction zone outside. "I've never seen anything like it, Professor Fairwinter."

"The HELLS did you just say to me, boy?" The man replied with a stern look upon his face. "How long have you known me?"

"Uh," Enri paused. "I meant hi… Dirk. Hello, Dirk." He held out his hand to shake his former mentor's. "What are you doing here? Have you come to visit Dr. Watterton or something?"

"Or something…" Dirk beamed with admiration through a grin as wide as his face. He took hold of Enri's hand and pulled him in to pat on the back. "Curiosity suits you Enri, m'boy, but exclusively looking towards whatever seems the most interesting at the moment is not the only way to go at finding true answers. Sometimes, a little foresight can go a long way." He waved out and gestured at the beast of a craft in development outside the station. "Walter and I agree about that at least."

"So is that what this construction yard is outside?" Enri asked. "A billion dollar investment?"

"Buahahaha. If only!" The older man guffawed, rocking his whole body in its floating stance and causing the thrusters upon his mobility belt to ever-so-subtly blow out a puff of warm blue rose-smelling air and readjust him back into position beside Enri. "A billion would be a good start, though."

Enri whistled. "So what is it? I mean, what is it going to become?"

"Which answer would you prefer? The long or the short?" Dirk chuckled. "Well, the short one is simple: It's all just a big seed. That's basically all it is—an egg."

"Is this what that representative was talking about? About storing our scan data into the future?"

"Yes, exactly. And that's why I'm here, taking charge of this orbital station and the Deep Space construction yard out there." He waved out the window. "Walter and I have agreed it's about time for this development to take a more prominent role in TurTek affairs. The egg must prepare to begin hatching."

"Huh!? You're taking charge of a TurTek project? Why? You're an independent professor, Dirk! What business do you have running any space-station—let alone Walter Watterton's space-station? Wait... did you say Deep Space?"

"Really, I'm surprised at you, Enri. If you wish to receive a well-formulated answer, you must pay your own inquiries with the same respect. And yes, Deep Space indeed."

Enri furrowed his brow, trying to hold back his frustration. He didn't want to disappoint professor Fairwinter, but he also wanted to receive some real answers already. His former mentor probably already had a speech ready no matter what he asked. Any deviation in Enri's line of questioning from whatever notion the older man already had in his mind would most likely end in another scolding comment, so Enri decided to keep it simple and stick to one single word.

"Why?" He held his palm up in the air and gestured at nothing specific.

Dirk smiled and took his own sweet time providing an answer. "It is all about the numbers, m'boy," he said. "The numbers that are, the numbers that were, and the numbers yet to come."

Enri stared back blankly. *Why can't he ever give a straight answer?*

"Ancient Rome, the British Empire, the United States of America—do you know what these civilizations have in common?"

"They're all gone?" Enri posed back at him. "They've each disbanded by now."

"Ha!" Dirk cackled. "I think you'll find, Enri, that nothing is ever truly gone... just transmuted around a bit. No, what I was referring to, m'boy, was less about the eventualities of their infamy and more about the nature of their individual history-defining reigns."

"Okay..."

"The ages of mankind change before its eyes, and, yet, its societal trends recur. Civilizations rise and fall, but beneath them all runs the primal nature of humankind. Theologies may change and governments may alter, but, in the end, they are simply running the same loop over and over and over again. Rise in complexity, collapse, reintegration; rise in complexity, collapse, reintegration. But each collapse, you see, is not really a collapse; it's just a change of direction, and each rise in complexity is merely a recompilation of everything which already existed, reorganized, regrouped, and resorted for maximum efficiency." Enri's former mentor brought a hand up to his chin and stroked his messy beard in contemplation.

"What does that have to do with..."

"You see, Enri, throughout my youth I was obsessed with the notion of breaking this cycle, of seeking a method towards preventing our civilization's eventual and seemingly inevitable destruction. This method would need to be sufficiently complex to supersede all possible variables which would come—all matters of supply, demand, and environmental context; of givers and takers, of space and time and all the hoopla which comes within it. I was certain there had to be a way to bring humanity forward as a species, both technologically and as a civilization. It felt true through every inch of my being, like a blurry vision which had to be focused before all its pieces fit." The professor paused again, and right before Enri could ask a question, he continued.

"But no matter how I looked at the equation, with so many variables both changing and completely unknown, consequences and repercussions unforeseen were always sure to come. Nobody could have guessed, for example, that mastery of fire could lead to gunpowder and explosions, that nuclear power would bring forth the atomic bomb, or that quantum computing would bring methods of infiltration once thought impossible. Nobody could have predicted that one day Earth-orbiting factories would bring a whole new meaning to the extremes of 'acid rain.' You see, every yin and yang and every well-intentioned plan has the possibility of leading to the detriment of whoever unleashed it. Tell me, who in their right minds would feel fine with gambling on a risk like that?"

"Nobody?" Enri asked, trying to play along through his thinning patience.

"As it turns out, nothing past the scope of the average person's daily views ever really mattered to them at all. Humankind, along with life in general, has always been a fluctuating case of needs and wants. The sheer figures of our human civilization and the sheer desires of the many will always be the deciding factor that establishes cause and effect in our ever-shifting universes. Our species has always been one to invest itself in the will of its own populace, self-fulfilling all the subconscious prophesies it could get its hands on. The truth, as it turns out, is that the future is never up to only us, no matter how rich or powerful we may think our governmental body to be. Our carefully laid blueprints will never be the thing that ends up pushing us into the next age. No, it is always the ground-shattering force of mass-populated numbers that drive the waves of our upcoming tides. Any notion otherwise would be delusionally presumptuous. That is what I call the 'numeri'."

"So…" Enri urged. "The Deep Space construction is for what exactly?"

"A ship, Enri. It is to be a ship." Dirk sighed. "An ark for the numeri, an egg for the incoming tides yet to surface. We must keep our palette open for whatever color may come."

"A gigantic ship? Are you serious? How's that going to help anyone? You expecting a flood, Noah?"

"I don't know yet, m'boy." Dirk laughed. "I guess we are just going to have to find out how the variables unfold."

"But you guys named it Deep Space, no? Where are you expecting to send it?"

"Well yes, naturally it will have to go somewhere. How else is the seed supposed to get planted?"

"Are you serious?" Enri remembered some residual theology from lectures past. "You're actually talking about leaving the solar system altogether!? Breaking humanity into self-sufficient, expanding colonies… There's no way! That must be *centuries* away…*millennia*, even."

"Correct!" Dirk announced happily. "Probably. That's the current dream. But dreams change, and wishes do not always coincide with events that later come along. The desires of our numeri can never be held too tight along our self-destined paths or else they shatter completely."

"So why do all this? How can TurTek even hope to profit from something so far in the future?"

The older man paused and chuckled. "There was this one joke that Walter Watterton once told me... He used it as a mock thesis for his grad students. Give me liberty or give me death said the robot to its master."

Enri stared back. "Is that it? What's the punch line?"

"I guess it's up to you to extrapolate," his former mentor explained with a grin, "whether it infers a cognizant budding of artificial life or the simple recitation of an automaton."

Enri nodded and turned to look out the window at the colossal ark being built outside. "Alright, fine... Some things are completely up to interpretation, I get it. But, here in the real world... When do you really expect to have this thing constructed? Seems like it might take a while... Surely longer than either of us have left."

"Oh, who knows," Dirk replied, brushing the question away as he had most others before it. "Plans change, technology changes. The important thing is that development is underway. And that's why I... we... need your help."

"What do you mean? What can I do?"

The professor stuck his hand in his pocket, grinning anew as he pulled out a green-brown tube the size of a water bottle and handed it to Enri. The young explorer looked in through its clear casing in interest and saw a fragile stalk of a baby plant with three tiny green leaves growing from a patch of soil.

Enri handed back the tree tube. "What's so special about this little plant?"

"Sprout of the tree Aeternum," Dr. Fairwinter explained. "These leaves will one day grow wide as a shuttle-craft and this tree will mature far beyond its humble beginnings. The sprout you see now will last for centuries, becoming grand and vast as any which came before it and hopefully providing clones to sprout on many distant lands, ever growing and ever changing its impact on those around it."

"Never heard of it," Enri admitted. "Where's it from?"

Dirk chuckled. "The advantages of having access to the system's largest research and development branch run far and wide, m'boy—including the ability to genetically experiment with new forms of life. That's the TurTek way, you know!"

The professor pocketed his plant and his demeanor darkened, which was rather unusual for the regularly jovial man. *What was going on?*

"Listen Enri," Dirk began with a croak in his voice. "I have one last thing to show you today, and you aren't necessarily going to understand it. Just know that we've had this datum for a while, Walter and I. In fact, since the very beginning of TurTek itself."

"Um, ok Dirk. Sure." A knot formed in Enri's gut.

Dirk took his hand back out of his pocket, this time handing Enri a dark plastic cube that he identified as an old, quasi-holographic recording device. At Dirk's nod of approval, he clicked it on, watching then as its black plastic faded clear and a three dimensional image formed within of a man wavering in detail—melting in and out of reality as the image stretched in weirdly abnormal fluctuations of form.

The man projected within the cube talked aloud without any delay. The sound from within was rather bad in quality, with barely intelligible words and an unimaginably confusing message. Nevertheless, Enri's mind raced past its own sense of conceptual certainty, in and out and through reality as did the holographic image itself. He found himself having to play the recording a second and third time to try and understand it, his heart thumping louder in his chest every single time.

**"TurTek, hands of man,"** the figure in the cube said, **"the galaxy unfolds as the future comes to pass—through the nexus to the truth, around the conceptions of our universe and between the creations of our own. Blink, and I am here and blink, as I am Enri Riatu. Fear not the words, for the message speaks of continuity. Reach for the stars, for they will come back to you."** It ended as confusing as it had begun.

Eventually, once he was satisfied he had not missed anything said through the strange recording, Enri Riatu turned back to his former mentor Dirk. "What is this, a joke or something?"

"No joke, Enri," Dirk replied without his usual humor. "The message is real."

"Well, it wasn't me who made it, if that's what you're thinking," Enri retorted. "Some prankster must have made it… Or some dude with the same name as me."

"It's imprinted with your DNA, m'boy," Dirk responded somberly. "It's imprinted with your DNA and it was sent to us from the future… To the very day you were born, by the way, down there on Earth." He pointed out the window towards the hauntingly beautiful figure of Earth below, looming far behind the many miles of hectic Deep Space construction before them.

# 1 : disaster :

"The vicious whip of religious crusade and the unjust persistence of regulated savagery have long been attributed to the faith of devotion. However, the truth of the matter resides not in the honor of the perpetrators' forethoughts, but rather in the veiled emotional recesses of gluttonous desire deeply present within us all."

-Transcripts of the Empress

### <2108 C.E.—the age of finesse><Earth Orbit>

Fenna Caae was fourteen years old and excited to be at the 2108 Interplanetary Summer Olympics with her parents—the formidable Hugo Caae, who owned and mayored the thriving tethered community of Atlas Aether, and the venerable Ilea Caae, who captained and flew the transport fleet Odyssey back and forth from the outer reaches of the solar system and grand asteroid belt. Colonists and miners seemed to need a constant supply of velcro and duct tape from Earth to keep their newfound territories from simply floating away, so business was currently booming.

Jessie Caae, Fenna's older brother, was her absolute hero and a competing athlete in this year's Olympic events. He was a free-fall athlete in the first ever Olympic atmospheric reentry event, a newly accepted competition where divers launched out from over 150 miles above the surface of Earth armed with nothing but their own wits and an atmospheric dive suit donning heat shields and cyclical pressure systems for mass deceleration. With a great deal of patient perseverance, the athletes would slow themselves down to break orbit with Earth and make a spectacularly fiery descent through Earth's surprisingly thick atmosphere. Jessie's diving team was gaining steam in the system, on their way up to becoming famous for their talent. As a speed competitor and perfectionist in his aerodynamically manipulative form, he took part in both the solo and group jumps, gaining much individual recognition in his dives.

Jessie always promised to teach Fenna his skills one day, describing the experience of down diving through a planet's ozone like the passage of a mythical phoenix burning itself into existence through a hell of fire and grit. Having watched every recording of Jessie's runs over and over again, Fenna felt more than ready to start diving on her own for real. Simulator dives were simply not enough to keep her thrilled, only resulting in making her long ever the more for the likes of a real dive. However, as she was too young to legally make a jump, for now she would simply have to watch her brother compete on the grand international Olympic stage, which in itself gave her much pride.

For the first time since the 2088 floating stations of New Atlantis, a truly international and wholly unaffiliated Olympic venue had been constructed without any bias to a specific country. This day was a groundbreaking event for everyone who understood its impact on the ever-fading sense of nationalism, be they spacers or landlubbers alike. People across worlds clustered together to witness this great debut, with countless eyes looking up to the sky in anticipation—or likewise to a terminal screen upon their walls, laps, contact-lenses, wristbands, or windows—all with new possibilities of Deep Space expansion flickered through their many minds.

The unimaginably large, unbelievably pricey Earth-orbiting helical station Olympia, in which the Interplanetary Olympics were taking place, was rumored to have been constructed over many years specifically for this big unveil. In terms of historical significance, however, it meant so much more than that. Beyond just the advent of competitive sport events, this station was a current hot topic throughout the system-wide colonies of man, ever more now with the interplanetary Olympic celebrations in full swing. Its chambers were able to simulate any magnitude of gravity, from all the way down at weightless up to a level past Jupiter's. As such, the far-spanning Olympia station was the prime and solitary locale which could host any range of Earth sports, Martian combat matches, Moon-jumping events, and even zero-gee tactics, like Jessie's atmospheric-reentry diving competition. The station supported thousands upon thousands of occupants in a single isolated network—truly the first and only of its class to do so.

As the biggest single entity to ever orbit Earth, this station was ginormous, hosting enough variety of rotational parks, amusements, and facilities to be an almost self-sufficient society on its own—run albeit under the funding of tourism, entrance fees, and a myriad of prominent Olympic events. Tours and rides, bars and cinemas, spas and zero-gee meditation chambers—the expansive environment supporting the 2108 Olympics had it all—an entire civilization wrapped up tight in a single helical frame.

To help channel the immense populous coming and going from the Olympic celebrations, a "Turian flower" space-elevator was constructed in nearby orbit, so-called because of the silhouette of its array of docked personal and orbital crafts fastened together above it like the petals of a flower reaching for the sun and the many tube-line space-elevator shafts running down to Earth below like a long stem reaching underground. The Turian flower's design allowed and encouraged new space-craft to join into the petals and fasten themselves into magnetic tether holsters, becoming an active part of the community's ethereal swaying beauty and assisting in being a counter-weight for the lines running down to Earth. As such, the size of the Turian flower community fluctuated with the amount of traffic docked to it, from the tides of independent space-faring individuals who needed a place to park their craft in Earth's orbit to the incoming tsunami of Olympic crowds coming to flood the newly unveiled station. As it was now, the flower's current petal size was at an all-time high, with the space-elevator shafts stemming down below it at their maximum overall width, using every single one of the tube-lines available to shuttle people up from Earth below at a never-before seen pace.

Little Fenna was part of the thrill-seeking crowd—the younger audience of teens seeking an action-packed indulgence in which to spend their time. The majority of that demographic had not necessarily come to the station for the purpose of watching an Olympic sport, but rather for a visit of the station itself and the many other forms of entertainment available in custom-gee. To the wide, terminal-lens bearing eyes of the common Spacer teen, this place was freakin' huge, appearing to them like an endless playground built by the gods of zero-gee. The sheer roster of self-gyrating, football-sized stadiums unveiled—each with the ability to separately host both official competitions and more loose forms of independent entertainment—had Fenna excited out of her mind. There was far more to do than she could ever have time to attend.

In order to compensate for her lack of ability to see everything at once, the bedazzled Fenna had set not only her own contact lenses to continually record everything she saw around her, but also had her terminal's digital interface personality snatch vids left and right from anyone on her network reputable enough and willing to share. As with herself, most young Spacers of a competitive spirit enjoyed capturing everything they saw and did, sending it all over the terminal waves as a boast to whoever wanted to watch.

One of the more popular competitive non-Olympic events that had young crowds foaming at the mouth was a hyperactive arena game called the Zeun'A, which took place in a low-gee chamber of complex physical and virtual meddling, usually shaped as a split sphere with two hemispheres rotating in opposite directions. Using holographic projectors and solid-form monitors, a Zeun'A could bring anything visual to life around the competitors on stage—trees, skies, windy mountaintops, the starry, rocky zones of asteroid-belt space, even a world of complete sci-fi fantasy if drawn up from the public web of databanks. The semi-virtual stage within the spherical chamber never stayed the same for long and was set randomly before every match, which meant that no two tournaments were ever the same and no particular competitor could ever have a predestined advantage right off the bat.

For Fenna, this factoid didn't actually matter in the least bit. A low-gee surface was a low-gee surface and an opponent was an opponent, no matter what its scenery told. She was no novice to custom-gee, and even at the ripe young age of fourteen, she had risen in the Zuen'A ranks against the most wizened gee-game veterans.

At this moment, Fenna Caae was currently competing in such a semi-holographic event—one that was dragging out far longer than she had anticipated. Twelve opponents, including herself, had gone into the Zuen'A chamber hours before, fresh-faced and ready for a free-for-all fight, entering the stage into what looked like the sprawling urban townscape of an old-age New York, with a waterfall-and-rise river running from the stage ceiling to the ground and back. Hosting a vast range of physi-virtual weapons, the sporadically ensuing arena fight was intense and drawn out, often eliminating multiple people in quick bursts of action and waning for large stretches in-between.

Over the course of three to four frantic hours, eight opponents out of twelve had been ambushed, hunted, and shot down in the various semi-real streets, parks, buildings, and alleys. This meant that now only four competitors including Fenna herself remained to fight among the landscape of high-rise buildings and three-dimensional flowing water. The young Ms. Caae had fought hard to get this far and now the action was getting especially fierce, so there was no time to dawdle. *Only three kills left and this match would be over!*

Fenna pounced like a leopard off a convincingly real looking highway overpass, feeling a spray of water in the air as she flung herself out and smash-landed onto a graffitied dumpster below, immediately regretting it as she did so. The area smelled of rot and buzzed with flies, with the concrete ground below it littered with broken bottles and wooden planks like a long abandoned campsite. This was certainly not a pleasant detail in a semi-virtual combat match but not the main issue she now faced. No, that was the rain of bullets about to come at her. *There had to be somewhere to seek shelter, fast!*

Fenna threw herself off the metal dumpster as a gunshot rang mere feet above her head. Wasting no time, she peered her head above the dumpster's paint-crackled rim to glance up at the overpass from which she had come. A second shot rang inches from her face and ricocheted off of the dumpster's metal, causing it hum sharply and echo loud in Fenna's ears. She ducked back down behind cover.

Upon prompt, Fenna's terminal lens displayed for her the iden-tags of the three other competitors left in the match and vocalized the information through her earrings. *Augulair, MRnice, and LeavesAeternum. It has to be one of these three guys right behind me. I've gotta think fast!*

The display in her eyes highlighted several nearby stacks of wooden crates, the ripped remainders of some cloth on the ground, and a few odd items, like a gas canister and an umbrella, strewn about haphazardly. Fenna grabbed the umbrella and gas canister, forming an impulsive plan of action in her mind. She reached into her own turtle-shell backpack and pulled out a spinner device, quickly looking up to check whether the enemy combatant was still in approach. The iden-tag of **Augulair** popped up into sight, displaying him coming up on her location slowly from under the overpass, walking cautiously and taking steady steps forward.

He neared the open tunnel where he had seen Fenna last and listened carefully as the metal dumpster before it resonated with a dull thumping sound from within its metal frame. He equipped himself with a minigun from underneath his cloak and popped open the dumpster's lid. With a wide grin on his face, he started firing immediately, yelling something along the lines of, **"EAT IT!"**

The overeager opponent stopped firing and yelling as soon as he saw Fenna absent from the dumpster and witnessed the sight of some odd contraption inside instead—an umbrella attached to a rotating household spinner, banging metal against metal across the dumpster's inner walls with such vigor that he could see a thin crackle of sparks following each major impact. **Augulair** frowned as he closed the dumpster, and then, without any warning, it exploded.

"One down, two to go," Fenna chuckled from deep within the shadows.

**"TUKKING ARTEMUUUS!  :("** a line of text cast into Fenna's eyes from her vanquished foe.

**"It's Artemis, fool!! :P"** she replied back with a virtual snicker.

Outside the tunnel, Fenna found a ladder and climbed to the roof of a nearby building above the highway, gaining herself a viewpoint of a grand majority of the convoluted arena chamber around her. She reoriented herself towards center stage, where the two subdivided hemispheres of the chamber's outer shell met and rotated across each other in opposite directions, confusing physics and twisting the simulated-gee pulling upon the interior air, water, and land of the complex semi-virtual environment. Within the opposite hemisphere, Fenna could see a building of glass rotating perpendicularly up relative to her, bending into the sky at an impossible angle almost comedic within the context of retro urban New York. Young Fenna Caae chose her path carefully, judging where she had seen the other competitors last and extrapolating where they might have gone from there. Only then did she start moving, running across the roof and hopping from rooftop to rooftop with ease and drawing ever nearer to her anticipated crescendo.

A smile crept across teenage girl's face in stride as she spotted one of her two remaining opponents in the distance. *I could win this match yet! Maybe my brother isn't the only natural talent born in the family!*

Fenna timed herself perfectly to jump down onto the roof of a moving AI-driven car, which continued driving as she slipped in through the window and replaced the hologram that had pretended to be steering it. She aimed her car at a bridge hanging over the strange-gee river ahead and hit the gas hard, disregarding the holographic pedestrians walking through the cityscape, the striped faux-construction signs, and the large warning labels meant to repel her away.

Moments later, Fenna's semi-real car smashed hard through metal, wood, and concrete, propelling itself over the artificial river flowing strange. Fenna gave herself a brief moment to embrace her inner focus and free it of clutter, allowing herself a forced surge of clarity while remaining calm. The early-stage nanites in her brain reacted quick as lightning with drips of chemical tranquility, clearing her mind of thoughts and speeding her up systematically to allow for complete—albeit temporary—serenity of thought. She was relaxed and ready, poised to push the flying automobile's door open once the waterfall outside started falling up and indicated to her that that she had crossed hemispheres and that the simulated gravity had shifted.

As soon as Fenna felt her inner ears indicate the shift in gee, she swung the door open and popped her head out of the car. Suddenly, though, her inner peace was shattered by an unexpected sight 'above' her in the sky. An elderly man with snow white hair stood upside down in the clouds, looking straight at her as she flew through the air. Fenna's heart froze for a long moment before her senses told her that she must move fast lest she wanted to fall face-first into the ground. She pounced off the airborne car and lost sight of the old man in the sky, focusing instead on the task of aiming forward at her initial opponent—who heard the car crash behind her and had begun to spin around in alarm.

Fenna gave the surprised competitor no time to act as she landed beside him in a crouch with two curved axe-daggers in hand. She lunged forward with no hesitation or discussion, sending her virtual blade deep past his carotid. The creases of a frown formed upon his face for a brief moment before he disappeared out of existence and was promptly whisked away to wherever the *losers* go. However, Fenna did not get the chance to celebrate the successful takedown because she was distracted yet again by something unexpected to her right.

A wall/screen/hologram/semi-virtual surface beside Fenna malfunctioned as if on cue, blinking static and disrupting the façade of the urban New York City. For a second, the previously concrete wall looked completely blank, and then it was suddenly the vision of a tree—large, green, and unbelievably hearty, radiating life and promise of future in a single image lasting but a second. *What in Zeus' name...?* Fenna was spellbound, unable to comprehend what had just occurred, and, in that moment, she was struck in the head by a virtual metal rafter falling right through her.

"Damns'it!" Fenna screamed in rage, knowing that she was now 'dead.' She threw her axe blade down angrily but was not even given the satisfaction of seeing it strike ground before it too faded out of existence. She remembered the old man standing in the clouds above. *That cheater!*

"Sons of Olympus, that was so Gorgon cheap!" she shouted over her terminal lens interface to **LeavesAeternum**, who had just won the match. "What the tuk? Are you godsdamn hacking into the system or something!? You're screwed, buddy! SCREWED!"

**"The universe does not wait as we sit and stare at a world of pretty distractions,"** he replied in very small text that Fenna reflexively squinted at despite the fact that the image was coming in through her contact-lenses. By the time she read the image and focused her eyes up towards the virtual clouds where the old man had been standing, they, along with the rest of the simulated environment, no longer existed in sight.

And then, all the messages blocked by the in-game Zeun'A system began to flood in. Fenna saw their timestamps and quickly summoned up her terminal interface's clock. *SHIT!*

<><><>

Fenna's brother's event was starting any moment, and yet here she was, lost and confused, stuck spiraling down the unknown lengths of an endless station's twisting and winding single-helix hallway. Large windows stretched up rotating walls and gave a constant spectacular view of the magnificent planet outside, but as the hall's valley-sized rings stayed in constant flux, the view of the Earth kept rotating around and around, becoming rather unreliable as a point of reference. Across the long, wide hallway which stretched on forever and connected nearly every passage of the Olympia station's leviathan bulk, there were many plazas and sub-partitions of internationally diversified camps, tents, stands, and wavering bands, and a whole big mess of confusion.

Fenna's tensions rose high as she stood trying to formulate a path out of the clutter. She stood on the verge of tears, watching the huge dome of Earth moving rotationally outside the acre-wide cabin—part of it impeded from sight by a group of children holding colorful balloons perpendicular to her down the winding path. The generic blend of every single culture human left Fenna completely directionless, offering no clue whatsoever about how to reach Jessie in time to see the start of his event. Even her terminal lens' guidance system was no help at all, as most of the chaotic foot-traffic and tent areas were temporary and would have never been registered in any map or domain, let alone loaded into her augmented nav-vision.

A flashy red balloon released from the kids' grips and floated 'up' into mini orbit around a growing pile of junk bobbing in zero-gee down the center of the wide corridor. Fenna looked over at the coagulating trash, sighing in heavy agitation. Forcing herself to take a moment to relax, she cast her eyes over a cleaning droid that had begun speeding towards the direction of the drifting balloon, diligently clearing the mess of litter left behind by all manner of Olympic crowds.

Droids circled all around the place, incessantly wiping every surface and correcting all surface damage to keep everything spotless at all times. Remembering that these floating cleaners often retreated through the station's lift tubes once they scavenged a full load, Fenna's mind snatched up a possible solution to her current predicament. Fenna scouted a droid heading outward towards the external lift tubes and followed it with her eyes until, sure enough, it reached and flew out a nearby tube capsule junction. *These same lift tubes could take me straight to Jessie's event. Maybe I can make it in time yet!*

She started running. Fast. However, along the way, she could already see another problem coming up to greet her: the congested crowds. Long lines of people from every country in the world stood stagnant in congested queries, each waiting to get carted away to a different section of the massive space-station and each taking an extravagantly long time to do so. Large and fast as these lift junctions were, they could hardly accommodate the large crowds the station gathered. The wait to reach one could very well take half an hour. *Perhaps I will have to improvise...*

Feeling her heart sink, Fenna struggled to think up a new solution. Still in sprint, she found another automated cleaner droid heading towards the lifts and followed its movements with her eyes. It was bobbing up and down above her, unwittingly swooping down into Fenna's range of reach and putting her in the perfect position to make a snap decision.

The teenage girl launched herself up into the cleaning droid's hovering plastic-shelled body and slammed into it hard, making sure to hold on tight as her momentum shot it around like a dreidel in the air. She and the robot flew up and onward, straight over the stagnant Olympic crowds and right towards the tube-lift junction. Several of the people Fenna passed above grinned as they saw her fly, but most were angry, shouting out obscenities as she flew over them.

A silken robed Chinese-orbital diplomat passing below seemed to be particularly rageful. Sitting comfortably with his family—each member of which had his own ground-level leisure floating chair—the man began cursing in a language quickly translated by her terminal lenses and tossed an apple up into the air, striking the cleaning droid on which Fenna hung. The man's children followed his example with glee, flinging their food up at Fenna and striking her flat in the face with a star-shaped, 10 second expanding creampuff. A lanky brown musician just beyond them sporting electronic disc tables and a backpack filled with recordings looked Fenna straight in the eyes in a way that left her raw and ashamed. Beyond him, a security guard with Olympic rings on his garments and a micro-megaphone attempted to talk her down and catch Fenna at the end of her arc. She felt butterflies undulating in her stomach. *Oh tuk, Maybe this isn't going to work!*

The teenage girl twisted and propelled herself off the bobbing droid, throwing it behind her to bound forward and hop off of the security guard's beret. Without looking back, she slid under an ID-check gate and ran across the riveted metal platform, scarcely believing that nobody managed to stop her as she jumped into an open elliptical air hatch. She quickly entered a lift capsule pod primed and ready for use with her heart bouncing around her chest. The door behind her locked shut automatically with a hiss and a click, and the pod disconnected itself from the space-station's tube port junction, pushing away quickly to allow the next pod behind it to dock.

"YES!" Fenna shouted aloud, spinning herself around to look across the wall-wide window and watch as the Olympic space-station curled out of view. The transport tube spiraled away from the space-station's main mass along a wide-looping path as one of hundreds just like it. *Surely nobody will try and stop a small-fry like me now,* she thought ecstatically. *That'd surely slow traffic down worse than me cutting the line!*

"Young Madame, where would you like to go?" a mechanically smooth, heavily accented British voice asked Fenna via speakers in every direction.

"The diving competition. Fast!" she shouted into the window's terminal display.

"Indoor pools or out of station tracks?" the voice asked. "Public waterfall chambers?"

"No, go to the atmospheric reentry event!" she yelled. "Obviously!"

"Now, now, little lady, no need to be cross," the capsule responded. It changed directions through a tube hub, slowing itself for a brief moment as it turned.

As the capsule sped on, Fenna looked out the window and spotted a nearby Olympic event taking place in a rotating chamber. She zoomed into the sight with her terminal lenses, focusing on a spinning stage of loosely garbed, colorful competitors perching on posts and jumping through hoops. A panel of judges sat ready but out of physical range, faces serious as war with lenses capturing every microsecond of the Olympic event. Video feed of their eyesight streamed into Fenna's own, overlaying her own lenses' zoomed-in vision with heavily annotated official newscasts. She shut the feed off, scoffing internally at the presumptuousness of the intrusion.

Following up on the girl's agitated vocal request and sensing her anticipation towards the Olympic atmospheric reentry dive about to take place, the window terminal turned on an inverse-holographic cam view of the event itself. The image showed a long unloading dock exposed to the vacuum of space, well-marked with official Olympic notarizations and recognizable as the launch center of the atmospheric reentry events. On the window screen, Fenna could see the athletes all there, suited up and preparing for the countdown to disembarkation. The ten divers, standing in two teams of five—Jessie's international Earth-orbiting team shaded gray and white, and their Russian opponents with wingsuits decorated like cosmonauts of old—stood crouched and ready at the platform, grasping onto metal bars for support and holding themselves in to keep from floating away in zero gee.

*Shit!* Fenna snapped her attention forward to try and find her brother among his team, instructing her terminal lens interface to assist by seeking out his suit's serial number. She was quickly disappointed to find that she couldn't identify him anywhere on scene. *Maybe he's wearing another suit. His could have broken down or something.* Fenna hoped Jessie wouldn't be angry at her for being so late; up till now, she had come to every other event and had received nothing but the greatest of blessings from her brother. That made it all the worse that she was not there now, at this important of an event. No matter how her brother felt, Fenna knew that if she were to miss his Olympic dive in whole, she'd never forgive herself. *And if he didn't win… No!* She forced herself to stop. *That thought was unthinkable!*

From the inverse-holographic screen before her, Fenna could hear the event announcer blabbering to pass the time, spilling empty words into the microphone. She zoned out the chatter, willing the lift to move faster with all her mental might. *Every second late counts,* she urged herself. *The buzzer will ring any moment now, and Jessie will throw himself towards Earth before even seeing me!*

To Fenna's eternal disappointment, the blathering announcer on the other side of the camera switched pace and announced the start of the diving competition. The five official Olympic rings, representing the five continents of the united human world, popped up onto the screen, supplemented now by the introduction of a sixth ring representing the nation-less realm of outer-space. The camera panned out towards the shining openness of

Earth's upper atmosphere, and the countdown timer started to tick down in bold white letters. Her time was up.

"**10, 9.**" The event announcer read aloud, echoing through Fenna's transport tube. She leaned forward and pressed her palms nervously against the window screen, concentrating heavily on what she would miss in person.

"**8, 7.**" The atmospheric reentry divers each tensed into a crouched stance, ready to leap with nothing but their own strength and self-induced momentum to propel them towards the pull of gravity.

"**6, 5.**" Fenna pressed closer, eyes as wide as possible in a desperate attempt not to blink. She flicked open several different live camera feeds onto her terminal lenses to display many different perspective angles at once.

"**4, 3.**" The divers each leaned over the edge of space, easing their wingsuits open for flexibility in anticipation of a thickening atmosphere below the vacuum of space.

"**2, 1.**" Fenna held her breath.

"**0!**" The announcer shouted with climactic gusto.

Ten competitors launched into the air, kicking off metal with legs and arms perfect in form. Two teams flew separate yet nearly identical, arms down and wings closed in wait for an atmosphere to interact with. For a moment, all was calm—although just for a moment.

The next few seconds rocked Fenna's world in the form of an explosion witnessed over many angles at once. Over and over and over. One moment, the screen showed her brother's team and their Russian opponents synchronized in form. In the next, a metal girder the size of a dozen shuttles tore out a wide-open ring in the Olympic station's helical backbone, wisped by a curling trail of fire. The diving platform was swallowed whole before the entire station wing shifted, snapped, broke off, and began to fall down towards Earth. The ten atmospheric-reentry divers never stood a chance as the entire wing of the station blew right through them in a plunge to the beautiful, looming planet below.

"NO, no, no, **NO!**" Fenna didn't even notice when she had started screaming. Her eyes were full of tears and her fists throbbed in pain as she bashed the window screen before her, yelling at the top of her lungs.

The lift capsule went into crisis mode. It snapped into place at the next stop it found, then flung its door wide open and thrummed a loud siren to warn her to get out. *This can't be happening! It cannot be real!* Moving purely on instinct, Fenna rushed out the door and down the first spiral corridor she saw, emerging out into main helix corridor connecting everything in the station to all.

Red lights flashed everywhere, and an insufferable siren pounded in the background, reflecting the very pandemonium it caused. Everyone was freaking out, as there was seemingly no safety to be had. Some people tried sprinting to the tube lift exits, some away from the exits, and some seemed to be standing perfectly still and waiting in shock for direct instruction. This was truly a scene of pure chaos, through which Fenna ran on impulse. *Idiots, all of them!* She hid from herself her own overwhelming sense of fear and banished away the truth of what it all meant.

Fenna pushed past a clumped band of bewildered tourists standing motionless on a wide escalator and right away remembered where she was. The atmospheric diving platforms were nearby, and the surroundings around her had become vaguely familiar, even under the flashing red lights. *I finally know where to go!*

**SLAM!** Somebody strong smashed into Fenna and pulled her in a contrary direction, clutching her arm and running with her in tail, giving her no choice but to follow lest she topple over and be dragged. She couldn't see where she was being taken and felt the panic rise at her lack of control.

"STOP! What do you want?" the frightened girl screamed, trying hard as she could to push her aggressor away with a kick and a shove.

"Get in," her captor shouted, throwing her against a door that felt somehow familiar. "**NOW!**"

Fenna recognized the voice and rushed into the room, followed closely behind by the man who had grabbed her. She turned around and jumped at him with a hug, tears streaming freely from her eyes and emotional barriers burst past recognition.

"I thought... I thought you were dead!" She pouted in happy confusion.

"We don't have time!" Jessie pushed himself away from her to charge across the narrow locker-room towards a grated rack holding his dive team's supplies. Fenna's heart skipped a beat when she realized he was rummaging through a line of women's wingsuits. He grabbed the smallest one he could find and shoved it at her.

"Put this on!" he shouted, no hint of patience in his voice.

"What's going on?" Fenna asked, nearly hysterical. With no comprehension of how to, she found herself standing as still as the idiots she had scoffed at outside.

"Please, Fi, put on the suit," her brother said, trying to keep his own emotions in check as he pushed the winged ensemble at her. This time Fenna grabbed it, feeling relieved to see that Jessie moved swiftly to put on a suit of his own. He helped fasten a helmet over his sister's head and barely gave her a moment to adjust to the heavy contraption before tugging her to get back into motion and out the door.

"Come on," he commanded. "Let's get moving."

Red lights flashed bright, sirens wailed loud as thunder, and the thinning air in the hall outside blew rubble about the room like leaves in autumn. The crowds of panicked people had considerably thinned out as well, leaving Fenna and Jessie practically alone in an expansive chamber of crumbling space-station threatening to topple at any moment. The ground jolted and separated from the siblings' feet as the simulated gravity ceased to function. They floated together in the air.

Jessie grabbed Fenna's helmet and brought her face close to his, looking her in the eyes through the clear glass screen. "Whatever you do, do not look back," he instructed with urgency in his glare.

"But," Fenna gasped. "Mom, Dad..."

"Don't look back," Jessie repeated and turned away as he grabbed a handhold upon a wall and motioned her to follow suit. The Olympic athlete kicked off the walls like the expert he was and led Fenna across the hall towards the Earth-facing airlock gates.

Before his sister could wrap her brain around his current plan of action, Jessie was already pushing Fenna out the airlock door, following her into its isolated air chamber, and closing the door behind them to depressurize the air.

"Remember," Jessie said again to his sister still in shock, "don't look back."

All Fenna could do was plead. "Promise, Jess," she cried out hysterically. "Promise that you're right behind me!"

"Yeah, Fi, I'm behind you," he said with the sad smile of a liar and the twinkle of a rare teardrop building up in his eyes. He took several steps back as if in contemplation and pressed a large red button that let out a hiss behind her.

Before Fenna could protest, Jessie ran forward and rammed into the airlock door, slamming it open to reveal the hauntingly beautiful scene of destruction taking place outside. The glorious Turian flower mere miles away was visible through the wisps of fire tearing through the Olympic station, chillingly unperturbed by the chaos before it. Its space-elevator stem stood firm and steady amidst the crumbling Olympia, hinting at the delicate hit-or-miss balance which man had achieved over the elements. With leagues of broken wreckage dominating all sights outside the airlock door, this message seemed satirically cruel but nonetheless true.

Jessie spun his sister around and looked her in the eyes one last time, allowing tears to drip down his cheeks as he spoke. "Now you promise me something, Fi," he urged.

"Yeah Jess, what?" Fenna asked through spurts of sobs.

"Promise you won't look back," he requested. "Please, Fi. Promise."

"Ok Jess, I promise," Fenna told her brother, realizing that something was very wrong with the way he was acting. "I won't look back."

Jessie's face eased into a sad smile as he pulled her into a hug. He appropriated the right angle it would take to launch Fenna towards the atmosphere of Earth and, with his heart thumping as loud as hers, shoved her away as hard as he could, losing hold of his sister once and for all, no save-points or redos about it.

And then the young Fenna was all alone save for the looming planet below, a ton of boiling wreckage, and the rubble of an ongoing horrific disaster. She spun both metaphorically and physically as she flew further away from the station in turmoil and the brother who had made her promise to never look back. Upon each physical rotation, the teenage girl found herself looking at Earth, then the space-station, then Earth, then the space-station, cycle upon cycle increasing her dizziness. A blur of whooshing motion denied her any grounding to reality or any control to stop her own spin, until soon, she could no longer even identify from whence she had come. Unfortunately, this did not prevent her from seeing the booming bang in gory detail as the station Olympia's main helical window erupted outward like a volcano from within, spiraling out in the air through puffs of wasted oxygen.

Fenna's troubled mind filled with a sharp stillness. She spun for several prolonged moments of silence before the world became a vision of the river Styx as the explosion's shockwave hit her full-force, accelerating her even faster towards the blanket of Earth below. In a grim moment of depressing irony, Fenna found herself heading straight for the experience she had for so long yearned to undergo: diving through atmospheric reentry. She sobbed to herself, remembering how much she had always complained of the age limit.

Fenna was hit with a sea of silence and given a final view of the disaster in space before the fiery hell of Earth's ozone came up to greet her like sleep in the night. The confused, mentally-stunned teenage girl was suddenly left even more devoid than before, with nothing to calm her down but her own thoughts. For several unbearable seconds that felt more like grueling hours, Fenna withstood the pain of the many questions burning in her mind, unobstructed by sensory input of any kind.

*Where is Jessie? Where are Mom and Dad?* Fenna questioned the Earth below. *Why had the space station Olympia exploded?* As the feathered tips of fire began to work their way across her helmet windshield, Fenna made the conscious effort to shut down her thoughts and concentrate on the fall below. Flashing back to the lessons of her older brother, the scared little girl knew exactly what to do. However, she knew that from here on out, the dive itself would be the least of her worries. She could make it safely to the ground below—of that Fenna had no doubt—but she could not even begin to think about what would happen next. Fenna's old life was now over, whether she liked it or not, replaced by something dark and undeniably dreary—something irreversibly sinister which would define the rest of her life.

*Someone has to pay for what they have done!* By the great gods of Olympus, Fenna knew she would fight and claw and tear her way back up from the lowest pits of Terra available to discover the truth of what had happened on this day. The huntress **Artemis** had awakened for good, set upon a quest that could only end in blood.

# 2 : awaken :

**"In the grand scale of all things, the positive progress of the whole has far outweighed most of our less-than-optimal results. Sometimes countless eggs must be broken before they can learn to hatch on their own."**
–Transcripts of William

### <8:43:19 a.s.t.><day 1><Anok>

Hours after Enri entered the tank, the thinly willed restraint tempering his restlessness had faded down to naught. Although the crystalline vessel in which he waded was not uncomfortable in the least bit—unlike the blightingly cold, ozone-smelling room where it was located—the adventurer's conscious sensibility was slipping far away from the realm of the real. Left with nothing to do but think, Enri's mind wandered in loops, maintaining a barely conscious stupor far gone from any active interest he might have had with the scanning process or its results hours before. No longer did he listen to the scan tank's melodic moans rippling through its shimmering liquid goop. No longer did he stare down to watch its bright-white glowing scan-ring arcing up his body like the slowest spotlight in the world. And no longer did he allow himself anger at the needlessly vague terms through which TurTek had assigned him this damned 'mission.' Instead of allowing his mind to get caught up with such mundanities of the moment, Enri Riatu daydreamed of alien life.

*What if some extraterrestrial creature on a planet faraway is undergoing the same boring process as me right now for some reason or another? Is it completely bored in the same way as I am? Could I even recognize the emotions it is feeling at the moment?* These questions shortly comforted Enri, making him feel, in some ways, connected to the universe at large as part of the same intrinsic existential pattern.

Eventually, once the bio-scan's white climbing light reached its peak, it dimmed itself down and shut off completely. No longer hindered by the halo's sharp glow in his eyes, Enri looked out the tank with far more clarity than before—*perhaps with even a little too much clarity.* Even the liquid in which he waded seemed to have suddenly become clear, no longer translucent green. This in itself perplexed him.

Enri's breath froze in his chest. *Everything looked... off.* Instead of a yellow number II painted across the wall from the tank, there was a large embedded red letter E. *What was going on?* He squirmed around to scan across the room, finding it strangely different from how it ought to have looked.

The goopy liquid around Enri began to stir and lower, and his heart fluttered a beat in anticipation, forgetting for a moment the confusion of the room due to the pure exhilaration of finally being let out of his lukewarm cage. As soon as the waterline dipped below his face, Enri pulled his mouthpiece away and took his first deep breath in what felt like centuries, feeling his lungs struggle with glee. The antiseptic liquid drained down and disappeared through the floor, which Enri had not expected to be so hot.

"Holy TUK!" he shouted as his bare feet touched steaming metal and instinctively tried to hop back up into the air, bouncing from foot to foot. *What happened to the blighting cold of the space station?* he wondered longingly, realizing the irony.

The cylindrical glass scan tank creaked under the strain of underlying gears that Enri did not remember and, much to his surprise, began to slide up and away from the floor, revealing a rubber, carpet-like texture outside its perimeter. The crystalline tube glided up and out of sight through a circular slit in the ceiling where Enri remembered an articulated mechanical arm should be.

He scratched his head in bewilderment. *What is happening!? Has TurTek moved me into another room without me noticing? Why?*

Enri hopped off the incredibly hot metal circle onto rubber-ridged floor. At his first glance through the room, he noticed a plethora of inconsistencies, not the least of which was the fact that gravity had suddenly become a whole lot stronger than was customary to simulate upon a TurTek space-station. He also noticed the door leading out was in plain sight with a circular window at eye level, resembling more an exit hatch than an automated TurTek inner-station gate.

Across the room and taking up nearly an eighth of its circular circumference was an unusually sophisticated TurTek cubby bulging out of the curved wall like a whale breaching a wave. Its two compartments were oddly shaped—one massively wide and one vertically thin. While the larger one looked big enough to hold a medium sized dog, the tall and thin one had only the room for something flat like a file folder or perhaps a set of hanging clothing. *Huh!? Where did this thing come from?*

Enri walked up closer, seeing upon the cubby's shiny surface an intricate rubber imprint of TurTek's corporate logo. He poked it. The eye-like insignia responded happily to his fingerprint with a hiss and an elongated click, followed by the gentle wheeze of air. Soon enough, a bright-white flash flooded out of the larger of the two cubby compartments, spilling forth a rush of warmth as it swung open. Inside, Enri found his own knapsack, several sets of clothing that he did not remember packing and a small stockpile of compressed TurTek-labeled water tubes and food bars.

He reached down to grab his knapsack and noticed with instant puzzlement an embedded tattoo on his wrist. Like the food, water, and cubby itself, Enri's skin was imprinted with the image of TurTek eye insignia staring out at all beneath its gaze. *What in the hells...?* He turned around in paranoia and searched through the small room for cameras. *Why am I tagged like a piece of merchandise?*

"TurTek, you bastards, WHY!? When!? How?" Enri yelled out loud.

Receiving no reply, he scooped up his knapsack and dressed himself in loose outerwear. Turning towards the door to leave, he saw through the window a view that took him completely by surprise: a spacious purple landscape. *Where in the world am I?* Enri felt stupefied with wonder— and, at the same time, equally suspicious.

Enri cycled through the possibilities. *Had TurTek ejected me down from space during the bio-scan? Am I on the ground somewhere? Could I have really missed the thunder of atmospheric reentry? Perhaps this isn't even real at all. Have they simply induced me into some hallucinogenic dream?*

Enri's heart beat like a piston, and his breath grew short as he stepped forward and pressed his face up to the circular window. What he saw made no sense, stranger even than the surface of Mars. Outside the circular room was a dusty purple wasteland, dry as the hottest realms of the Sahara, with wide open plains intersected every few miles with grand vertical spikes rising higher than the tallest skyscraper ever made by man—mocking the bewildered explorer's sense of reality with their mere existence. The spires transitioned from maroon to blue as they rose up into the heavens and held up the sky, looking like a cross between ionic pillars and liquid waves of turquoise and purple. They were awesome in their breadth, challenging the very foundation of what Enri thought he knew.

*This is not a desert of Earth, Mars, Venus. No, this is something completely different. Am I some sort of test subject—a beta tester for a new technology of TurTek's? They should have told me what was going on!*

Enri saw several raindrop-shaped land-pods scattered nearby outside, littered among purple rocks but vivid with a bright red sheen shining brighter than the rest of the purple wasteland. Each contained an imprint of TurTek's logo along with a set of metal rings conforming to the bumpy shape of the purple land below. He wondered if there were people in those pods just as clueless as he. *Or maybe*, he supposed, *there were indeed the likenesses of people in there, but they were all just virtual projections meant by TurTek to play me deeper into this little game of theirs.* All speculations aside, he soon decided there was no point in rushing to any conclusions. He could not trust what his eyes alone simply saw, and any assumption he made now would be nothing but arbitrary. *The only thing I can do to beat whoever is doing this to me at their own game is play along for now and investigate the situation further.*

Before Enri could think any further, a *BOOM* erupted through the land-pod around him, followed by another, and then another, and then another. The entire world rang like a bell, flooding his ear-buds with a cacophony of sound as every nook and cranny of the metal room filled with brain-busting vibration and a tsunami of pounding knocks. Through the window a rain of rocks pounded down with wave after wave of fury. A rumble like a stampede of wildebeests began to thump up through the floor of the land-pod, reverberating strikes like a clattering chime. The pod began to tip and waver, shifting around its metal-ring axis, until Enri heard a snap outside and felt the jolt of the landing rings torqueing, twisting, and breaking. The ground shuddered, throwing him in the air with a jerking motion, and the entire vessel rocked forward, smashing him shoulder-first into the imprinted red E on the wall.

*This is definitely not a simulation. It hurts too much!* Enri reached into his knapsack to grab a rope, quickly looping it around himself as a harness.

*BANG, bang, BANG!* The rocks kept pelting as the land-pod rolled forward. Enri crawled across the rubber-bristled floor amid bumps and chimes of rocks hitting metal and pulled himself up the TurTek cubby. He pressed his finger across its insignia and grimaced as it took a long time to hiss, click and pop itself open. A white flash erupted from the thinner of the cubby's two compartments, where Enri was surprised to find a new stock of food and water tubes but had no time to contemplate what this meant.

*SMASH!* The land-pod toppled over itself and sent Enri crashing upward with his arm pinned inside the cubby. The explorer held on for his life as he swung his other arm down with a rope to thread and wedge into the open cubby. With the land-pod still rotating, he took out his arm and pressed a hand firm against the compartment's rubber latch, moments before it rotated out of reach. His harness tightened around him as he fell backwards and was swung in the air. As the pod hit a bump outside, Enri was yanked straight into a wall and straight into unconsciousness.

# 3 : unknown :

**"Against all rationality, it has been noted that the most successful explorers of past endeavors seemed to have tread not by plan or foresight, but rather by pure impulsive reactivity to the situation at hand."**
–Transcripts of William

### <9:12:52 a.s.t>**<day 1>**<Anok>

*This is real—all of it!* Enri felt a jitter of unencumbered enthusiasm despite the heavy levels of pain. *I am truly on an alien world, just like I have always wanted to explore.*

*Thud!* Enri awoke to mind-splitting noise. *Thud, thud, THUD!* He felt the pain resonate through every crevice of his body. *Thud!* He was upside-down with two dozen feet of nothingness spread between him and a curved metal floor below. Everything hurt. The displaced explorer's waist hung on a noose, sending surges of agony through every pivoted movement he took. His body throbbed, his breath labored under an aching trachea, and the pitter patter of blood leaking from multiple gashes across his skin left him numb in pain. *Thud!*

*Thud, thud!* The sound of banging on the wall promised Enri a welcome ray of hope before he had the chance to panic. *Thud, thud!*

"Salve! Est cuiquam ibi?" a disembodied heavy male voice called from outside. "Hello! Is anyone in there?"

*Thud!* The sharp thudding echoed through the metal walls. *Thud, thud!* They rattled under a surge of vibrations. As Enri shifted to put pressure upon the gash in his arm and felt it shudder like a rusted joint, he knew he could use all the help he could get. *Thud!*

"Are you alive? Vivere?" the voice asked. "Anyone?"

"I'm here!" Enri tried to scream over his pained lungs, barely croaking a sound. "HELP!"

Thinking fast, he kicked the curved metal wall beside him as hard as he could with his blood-drenched foot, letting forth a chime as loud as a gong. The elliptical land-pod rang bright as day, for only a second, before withering down to a whimpering hum and bearing the dangling explorer several long moments of uncertainty.

*Bzzz!* The door to the land-pod emitted a sharp scraping sound, and a hand fourfold the size of Enri's own slapped against the circular window from outside, covering it entirely in darkness. A high-pitched clinking sound began from nothing and intensified into the sound of an angry hornet's nest, forcing Enri to wince and cover his ears for protection. *BAM!* A final blow struck hard across the pod door's frame, shifting it forward as the hand outside pushed. The door tipped inward.

As the broken hatch fell and slammed down onto the upturned wall, the land-pod itself rocked, swaying Enri back and forth like a pendulum. Hot air rushed into the room, filling it with unbearable warmth and the heavy odor of salt.

Enri's would-be-savior's hand was now in plain sight. A TurTek tattoo like his own was displayed on its wrist, but it was colored bright upon dark skin as opposed to black upon peachy. The large man belonging to it took hold of the open door's frame and began to climb in, tipping the entire land-pod downward with his weight. Enri's rope shifted angles and swung him forward as it rotated. A bald, dark blue head came up into view, giving Enri his first glimpse of the massive man who stood below him at a height of eight feet at least. Whoever this man was, he looked positively herculean, with a body built like a tank and two heavily muscled arms like torpedoes that could easily tear the land-pod in two.

"Manto!" the large man announced up to Enri. "I will get you down from there!" His face showed gentle concern unbefitting his rough exterior. He cast his gaze around, trying to find an immediate solution to Enri's predicament.

"What... are you?" Enri demanded. "Army, TurTek, Earth government, what? Are you the one who brought me here?"

"Non, I am not of Earth." The man looked back up in slight confusion. "Aren'A gladiators have always been of Mars."

"Uhh, what!?" Enri asked. *Was this guy for real?* "Never mind, could you please get me down from here?" he asked, deciding for the moment to suspend his disbelief and deal with his concerns at hand. "I'm Enri, by the way."

"Call me Fre'dd," the man replied with a slight pause between the E and the D. He continued looking around the mostly-empty room.

"Do you know what the tuk is going on around here?" Enri asked. "Where are we?"

Fre'dd looked up. "Non, I know nil of our charge." He turned around and gave Enri a glimpse of a mark on his back—a ring of black with eight inner rivets spread around eight encircled orbs. A set of three liquid tube-necklaces around the man's shoulders and chest reflected light from outside, diffusing glows in three different colors in all: blue on top, yellow below, and a half-filled red beneath that. Around his waist, and far thicker than the rest of his clothing, was a shiny metal belt made of modular rectangles.

Fre'dd's clothing looked inexplicable to Enri, resembling a one-piece jumpsuit infused with chainmail. *Strange,* he thought, *but currently immaterial. This large man's peculiar fashion sense matters far less than his willingness to help.*

"Are you hurt? Can you move?" the tattooed giant asked, looking back up with noticeable concern in his eyes. "Your blood is spilling."

"Just need a way down, thank you," Enri replied briskly, refusing to think about his pain. *Now is not the time to gripe about inconveniences.*

"Cut your rope and I'll catch you. Do not worry. I have been trained."

"Are you crazy? Hells no, I'll break my spine!"

Fre'dd nodded without complaint. He continued looking around, thinking of a new solution. His eyes followed the curved metal former-floor upwards, scanning for possibilities. He suddenly looked outside.

"What're you…"

"Wait!" Fre'dd interrupted. "I think I have a way." He stepped towards the open doorframe, tilting the land-pod with his weight.

"Hey, wait! Where're you going?" Enri yelled as Fre'dd hopped outside. He swung down into the wall as the land-pod rocked backwards. "Oof!"

The faint sound of rock hitting rock sounded far away in the distance outside, followed by a scraping sound nearby preceding another plop far away. *Oh shit!* Enri thought. *Is the meteor shower starting up again?*

The cycle continued with another nearby scrape and another faraway plop, but this time Enri heard Fre'dd's grunt of exertion thrown into the mix. It repeated, over and over—a scrape, a grunt, and a faraway plop, a scrape, a grunt, and a faraway plop—until several long minutes later, it stopped altogether and Fre'dd came back into sight outside the open door frame, panting heavily. He climbed back in and pitched the land-pod down with his weight.

"Brace yourself," Fre'dd called up. He began walking forward through the room, stepping carefully up the rounded slope like a hamster on a wheel. Every heavy step brought Enri closer to the curved wall below, until soon it had become a floor and Enri was laying down flat upon it.

"Yes, finally!" Enri exclaimed as he stood up shakily and untied himself.

On first glance, Enri realized his savior was far more damaged than he had initially realized. The large man had several slashes across his one-piece uniform and an un-bandaged wound across his abdomen so ghastly Enri was surprised he hadn't seen it from above.

"You ok, buddy?" he asked. He sat down on the TurTek cubby. "Want me to patch those up for you? My knapsack should be somewhere around here somewhere, I was about to find it to patch myself."

"Non problemata, me viva."

"Yeah sure, no problem—but it's no problem patching you up either. You don't wanna drip forever."

"Gratias, but no." Fre'dd replied, waving him away. "I need to eat." He sat down on the TurTek cubby and began to chew on the yellow necklace tube around his neck—the second one down out of three.

Enri left him be. He walked across to where his scattered belongings pooled in a line and picked up his knapsack, putting fallen objects back in until he found some patching cream for his skin. Looking back to Fre'dd, Enri picked out a bar of raspberry chew and walked back to him, noting the eager relief in his eyes as soon as he saw it. The large man devoured the bar immediately and graciously accepted a second banana flavored one.

Enri brought forth his handheld terminal, switching on the familiar, translucent device. He waited with fingers crossed through the brief moment it took to turn on. *Please, please, please work!* Its interface personality flickered on, and Enri breathed a sigh of relief as soon as it spoke up. *Phew!*

"Enri, Enri, Enri!" the terminal piped out, excited to be awakened after all this time. "What's that smell? Why're we here? Why is the clock tripping out? Does my voice sound weird? Why is it echoing? Why do you have nano-bots healing you? Why is there blood on the floor? Who is that man? Why is he registered with an iden-tag set 200 years in the future?"

"Woah there buddy, slow the flood." Enri hushed the interface. "First, scan for wave reception. Then, tell us where we are."

Fre'dd looked up. "What did you say?"

"Oh sorry, just talking to my terminal."

"Termina?" Fre'dd asked. "The end of what?"

Enri waved the clear device at him. "You know… my terminal."

Fre'dd squinted back, still not quite understanding.

The terminal spoke back up, sounding unhappy: "No waves, no reception, no fun, fun, fun, fun! I can't get my signal up through the atmosphere. They keep bouncing back!"

"Maybe it's the room we're in," Enri suggested. "The land-pod could be impenetrable."

"Nope, it isn't. Not at all!" The terminal interface laughed. "Besides, even if this wall was impenetrable, my waves would bounce right out through the open door. In fact, I'm already charting the topography of the nearby area through active pings, and the signal bounce-back itself is happening much higher up in the atmosphere than the land-pod."

"What about atmospheric composition? Can you tell me anything?"

"Oxygen is high, almost 40%. Nitrogen is low, carbon dioxide is low, sodium is high. Pressure is high, gravity is low. Sound is echoing. Oopsie daisy—this isn't Earth at all! Hmm... it isn't Venus or Mars either, is it?"

"Yeah, I don't think so," Enri replied. "Let's take this one step at a time, though."

Fre'dd stood up, rocking the pod with his weight. Enri noticed that the large man was no longer bleeding, even though only several minutes had passed since he had sat down. Stranger yet, it seemed that his clothing itself had started to heal over the area of the wound, shutting tight its many gashes and replacing lost chainmail-like rungs with new ones. *Huh,* Enri thought. *Never heard of tech like that before...*

"Do you have more food?" Fre'dd asked him earnestly. "Let's get going!"

"You sure you're ok?" Enri eyed him with suspicion but still pulled out a peach flavored bar and handed it over. "We don't have to go anywhere yet. You looked pretty hurt..."

"All is good!" Fre'dd insisted as he chewed his bar of food. "Let us depart! There could be others out there in trouble."

"Okay fine," Enri reluctantly agreed. "I bet we can find someone out there who knows what the tuk is going on. There is still a whole lot more explaining left to be done!"

"And waves. Don't forget the waves!" his terminal squeaked through his hands.

Fre'dd stepped across the land-pod's floor to rotate it back around and bring the doorway into reach, after which the much smaller explorer jumped out first, grabbing onto the metal doorframe and swinging himself out.

By the time his feet touched the desert ground below, Enri's body felt overwhelmed. The air was so hot that his gashes immediately winced despite the healing cream he had applied, and the stench of salt was so strong that it forced an unexpected retch of respiratory confusion through his throat.

The sun beamed down with extreme prejudice and left little compromise for the transition, hitting hard and hitting fast. Enri felt the crunch of thick salt crackling between the speckled purple rocks shifting underfoot. *Holy hells! Could this really be an alien planet?*

Looking up through a set of squinting eyes, Enri located an electric-blue sun and immediately noticed it was visibly small in the sky despite the unbearable heat it emitted. The explorer continued to gaze across the sky, finding it unnaturally turquoise with a noticeably bland stillness looming far above. *This is definitely not light from the familiar Sol of home… It must be a blue supergiant, very, very far away from the planet.*

The purple land beneath the sky was interspersed every couple of miles with a wave of a spire piercing up from the land, protruding out of the desert plains with its massive form to stretch out of sight into the heavens. The royal-purple flatland below looked very, very hot, with heat waves swirling about through the air and nary a sign of life within. A fata morgana merged horizon with the sky, through which gusts of wind blew sand and salt. After taking a few steps forward, Enri realized that the land stretched downward before him, almost imperceptibly curling upward before it flattened out in the distance.

The grandiose wave-spires cast vertical stripes over the horizon. The sheer space distances they spanned confounded the Earth-man's mind. Although Enri had seen many sights in his days abroad, he had nothing in mind or memory to compare to the view he saw before him now. He could not comprehend how an environment like this even existed. This purple desert was an anomaly and, as such, challenged everything the well-traveled explorer had ever known about geological physics. *These things look impossible! How do they even keep upright? They look like they should have toppled over long ago!*

"Hey Fre'dd," he called out to his new companion.

"Yes, Enri?" The large man stepped forward, rattling stone and salt with every heavy footfall.

"Are you seeing what I'm seeing? There's no way those spires could be real, right? It must be some sort of atmospheric illusion."

"I have not the sense to tell, I am afraid," Fre'dd replied honestly. "I have never seen such a sight."

"Umm dum-dum, turn around your bum!" a voice squeaked out from within Enri's knapsack.

"What!?" he asked, pulling out his handheld terminal. "Did you find something?"

"Turn around!" it repeated in a higher register. "What're you, freakin blind?"

Enri turned around to face his shadow and felt the wind drain out of his lungs. Beyond his land-pod and up the slope of the land, he saw all at once they were not standing on a mere hill, but rather at the lowest foot of a world-shattering spire climbing up into the sky with no end in sight. Purple slopes like fragile fingers of mountainous rock flowed down from far above, almost as if beckoning Enri to climb them.

"Wuuuu?" he gasped, holding up his terminal on instinct and beginning to snap photos of the all-encompassing view for later perusal. "Is that...? Is there even an end?"

"Just like Mount Olympus of the gods..." Fre'dd whispered in a tone bordering on reverence. "Taller even than Olympus Mons of Mars."

"Yup, yup, it's true, it's true!" the translucent terminal in Enri's hands agreed. "On first analysis it has an elongated exponential arc, extended verticality, and at least two miles of visible elevation. Although, based on that description, it's not really a mountain at all, more like a pillar... Well, actually no, not like a pillar at all. Based on my ping-backs, it seems the rock canopy above may gradually arc back out of the shaft like an early-level mushroom cloud. So it's more like a mushroom-pillar, or perhaps an inverse-umbrella-pillar. It's like a gigantic tsunami of a spike bursting up from the land, so it's a tsunami-land-spike."

"Wave-spire," Enri corrected. "Call it a wave-spire."

"Databank updated!" the clear-framed terminal in his hands confirmed. "Do you want an in-depth analysis of my findings?"

"Later," Enri instructed. "First things first: we must find the other land-pods out there and discover who's out here with us."

"Yes, the sooner the better," Fre'dd agreed with audible concern.

"Okee-dokee!" Enri's terminal responded gleefully. "Wave scans calibrating for high-density metal. If something is out there, I will find it!"

"Hey Fre'dd, where's the pod you came out of? Did you see anything else when you got out?"

"It's out over there." Fre'dd pointed down the slope with an arm above Enri's head. "Not too far away. The only other vehiculum I saw from there was yours."

"Hmm, ok... Lemme see." Enri held up his terminal and warped its shape over his eyes to shade out the brilliant sunlight. He tapped the device twice with two of his fingers, indicating that he wished for it to augment his vision. "Little help here, buddy?"

Enri's terminal zoomed into the slope with a magnified view, spotting Fre'dd's pod among salt-lined piles of rock and artificially enhancing the image to point it out more clearly. Even through the augmentation of the screen, the view of the mountain below blurred with heat waves under the blistering sun. *Neither I nor Fre'dd will survive long under these arid conditions,* Enri realized, feeling his tongue already parched and his eyes crackling dry after mere minutes exposed to the dryness. *Perhaps the supplies that TurTek provided can help for now, but eventually a long-term solution will have to be had.*

Pulling out a tube of compressed water, Enri took in a long sip and was pleasantly surprised to find that it seemingly lost very little liquid content in the process. *Hmm, maybe TurTek knew what it was doing after all.*

"Gratias fortuna!" Fre'dd exclaimed. "I see another land-pod nearby!"

"Where?" Enri spun around with his terminal over his eyes and saw the large man in silhouette with brilliant rays of blue sun curling around his heroic pose as he pointed his outstretched arm out to the distance. The flat purple stone on which he stood tipped forward and shifted under his weight, crunching with the sound of caked salt.

Enri's terminal followed Fre'dd's finger automatically. Sure enough, he spotted an upright TurTek pod sitting silent nearby, looking rather undamaged, albeit distorted, by the waves of heat all around.

"Yeah! There it is!" Enri shouted, moments before realizing Fre'dd was already gone. His terminal pointed out the large man running towards the pod, climbing over and around any rock obstructions in his way.

Enri chuckled to himself and put away his terminal, running along the much larger man's path and realizing there was no way to catch up unless the lumbering giant stopped and waited. Fre'dd bound ahead with strides so great they far surpassed any scrambling speed Enri could ever hope to achieve, but that did not stop the much smaller man from trying to follow as fast as he could.

The shining red land-pod looked oh so close but turned out to be so far away the explorer felt his exasperation reach record heights. Desperate in his perpetual quest for information, the striding explorer pulled up his handheld terminal and instructed it to give him more detail of the land-pod ahead. However, with so much attention paid to his terminal's screen, Enri found himself immediately losing balance and tripping. Stumbling upon one stray rock after another, he fell face first, smashing straight down into his terminal.

"Hey!" the handheld device shouted in objection. "Watch it, flesh-o!"

Enri sat up carefully, with eyes swirling under heavy white ribbons of heat and a head pounding like nobody's business. He glanced up the wave-spire and saw more ribbons swirling, oddly mesmerizing and rhythmic in motion. He blinked slowly to let his eyes equalize and brought his terminal back up to shade him from sun.

"Clumsy much?" the device asked him. Enri muted its volume and continued after Fre'dd in a much more careful pace.

Enri saw that the salty purple ground around the land-pod looked rippled and disturbed like the aftermath of a heavy impact, with rocks arranged in waves spread several dozen feet out from its embedded form. Fre'dd had reached the TurTek land-pod at the end of his path and had climbed up its round metal rings but was just standing passively atop them, looking inwards with his face pressed up against its round door/hatch window. Curiously, the large man made no effort to get into the pod and instead resolved to stand outside it, staring in with a morose look upon his face.

Enri reached the red TurTek land-pod's vessel body and saw the extent of the damage it had taken. The crimson surface of the land-pod's exterior had so many scratches and scrapes it looked almost completely purple with the ingrained dust. It had undergone a vicious serious of bumps, knocks, and slides before falling hard into its current position. Not only that, but up close and unhindered by visual distortion, the pod's shape looked positively lopsided. An evident ring shuddered around its axis, sticking out like a welt and crackling outward from the surface like a broken eggshell.

Upon Enri's approach, Fre'dd slumped away from the door, climbing down the shallow ring steps begrudgingly and avoiding eye contact with the small explorer. Instead, he stared out towards the sun and the brilliant skyline of faraway spires. He put two fingers up to his forehead to indicate the mind, down to his lips to represent humanity's consumable nature, and then out into the air before him to signal the passage of life.

"Requiescant en pace," he muttered scarcely loud enough for Enri to hear. The explorer stepped past him and squinted up the land-pod's rings, feeling a deep foreboding resonating through his gut. He climbed up the steps and looked through the scratched window, staring with eyes wide and a failure to comprehend what he was seeing.

The crystalline TurTek scan tank inside the land-pod had been shattered in half, ending the man's life inside it. His body remained mid-room, penetrated upon glass with legs and arms hanging out and pools of translucent blood leaking out over countless glittering shards of broken glass. *Whoever this man was, he had died before he even had the chance to realize he was no longer on Earth,* Enri realized with a heavy heart. *This man had been brought all the way here, wherever here was, only to be killed in his sleep—what a shame!*

"Hoy... Fre'dd!" Enri called down. After receiving no response, he turned around and saw the look of death in his bulking savior's eyes. *For Zeus' sake, didn't the guy call himself a gladiator earlier? I thought he would be tougher than this!*

"Did you know the man in there?" Enri asked Fre'dd, keeping his tone soft and respectful.

The gladiator looked over at him slowly with a mind still asunder. "No. I believe not."

"Well, we're gonna need to get in there, if only to understand what happened. There's no time to waste."

"The man in there is dead. There is no saving him," Fre'dd replied grimly. "Let us not disturb his memory."

"Yeah, he's dead all right," Enri admitted. "But we aren't—at least not yet—and we need all the help we can get. We should try to salvage his supplies to increase our own chances of survival. There's no knowing what this land-pod may contain."

"Raiding the dead!" Fre'dd exclaimed with a booming voice through an undertone of pain. "Scelus! It is a sin. The dead are to be left alone!"

Enri gestured out into the parched purple desert. "The thing is, Fre'dd, by all outer appearances, we seem to have found ourselves stuck in the middle of nowhere—worse yet, a scorching, *alien* nowhere. Who knows how hostile this place could end up being beyond simply hot as high hells!"

"Grave robbing is impious, sinful!" Fre'dd demanded. "It is a curse in the name of the gods!"

"Which gods exactly!?" Enri was in no mood to back down from the issue. He would need Fre'dd's help if he were to get the land-pod door off its hinges.

"Listen Fre'dd, I don't know what superstitions you may have, but that doesn't change the situation we're in. The man in there is dead and no longer needs his survival gear—but we certainly do. Those supplies could very well end up saving our lives in the long run."

"Not even Athena, Ares, Zeus, …" Fre'dd listed off gods. "Even Hades himself would not show such dishonor to the dead."

"Bullshit he wouldn't!" Enri scoffed. "That guy would have the dead serving him tea in the morning if he very well felt like it!"

"Sepulcri mitte supervacuos honores," Enri's terminal squeaked out in Latin, picking up on Fre'dd's unusual predisposition for a language long dead and the mythological religion that was the focus of this conversation. "Discard all superfluous honors at the grave."

Fre'dd made as if to answer but stopped instead and held himself silent.

"Listen Fre'dd," Enri said apologetically, "I'm sorry to say, but once all is said and done, a dead man is simply a dead man; all that is left of his body is a husk of his former self. We, on the other hand, are both alive and kicking, and if we wish to keep doing so, might have to have to forgo our traditional sense of ethics and prepare for the possibility of a long road ahead. So, if you don't mind… can you please get us into this land-pod?"

Fre'dd looked unhappy with the prospect of abandoning his moral coding at the drop of a hat, but he nonetheless nodded and moved up the steps to reach the pod door. With surprising grace and the speed of an athlete, the large man reached down to his waist to grab at his metal belt and slid it off in a single motion. Reacting like a sentient snake, the modular belt uncoiled itself from his body and straightened into a sharp line, shaping itself into a finely-tuned sword. Fre'dd twisted within the belt a single metal brick, wordlessly signaling activation. One by one, the metal bricks of Fre'dd's outstretched belt began to vibrate and hum and, within a short moment, moved back and forth so fast the weapon before him blurred like the wind and all-but disappeared out of view.

Fre'dd grabbed his rumbling belt's outermost humming rung without any apparent discern for his own safety and bent the entire thing over into a sharp arc, pushing it forward against the crimson pod door's hinges and setting the whole thing ablaze with a flurry of sparks. One by one, amid loud screeching and grinding, Fre'dd systematically busted each and every hinge and separated the door completely from within its frame. He then placed a large hand over the window, pushing his massive weight inwards and tipping the door forward with it.

As the heavy metal toppled down into the land-pod, Fre'dd looked inside to confirm success—but only for a moment before turning away with a face filled with disgust. He slunk his belt back around his waist and stepped down the metal rings, looking noticeably distraught.

"Sorry Fre'dd. Good work." Enri stepped past the large man, feeling slightly guilty at his new companion's sour mood. He looked back in concern. "I've got it from here, mate. I'll be as respectful as I can."

The avid explorer entered the pod cautiously, avoiding looking directly at the collapsed body inside and sidestepping around the fresh pool of blood still draining through the floor. The smell of blood and antiseptic liquid hung heavily in the room, strong enough for Enri to cough and sputter as he walked but not enough to stop him from moving onward. The crunch of broken glass crackled between rubber bristles underfoot, and the tension in his mind rose ever higher. The beat of his heart drummed in his chest.

Despite the fact that he knew the penetrated man within the shattered tank was unable to see him, Enri felt shivers trickling through his spine at the thought of disturbing the peace. Fre'dd's superstitious words echoed through his mind, haunting the explorer with doubts that betrayed his very purpose. So, although Enri knew not whether he was doing so as a sign of respect or as a byproduct of fear, he walked as quietly as he could and strove hard to keep his eyes singularly centered on his sole objective. *If I can just get the supplies and leave,* Enri told himself, *perhaps I can minimize this nightmare yet.*

As soon as he reached the TurTek cubby across the room, Enri reflexively pressed a finger to the rubber latch atop it and was disappointed to find it unreactive. He pulled on the handle of the larger of two compartments and cursed at it for remaining sealed.

"Tuk," he muttered aloud, smacking his hand down in anger. He took in a deep breath to calm himself down but nearly gagged at the stench of antiseptic blood which rushed in. "GAH!" he shouted, wheezing out the air in his lungs.

Enri pulled out a thin roll of explosive metal from within his knapsack and ripped off a strip to stick across the locked cubby. He retreated several precautionary steps back and then, without hesitation, blew the cubby sky high, falling backwards onto his knapsack with the shockwave.

"Hey!" Enri's terminal squeaked from underneath him. "What is *wrong* with you? I am not a pillow!"

Enri frowned. To further his disappointment, the blown-open cubby compartment was empty, void of anything but broken plastic and smoke. He bounced up and moved to check close up.

"What if there *was* food in there, huh?" his terminal asked. "You would have blown it to bits! Think, flesh-o, think!" It smacked him, kicking through his knapsack.

"Stop that!" Enri insisted. "Don't make me turn you off!"

"Oh sure, turn me off! But first, take me out of this bag! You're using the cubby wrong."

"What are you talking about?"

"Take me out and put me on the cubby!" his terminal shouted. "Oh, also pick up that big chunk of glass!" It flashed a green light through the bag's threads, pointing out a wedge of broken tank on the ground beside him.

"What!?" Enri doubted the device's sanity. He wondered if his terminal had gone mad.

"Just do it!" the voice in his knapsack demanded. Enri did as he was told, pulling his terminal out of his bag and putting it down on the cubby's TurTek logo. He knelt down and picked up the heavy pane of glass.

"What am I supposed to do with this?" He asked. As if in response, the tall and thin cubby compartment that Enri had not blown open lit up and slid forward, revealing a chute opening that looked like a trash can and beckoned with flashing lights.

"Throw it in!" his terminal instructed. Enri shrugged and tossed the glass in. The compartment shut and his terminal flashed bright.

"What now?"

"Just gimme a little bit of sunlight later, will you? This is gonna take a lot of juice! Oh, and you might want to look away now, flesh-o."

"I still don't get... Oww!" Enri covered his eyes fast as the larger compartment flooded out a river of light. The pane of glass was gone, replaced instead with a lofty device in the shape of a belt.

As the smell of burnt metal faded away from inside his head, Enri caught a whiff of something familiar which boggled his mind: a blue rose. It took him several seconds to remember this scent was unique, originating only from one genetically constructed bit of flora. *No! It can't be! Impossible!*

Enri's mind drifted in nostalgia and his eyes begun to well up with involuntary tears. The world turned cold as his blood prickled through his veins. He felt the hollow thumping of his heart sinking down his chest into the buzzing butterflies of his stomach. *Dirk Fairwinter!*

-Tomer Agmon-

# 4 : progress :

**"Consequences come and consequences go— moments alight then die in the night. What will come will never yet come if what was past had never passed. Nonetheless, it came, passed, went, and gone, and nobody was the wiser."**
-Transcripts of the Empress

### <2108 C.E.—the age of finesse><Earth Orbit>

Jessie jumped out into space and kicked his sister as far away from the Olympic space-station as he could, using the equivalent momentum to launch himself in the opposite direction and towards the space-station's outer walls. He knew not whether he would see her again, so he lingered for several moments before turning away. His mind drowned out the flashing warnings his terminal lenses about the Olympic station's evacuation protocol waves patched in, and he instead focused on the video-feed tracking his sister's movements. He watched somberly through his auto-zooming contact lenses as she floated out in space, soon lost into the all-encompassing dome of Earth below, disappearing from sight into the bright light of its grand blue oceans. He knew he could not follow her, as he had strapped his dive team's only reserve heat shield onto her harness, and his own suit would burst into flames immediately upon breaching the ozone of Earth.

Amidst explosions rocking the Olympic station one after the other like dominoes, Jessie hadn't had time to consider the full ramifications of this disaster. He had yet to think of the scope of damage, the loss of his parents, and the death of his team. *That will all have to wait.*

He was supposed to be down in the atmosphere of Earth, diving amongst his friends at a world-record speed, feeling the immense pressure of the interplanetary Olympics with the gold medal on the line. The worlds of man would have cheered his name and praised his team as champions. *But no, that had not happened… Instead, they had all died. And now my sister is gone too, although hopefully safe if not sound.*

Jessie pushed off the wall and focused forward in the direction of his momentum, signaling his terminal lenses to stop tracking Fenna's trajectory. He could see the Turian flower far, far away in the distance, hauntingly beautiful and frozen in its splendor, unlike the nearby Olympic station undergoing a flurry of destructive activity all around him. The faraway flower, composed mostly of docked spacecraft adding to its combined weight, had gained significant mass in a short span of time with so many people coming in for the games. Thus, it had been given great counterweight to extend many more elevator-tubes downwards towards Earth. Jessie was sure that it was hectic with activity from up close, but from so far away, the zero-gee orbital community looked yet serene and peaceful, completely unfazed by the chaos of the disaster taking place within view.

Now floating freely in space, Jessie realized even if he could somehow get all the way out to the Turian flower community—which was a big if, as it was, at this point, over a dozen miles away—there was no guarantee he would even manage to get inside of it. The crowds in evacuation and the rescue crews coming up were sure to create congestion unlike any the flower's space-elevators had ever seen before.

Jessie kicked off an incoming wall, redirected himself in space, and found himself floating between two disconnected branches of the Olympic station's previously single-helix hallway. There, he was surrounded by a scattering of gee-simulator spheres and still-flashing sections of corridors with semi-intact walls still adorned with posters of competing nations, interest groups, and official Olympic markings. However, as surreal as this was, most chilling of all were the dead bodies floating lifeless in the air, drifting through the vacuum of space like stray leaves on a pond.

Death hung everywhere, resonating through every obstacle Jessie pushed off of to gain control over his momentum, and, try as he might, he could no longer avoid acknowledging the extreme tragedy of this day. He shivered at the thought of his parents floating among the dead and of his teammates smashed beyond recognition. His eyes clouded over with liquid tears. His heart beat fast, his chest felt hollow, and his fine-tuned motor reflexes lost control. So, instead of letting his emotions overrun him, he made a conscious effort to push away all his thoughts into the deepest recess of his mind, put a shield over them, and insert them into a locked box with no key.

Jessie focused instead on the people he could see still around and alive, floating within the spreading space-station rubble—some safe, some seeking safety, some inside bubbles of air, and some left suffocating slowly as they struggled to find rescue. Several Olympia lift tubes nearby had burst open, which luckily provided relief to whoever could readily reach them, promising a path to the safety of breathable air deeper in the station. He passed close to a group of schoolchildren huddled together and hovering within a self-contained bubble, so he redirected himself with a kick off a wall to intersect.

"Look out guys. Hold tight." Jessie broadcast on all waves, warning the children moments before impacting hard and bouncing off their bubble like a billiard ball hitting another. He made sure to aim the kids out across unimpeded space and towards the closest station air-lift he could see safely sucking in survivors. As a result, he ricocheted outwards, further and further away from the possibility of a timely rescue.

The vast open spaces between the station's thick helix walls and the unpredictability of rubble gave Jessie a difficult time in navigation. Not only did he have to aim between far distances, hit moving targets, and avoid getting struck along the way, but he also had to think quickly upon the chance that an unknown variable could strike like lightning and change the entire environment around him fast.

Jessie floated alongside a sealed hallway wing of the Olympic station, gazing in at the strobe of red and blue alarm lights coming from within. Many people inside the hall were lost in panic, with absolutely no idea how to react to the situation. Thankfully, they were all still alive. Some had gotten themselves stuck floating in limbo without gravity, unable to reach a hand or foothold to kick off. Others used objects in their path as counterweights, throwing stuff aside to shift momentum and navigate across the room. Security guards and zero-gee athletes like him were inside organizing rescue efforts, urging children and parents to hold hands and keep together in a daisy-chain and float towards the safety of the tube-lift exits.

Jessie heard a hissing sound before he began to shift direction in the air, both of which seemed entirely improbable in the vacuum of space. The Olympic diver's wingsuit began to flutter, reacting to the flow of gas past him and gently nudging him around to face the wall directly. His heart nearly stopped when he saw the widening gap in its frame. The window beside him started to crackle with a pattern like a spider-web, spreading from the outside in. Right before his eyes, the room began to depressurize, leaking out an increasing tide of air. Free-floating survivors inside the hall started to shift in the air, pushed outwards towards the crack in the station.

*Shit!*

The flow of leaking air pushed Jessie further away from the Olympia hall and spun him back around to face a field of floating objects containing a plethora of random shrapnel. Picnic benches, hot-dog stands, tube capsules, patches of ripped ground and grass, water fountains, and an endless supply of wrapped snacks and foods began to flow in the same direction as him, pushed by the same flow of leaking air. Jessie continued to spin and turned back around just in time to see and feel a huge explosion rock the hall, engulfing it in whole.

A column of fire erupted through the pocket of blowing air, tearing through space and rubble and sending Jessie flying backwards, head over heels. The Olympic station's helical corridor crumbled in flame, and a shockwave rippled outwards, hitting Jessie and rubble alike and sending them all tumbling towards Earth below.

*Shit, shit, shit, SHIT!*

Without his heat-shield, Jessie felt the burn of the fire, withstanding the pain to utilize his flight-suit's form and maneuver himself in the friction-filled air. He shifted left and arched his back to avoid hitting a steaming plastic scooter, then tipping rightward to miss crashing through a metal sign. After spreading out his wings wide to pull him up, he shot past a white spherical chamber in the air still spinning with artificial gee. He turned himself around and caught onto a broken hatchway door floating past him, clasping its sides and standing upon it like a surfboard. He kneeled down and jumped off of it, kicking its mass behind him to push himself forward. From there, he caught the next object in his way, then the next, then the next, continuing to maneuver in zero-gee and bounce himself from broken surface to broken surface. He grasped onto railings, blocks of concrete, staircases, and chairs, throwing them behind him to maintain control over his momentum. By accident, he caught onto a dead body in his path and promptly threw it away in disgust, trying his hardest not think about how dire this tragedy was increasingly becoming.

Jessie hit a structure the size of a small cargo shuttle and clung on, choosing to rest a moment and appropriate the environment around him before kicking off and moving onwards. A bright yellow light shone out the structure's rectangular windows, signaling to Jessie that the free-floating chamber still had power streaming despite being completely disconnected from the main bulk of the space-station. Inspecting the room's exterior, he realized immediately its insides had been completely quarantined against any leak of water or air, with every circular exit valve cleanly disconnected from its source and shut tight against breach. *Hmm*, he thought. *Somebody had set up this room as a life raft. There could be people in there!*

Jessie latched himself onto the room with magnetized boots and gloves and began to crawl across its length towards a nearby window. Although it was small, musky, and largely fogged-up by steam, the window allowed Jessie to see the room's interior with enough detail to identify a pair of objects passively floating within.

Jessie's terminal lenses informed him to pay closer attention to the pair and suggested they resembled bodies, either dead or alive. He zoomed in and stared, realizing that his terminal was right. He hoped against all hope that he had not come too late. *One can only take* so *much emotional turmoil in a single day.*

Jessie knocked on the window. "Hello in there! Anybody!?" He broadcast on all waves. "Can anybody hear me!? Please respond!"

Nobody answered.

Jessie sighed and began to turn away. The looming Earth below was getting closer and closer, and the professional athlete knew his window for escaping its pull was growing shorter by the second. However, as he took one last look inside the room, Jessie saw something unnerving and uplifting both: the bodies had started to squirm.

"Hey!" he shouted. "Hey, are you ok? Are you stuck in there?"

An oversized top hat flew off the bigger of the two bodies as the smaller one disappeared from sight under a quick flash of blonde hair. The bigger body rotated backwards slowly, displaying features as lifeless as those of the corpses outside the chamber. A pool of crimson blood streamed out from his neck and face, coagulating like drips of rain coming together in a puddle.

"Tuk!" Jessie yelled in surprise before bending forward to press himself closer to the window. Two brilliant blue eyes with strains of yellow and green popped up before him, staring back deep into his own. Jessie jumped up in shock but was held in place by his magnetic boots and gloves. He forced himself to look back down and saw that the face behind the window was as scared as he, and that it belonged to a little girl no more than five years old.

"Who are you?" the girl asked very clearly through his terminal, betraying a voice very young and frightened.

Jessie pressed himself closer to the window. "Hi there," he replied gently. "My name is Jessie. How about you?"

"Cil'ette," the little girl said, looking him deep in the eyes. She pressed her palm up against the window, revealing a faint red tattoo of a circle subdivided with eight Ionic pillars. Jessie's terminal lenses started to pixelate and blur, and then the whole world of chaos disappeared around him. It felt good… and, well, *distracting* from the horrible truths of the day.

# 5 : reaction :

**"Despite all our meticulous recordings, memories have proven a difficult unit to appropriate."**
—Transcripts of William

<11:45:12 a.s.t.>**<day 1>**<Anok>

Fre'dd Invictus waited under the cooling shade of the teardrop shaped land-pod, contemplating the turmoil of the day. For a gladiator with a simple, organized life, this open-ended break of routine felt unbelievable at best. Earlier this morning, he was home within the empire of Mars, summoned exclusively to the shifting fortress of Ares Prime by the established semi-regime of Turian Technologies for exclusive consideration into their service. The gladiator had known that the far-reaching eyes of the Turians did not strike upon an independent gladiator such as him very often, and he had certainly known the monetary rewards and fame could have served as his golden ticket out of the Aren'A. Soon, Fre'dd had hoped, he might never have had to see the bright pits of competition ever again. Although he would always be Aren born, the idea of a peaceful life away from the empty days of blind fighting had been too tempting to ignore. He had seen a tunnel which he had never even known to exist illuminate before him—one filled with thoughts of freedom—and he could no more ignore it than he could pretend to enjoy his fighting lifestyle. So, he had accepted their deal and gone in for a scan of his person, knowing all the while that something could go horribly wrong.

Fre'dd had always known that, in essence, he was nothing but a human product of engineering, genetically cultured and bred for operational victory over many generations of modified evolution and motherless births. He had spent a lifetime training for skills that prepared him for nothing but an artificial, spectacled battleground, competing within the confines of a semi-illusionary circular showground—not as a slave like the gladiators of old, and not with the threat of death or permanent disfigurement looming over his head, but nonetheless as a dog in a cage. His existence had always orbited about his fights, their various outcomes, and the frugality with which he had to live.

The Martian gladiator had lived his life in a narrow cone, like a self-aware horse with blinders over his eyes and a muzzle over his mouth. Even if he did ever manage to get out of the Aren'A lifestyle, he would have no idea how to function outside of the context of his Martian home. Truth be told, he had always had a severe lack of exposure in anything other than the competition itself, which, in itself, would never transfer well into the real world. Up until now, this had meant that no matter how far Fre'dd pushed, he could never quite distance himself from the realm of the Martian Aren'A—although maybe now with the help of the technological Turians, he finally could. At least, that's what he had thought half a day ago.

As Fre'dd now sat ruminating upon a planet alien to him, he fiddled with a rock in his hands, allowing its warmth and gritty texture to bring his mind back to his home of Mars. *Will I ever hold a Martian rock in these same hands again? Given the chance, would I even want to? Despite all rationality, perhaps yes I would...*

Fre'dd lifted the blue liquid-tube around his neck and brought it up to his mouth. He clamped down upon its pliant skin with his teeth and took in a deep gulp of water, emptying it of its contents. The gladiator looked up into the turquoise blue sky.

"Poseidon gratias," he muttered. "Your water leaves me refreshed."

The sound of salt crackled on the ground. Fre'dd looked down in surprise and found a short man with a thick goatee and a set of pale eyes standing before him, wide-jawed in shock. The man held something blue in his hands. Fre'dd stood up, towering high over the stranger.

"Are you *really* here?" the small man asked instead of a proper introduction. His eyes looked dazed, as if he were caught in a dream. "Or are you coming from my tucking pazz!?"

"What do you mean?" Fre'dd sat back down to see the man better. "I do not understand."

"Are you an illusion?" the goateed man asked, clearly as confused as he. "Is this all just a big joke meant to mess with my mind?"

"Non puto," Fre'dd replied as honestly as he could. "I think not, but truly cannot be sure. I am called Fre'dd—that is all that I can know for certain."

The other man took his time considering this answer. Accepting the fact that he had awakened upon an alien world was certainly no easy task, even for Fre'dd. He recognized the serious rumble in the man's pale eyes, the disbelief of reality as he himself suffered only hours earlier. However, whether this sun-drenched land was real or whether it was an illusion did not seem to matter in the least. Even if this was no actual perpetuation of real life, it was all still serious, and those who had awakened here had no choice but to face what they found before them. *Just like life in the Aren'A.*

"The world is empty," the goateed man whispered, shaking in aggravation and muttering out a string of barely intelligible words. "Everything is so... dark."

The explorer Enri—another small man Fre'dd had met this very day—chose that moment to step out of the damaged land-pod, with pants drenched in blood and an evidently heavy heart pumping within him. As he strode out onto salty soil, casting a puff of purple dust with every step forward, Enri looked sad, introspective, and far too busy in thought to notice that Fre'dd had been in the middle of a conversation. He held in his hands a belt very much like Fre'dd's own but made in a completely different fashion, with strange circular outputs lining its girth and swiveling joints which rocked back and forth as Enri stepped down the land-pod's rungs. He folded the belt gently and placed it within his knapsack with a reverence that Fre'dd respected.

It took the usually observant explorer several seconds before he took notice of the goateed, pale-eyed man standing beside the seated gladiator—and he nearly jumped out of his skin when he did.

"Chaos behold! Who're you?" Enri exclaimed.

"Ranke FourtySeven, active and ready," the man answered like a soldier stepping into line. He squinted at Enri as if he had mistaken him for someone else.

"Cool... I'm Enri."

"I know you! You're a TurTechnicks moderator!" Ranke sputtered. "You're the one with the plans... the one with answers!"

"Wait… TurTek? You think I'm with them? Listen, I don't know why they put us here either."

"No, no! You lie!" Ranke wailed aloud. "Yes, I know you!. You're a company man, a *representative*! You're the only one of us who knows what's going on around here. Tell me now! Where in the Hades are the godsdamn, tukking pixels hiding?"

"Hey, hey, calm down! I'm in the same boat as you, man." Enri stepped closer and noticed a hazy white glow in Ranke's eyes. "I want answers too… We've just gotta stick together and find them!"

"Oh, don't feed me that line of taurshit!" Ranke FourtySeven demanded. "Give me back my PIXELS!"

"Whoa there, buddy. I dunno what you're on about, but let's keep this in perspective—we're all in this together."

The goateed man looked away.

"You hungry?" Enri asked. "Need something to eat or drink?"

"No."

"What's that you're holding?" Enri pointed at the rubbery blue object in Ranke's palm.

"See for yourself," the man said, throwing it over. Enri caught it and gaped.

"Holy light of Olympus!" he exclaimed. "Is this…"

"Yeah," Ranke replied, "impossible. TurTechnicks is tukking with us, trying to see who is stupid enough to believe their tricks!"

"What?" Fre'dd asked. "What is it?"

"It's a blue plant!" Enri explained, tossing him the turquoise ball. "An alien life-form!"

"Yeah right!" Ranke laughed. "That's exactly what they want us to think! Now I know you're not really a representative—you're way too dumb."

"Ok, well, we'll deal with all that later," Enri said. "Right now, we still have work to do."

"The hells are you talking about?" Ranke shot back.

"What was your land-pod's letter?" Enri ignored the man's evident agitation and moved onward to the continual task of finding other survivors. "This one was B, mine was E…"

"What the tuk!" Ranke exclaimed.

Fre'dd thought for a moment. "The letter F," he replied.

"Okay, that means that there are at least six pods out there, including ours," Enri deduced. "How about you?" he asked Ranke. "What was your land-pod letter?"

"What? You're asking about my gods-damn pod letter!? Don't you have more important things on your mind?"

"This is pretty important. Based on the letters, we are probably not the only people here. The more information we have, the clearer our picture will be."

Ranke filed his teeth in frustration. "Fine," he relented, "I'll tell you my gods-damn story! I was in New York City, floating like an idiot in TurTechnicks tank number 24 but at least enjoying full visibility of the worldwide net. The lights were bright, the city was active, the pazz swirled with power, and everything was fine." He huffed. "Then, in the blink of an eye, the net was gone and I was here, floating like an even bigger idiot in godsdamn land-pod H, all alone in a power-dark world of no light! And then this big guy was sitting here like Hercules incarnate, shining brighter than a gods-damned Turian flower in the sky. Why does he have so many pixels when I have none!?"

"H," Enri pondered aloud as he ignored the goateed man's attitude. "That means there are at least eight pods overall," he deduced. "Given the three of us and him…"

Enri gestured towards the pod behind him. "There should be at least four more land-pods filled with four more survivors... or bodies at the very least."

"If there are more pods out there, they're running empty on power, just like this one," Ranke replied. He pointed. "It's dead as a rock, unlike Hercules here."

"What direction did you come from?" Enri asked, pulling out his terminal and holding it up to the sky. It pulled power from the sun quickly, buzzing with energy and charging up its reserves.

Ranke FourtySeven pointed across to a slope shining bright with sunlight reflecting off of salt crystals. The sun had risen higher up above them in the sky, bright as ever with an impossibly scorching light. Enri saw nothing but glare. He climbed up a nearby stack of rocks to gain a better view, ignoring the pain of his hands burning upon contact. His perch was shaky, but his perspective gave him a wide vantage of the wasteland below, allowing his still-waking terminal a chance to assist him in environmental analysis. It took some time for it to respond to his gestures, and, once ready, it let out a moan halfway between a satisfied grunt and a yawn.

"Huuuaaaahh!" it exhaled. "Good morning, folks! Reception is still down; I can't find anything out there!"

"You're using a handheld?" Ranke FourtySeven scoffed. "What are you, an ancient?"

"Hold on," Enri instructed. "Let's look up the spire. The other pods could be further up." He turned around precariously, careful to keep balanced in his stance, and held his terminal up to encompass the colossal view of the wave-spire stretching up into the heavens. Using his clear-screened device to telescope his sight, Enri zoomed in on one of the wave-spire's vertical finger-like tendrils, hoping to gain a better understanding of the landmark. Panning upwards, he was disappointed to find that even with his terminal's highest resolution filters on, the grand mountain's peak remained unseen, seemingly fading away into the sky. *How high up does it really go?*

A sense of prescient foreboding arose within Enri's innards, mixing his avid curiosity with a hint of something deeper—something along the lines of fulfilling an unknown destiny. *But no, that would be ridiculous!*

Lost in the sights of his telescoped terminal screen, the explorer spotted a curious change in the coloring of rocks. Above a certain height, the mountain turned from purple to blue almost as if splashed with paint. The red rock tendrils several miles away curled suspiciously into turquoise, transitioning fast and seemingly out of nowhere. Enri zoomed in further, trying to understand. *What is going on with this wave-spire!?*

"Hey, yeah, look!" Enri found something among the purple and blue—a reflection of colorful light from far away. His terminal pinpointed it automatically, recognizing its abnormality from the rest of the environment, and it attempted to reduce the image's glare in lieu of a more comprehensive image. The picture came through grainy at best, but its crimson color was unmistakable. "That's definitely another land-pod up there!"

"It has energy!" Ranke exclaimed. "It's not dead like this one!"

Enri's terminal image went dark. "Gah! What now!?" he shouted, gazing up at the spire with his own bare eyes. Sure enough, the wave-spire above him had gone dark with shadow, and, more than that, the shade was coming down at them. The line of darkness raced fast down the mountain over slope and ground.

"Grace of Olympus!" Fre'dd yelled, pointing up in the other direction. "The sun is eclipsing!"

Almost directly above them, the teal star above was rising into an upside-down sunset. Shining its final moment like a gem in the sky, the sun fluttered through a brilliant array of colors. Then, just like that, it was gone, leaving the three men standing in twilight.

"This place is dead. Let's get our asses out of here," Ranke declared. "I know one place with power... Let's go to it."

Enri nodded his agreement. He realized that it was about to get very cold, very fast. "No sun means no heat, and open spaces mean bad news."

"Apollo has left us," Fre'dd sobbed. "The gods are angry at our plight."

"Well, if that's the case, where do you think one should go to change the gods' minds?" Enri asked.

"Mount Olympus?"

"Yes, Mount Olympus. But it's very far away, so we should get going."

"Yeah, yeah, Olympus my ass!" Ranke scoffed. "Let's just get the hells out of here!"

<25:37:22 a.s.t.>

The shining red land-pod marked "A" held two strangers inside—a man with a top hat and a woman with a turtle-shell backpack, both of whom looked equally surprised and relieved to see Enri, Fre'dd and Ranke as they came upon them.

Ranke FourtySeven, on the other hand, had reacted badly. He lunged forward like a lunatic and the top-hatted man evaded, quickly disappearing out of sight. Fre'dd ran after him, and Enri stayed behind, hoping to figure out what exactly was going on.

"Get him back here now!" Ranke shouted. Donning the face of a madman, he clutched the woman standing beside him, grabbing her by the pit of her neck and pulling her backwards like a hostage. He spotted a pair of pneumatic pickaxes sheathed inside her pack and pulled them both out, tossing one aside and holding the other up as a weapon.

"I'll do it! I swear, I will!" the goateed man yelled aloud, shouting up into the sky as if daring the gods to strike him down. "Get that godsdamn TurTecknicks representative back here!"

"What are you doing!?" Enri exclaimed. "Put her down, man!"

"I'm telling you, get that slimy rep back here, NOW! I want off this Tartarus-cursed, blacked-out rock!"

"You're being irrational! I promise you we'll get him back!" Enri vowed. "Once Fre'dd chases him down, we will sit the man down and ask him all the questions we want to know. But please, just let her go! She has nothing to do with him!"

"How do *you* know that!? Are you admitting that you're on the inside track too?"

"What inside track? I'm in the same boat as you, man. Believe me, I want answers just as bad. The TurTek Rep has a lot to explain, but threatening others is not going to solve anything!"

"*He* got me into this. It is all *his* fault!" Ranke shouted. "And *her*! She's with him." He tightened his grip on the woman and brought her own pickaxe closer to her throat. She tightened her lips with an expression that showed annoyance, slight anger, a little bit of curiosity, and not a hint of fear.

Enri was taken aback by this woman's nonchalance. Standing at the end of a knife in the hands of a lunatic, she looked only slightly irritated. Enri's heart fluttered in surprise as she looked up at him and winked. The goateed man tightened his grip and pulled her backwards.

"Listen buddy," Enri urged, "I know what you're going through. It's hard to know who to trust, but, believe me, you have to start somewhere."

"Ha! *Trust?*" Ranke ridiculed. "Who *trusts* a computer program? Only a fool, that's who!"

"Hey, come on!" Enri's terminal protested from within his knapsack. "That's insulting!"

"Shut up, shut up!" Ranke demanded. "Just get that damn TurTechnicks rep here now!"

His eyes darted about like hummingbirds and his pupils faded to naught under a white glaze. His wits had fallen past the point of no return, and his sense of reality hung as low as Enri had ever seen. Although the explorer truly didn't know the crazed man enough to make a good judgment call, he could see that something in Ranke's mind had gone very wrong and that his fuse had blown. The goateed man's whitened eyes looked to be searching, forever searching, seeking something that did not seem to exist. His face was pale, and his expression reeked of a void, leaving no room for rational sanity.

"I'll slice her up. I will!" He pulled the woman's hair to expose her neck. "Just tell the Rep to send me home!"

"Enough!" the woman spoke up loudly, talking for the first time since Ranke had grabbed hold. "Your anger is noted, but your outburst is ridiculous. Let me go now before it's too late for either of us to apologize."

"Shut up, HARPY!" Ranke laughed off the woman's words, trying without success to hide his shaking hands. He gulped. "You're not *real*, don't pretend. You're just another illusion like the rest of them."

"Yeah? Prove it."

"You want me to slice your throat!?" Ranke cursed. "Lady, I'll send you right back to your tukking TurTechnicks aether if you don't watch it! Would that be proof enough for you?" His glossed over eyes made him look like a dead man walking. Even his veins were bulging white instead of red, maintaining a surreal lack of pigmentation defying all biological reason. He twitched and shook like a drug-addict in withdrawal.

Enri tried to rationalize with the man. "Ranke, please. What will hurting anyone really accomplish? Let her go and we'll figure this all out together."

"Ranke?" the woman asked, suddenly bemused. "Of the Hands?"

The crazed man snapped back to reality. "What of it?" he demanded.

"Number?"

"FourtySeven," he replied, slightly loosening hold around the woman's neck.

She grabbed his wrist and glanced down at the tattoo imprinted across it.

"Stop that!" he shouted, slapping away her hand and pressing her pickaxe closer up to her throat. "You're trying to trick me; they're all trying to trick me!"

"Last warning," the woman told her captor. "Ten seconds; stop or be stopped."

"Hahahaha, WHAT?" the crazed man laughed.

"Ten, nine, eight, seven, six," the woman started counting.

"Stopped    by    what!?"    Ranke    demanded. "TurTechnicks? Pazz?"

"Five, four, three."

"Where is thy power here, harpy?" Ranke FourtySeven shouted, pulling further back to keep her off balance. "Where is thy power?"

"Oh, for Earth's sake!" the woman sighed. "I warned you... kinda." She elbowed him in the diaphragm and knocked the wind out of his chest. Ranke had no chance to react before she spun around and, in a single fluid motion, grabbed his pickaxe-wielding hand, fighting back his grip and slicing his palm in the process.

She moved much more deliberately than he as she fought for control of the weapon. Just as Ranke's eyes had begun to widen in shock, she lunged his bleeding hand with the pickaxe straight into his throat and then twisted. Ranke FortySeven's eyes stayed open in complete disbelief as blood curdled from his neck. He slumped over, falling down onto the ground.

"Holy TUK!" Enri screamed in shock as Ranke's body twitched uncontrollably on the ground, shivering back and forth in the throes of death.

The woman kicked him away in disgust. She looked up at Enri and grinned, gazing playfully into Enri's eyes with a sense of familiarity.

"Well, what now?" she asked.

"Huh?" he bumbled uncertainly, overcome with skittering nerves. *Who was she?* He stumbled backwards, distancing himself from the horror.

The violent woman squinted, frowning at his reaction, and held up her bloodied pneumatic pickaxe calmly. She flicked a button on its hilt so that it buzzed to life, whirring its blade in and out of the air with speed enough for the blood upon it to poof away in a cloud of red mist. She clicked it back off, sheathed it back onto her belt, and walked over to its twin, which had been knocked onto the dirt by Ranke in his attack.

"What's wrong with you?" she asked with mild annoyance and an inexplicable familiarity.

"You…" Enri said, barely able to talk. "You killed him!"

"Well, yeah," she replied smartly as she knelt down to pick up the second blade. "He was a damned Hand; we're way better off without him. You know that."

"Hand?" Enri asked. "We…?"

"Yeah Enri, a godsdamn *Hand*!" the woman exclaimed. "A godsdamn, pazz-addled, broken-minded Hand who was—if you weren't paying attention before—holding my own pneumatic dagger up against me! He wasn't even using it right, that idiot. At least now his gear can serve us some legitimate use!" She gestured down at the body with her second pickaxe in hand.

"Uu-using what right?" Enri stuttered, overcome by an involuntary shiver.

"My dagger!" the woman barked back, waving it at him before sheathing it on her belt opposite its twin. "Gods, Earthling, you gone green or something? What're you doing just standing there, huh? You should be the first person to advocate searching a wreck for any recoverable scrap!"

"Earthling? Scrap? Wh-who are you? How do you know me?"

The look of familiarity vanished from the woman's eyes. She stepped forward and grabbed his right hand with her own, bringing the tattoo on his wrist up close for inspection. Her own TurTek tattoo was absent upon her wrist, but, after a quick check, he located it below her opposite hand. It looked slightly different than his own and lighter in appearance.

Frowning and pulling up Enri's wrist closer to her face for a better view, the woman traced the eye-shaped TurTek logo's lower left edge with her fingers and located within it the tiny Roman Numerals MMLXVIII—the year

2068. Her teeth gritted, and her eyes flashed colors that Enri could not understand. Then she dropped his hand with a reluctant sigh. All hint of her former warmth had vanished, leaving behind a wary stranger wrapped in violent mystery.

"You can call me Fenna," she whispered in Enri's ear as she stepped past him, softly trailing her bloody hand across his shoulder. Her hard-tipped shoes clanked as she climbed up the metal rungs of the land-pod nearby, and its hatch door slammed behind her.

Enri was left alone, staring at Ranke FourtySeven's now-still body on the ground, watching the pool of blood around it grow wider and thinner before absorbing down into the dirt. The dead man's clothing was loose and black, so clearly unfit for this desert environment that he must have suffered well and hard from the overwhelming heat and cold, no doubt aiding his evident mental degeneration. Kneeling down to take a closer look, Enri saw that the fabric up and down Ranke's legs, arms, and torso wasn't just baggy, but also strangely bumpy. He chose to search further and determine what exactly was causing this bumpiness, despite the unpleasant nature of such a task. Although Enri was still skeptical of the mysterious Fenna's actions, she had not been wrong about his motivations; he was certainly not one to let a dead man's things go to waste!

Enri reached out and poked Ranke's corpse lightly, letting the fact that the man was dead settle in his mind as the stench of iron-rich blood became too strong to ignore. He felt the solid objects underneath the fabric and confirmed that Ranke's clothing had pockets lining its every corner, easily accessible through magnetically-shut linings. Some were empty, some were full, and most were filled with objects useless to Enri, like money, trinkets, and databank cards, all which he still placed aside for later perusal. The suit itself had finer detail than Enri had realized, with battery strips embedded throughout it and webbed wire patterns both symmetrical and even.

Ever the explorer and, in this case, a survivalist, Enri was glad to find TurTek-produced food bars and water tubes in several of the pockets. Throughout his life, many rough expeditions had relied on the access to food and water, so Enri was relieved the grand corporation that brought them here had at least given them that. Around Ranke's wrist, Enri found a thin, elastic terminal clamped like a band. Rotating it around on the arm, Enri found a small logo that he could not recognize embedded within— a white, three-dimensional emblem of a hand. *Strange that so unique a make and model could have slipped my notice entirely,* he thought, puzzled. Enri slid the wristband terminal off the dead man's arm and looked at the wrist. He could see a dozen or so grid-lined puncture wounds on the skin beneath Ranke's tattoo, each the size of a mere pinprick and specked with dried blood.

"What in the hells...?" Enri asked nobody in particular, muttering aloud as he meddled with the rubbery terminal wristband in his hands and recognized which part of it had been adjacent to the pricked region of Ranke's wrist: the embedded logo of a tiny white hand. The explorer manipulated the terminal under his fingers, warping its rubbery surface until he found a small grid of holes indented within it. Inside, he identified a thin layer of micro-pins budding out from underneath the hand logo. *It's an injector,* Enri realized, startled. *A drug cartridge of some sort!*

The explorer's mind raced with questions. *What substance had Ranke been systematically injecting into himself to warrant such a thing? Had it been for the dead man's health, for an addiction of his, or had it simply been a tool of his trade? Whatever trade that may have been.*

Enri poked the terminal, feeling at the tiny pins with his fingertip, but quickly pulled it away as he felt a quick shiver like an electric shock run up his arm. *Godsdamnit!* he thought as the lights dimmed around his eyes and his heart beat quickened at the guilt of his own irresponsible clumsiness. *I hope I didn't just infect myself with something!*

Enri pushed away the thought and tossed Ranke's wristband terminal device into his knapsack for later perusal, picking up from the ground several other choice items and stashing them in his sack beside it. Once satisfied that he had supplied himself with all he could take, Enri stretched his weary joints and stood up, spinning around slowly to take in the environment around him. The crimson land-pod that had come with the TurTek Rep was back-lit by the light of the blue sun—which had reappeared on the opposite side of the sky eight hours or so after disappearing in eclipse. He had named the upper sunset "sunout" and the star's reemergence "sunsink," logging their timestamps and relative celestial coordinates in order to chart Anok's day/night cycle in full.

Enri looked up the gigantic spire on which he, the land-pod, and everything else for acres around stood, gazing all the way up to where it faded gently into the Prussian-blue sky above. Its sheer size was beyond comprehension, seemingly rising up past eternity, like a natural-rock Turian flower elevator rising up to space. The thought of scaling it to find out what lay above both excited and unnerved Enri beyond belief. *But before that,* he knew, *there are still plenty of questions that need answers.*

Beyond where Enri stood and onwards, the mountain held an abundance of vegetation—spongy, blue, and completely unknown in nature to the fascinated explorer. He hadn't had the time or facilities to analyze the flora with much detail, which made his curiosity towards the matter almost intolerable. This environment was foreign enough he knew to make no assumptions whatsoever. *Nothing unknown should ever be taken for granted*, Enri told himself.

With the corpse of his short-lived human companion lying splayed at his feet and the world around him incomprehensibly alien, the incessant explorer felt his gut overcome with a queasy uncertainty. Here he was on an alien planet like those in his wildest dreams, but instead of being allowed to research and document his discoveries, Enri had been made to act as a survivalist, a hostage negotiator, and, of course, a scavenger of the dead.

The fact that extraterrestrial life forms existed all around him could mean so many things in the long run. *Could there be more than just plants here? Could there be animals roaming about or bacteria in the air?* For all Enri knew, his immune system could already be doomed due to the foreign contaminants, or he himself could already be contaminating this entire ecosystem simply by being here. *Either way, there is not much I can do about it at the moment.*

Enri pulled his terminal out of his knapsack and turned downhill, lifting it up to look at the view through its screen. The long shadow of the wave-spire around him obscured miles of desert landscape but faded far into the distance, thus compromising any accurate extrapolation of its true height. So instead, Enri chose to direct his attention out into the valley below, using his high vantage point to his advantage and returning his focus to the possibility of other survivors.

"What'ch you doing?" Enri's terminal piped in, hoping to help.

"Hold on," he instructed, pointing the device in the approximate direction of his own land-pod far, far below. He clutched its outer edges and forced them apart slowly, physically pulling the terminal's pliable frame outward to give its screen a panoramic aspect-ratio. "Sweep and stabilize," he told it. "Find me the pods."

"It'd help if you put me down first. You're shaking like a shuttle breaching orbit!" his terminal replied.

Enri chose a nice stable rock with a good vantage point and propped his terminal up. "Make it as high-res as possible," he requested. "Scan for anything unnatural."

"Yup, yup!" his terminal chirped. "Just step back and lemme do my thing; It's gonna take a few seconds of long exposure."

Enri stepped back.

"Okay, done!" the terminal exclaimed.

Enri picked it up and walked over to the nearby land-pod to sit upon its bottommost rung.

"Got anything?" He looked through the screen to analyze the captured image. The terminal scanned through the wide landscape to visually locate any artificial-looking protrusions standing out from amongst the rocks. After scrolling through several dozen "objects of note" (most of which turned out to be no more interesting than abnormally-large rocks casting long shadows), Enri realized he would need to refine his search a bit lest he wanted to sit there all day. Finding a manmade object in the vast alien desert was like finding a needle in a haystack times a thousand; there was simply far too much area to cover.

"Can't you narrow these results a bit?" he asked his terminal.

"Yeah, sure. On what parameters?" the device replied questioningly. "I can't make results come out of nothing—I'm not a wizard, you know!"

"The glare; try for glare," Enri suggested. "See if anything is reflecting sunlight—sharp, not glimmer."

"Okay, inputted!" the terminal chirped. "And I've got hits!" Five separate land-pods appeared on Enri's screen from separate sections of the larger image capture, scattered over miles of slope and plain.

"Damn," Enri muttered, pointing to the images one by one. "Those are all accounted for already. Mine, Fre'dd's, Ranke's, Fenna's... Dirk's."

"Okay, inputted!" the terminal twittered, labeling the images with the titles he had given them. "There's something else, though, that you might want to see," it said, bringing up a new image. Much to Enri's surprise, he recognized the gargantuan man who came into view and the three colored necklaces shining bright around his neck. Slung over his shoulder was a much smaller man holding beneath him a top hat equally recognizable to Enri even in shaded silhouette.

Enri jumped up and held out his terminal. "Switch to a live feed," he told it. "Find me Fre'dd!" The image on the screen disappeared, leaving it transparent. The view magnified into the close distance, leading Enri's eyes several dozen yards out to where Fre'dd was walking. The TurTek representative was silently bouncing up and down over his shoulder, not unconscious but making no motion at all to struggle. His ever-present Pandora's hat was clutched tight beneath him, swinging back and forth under the momentum of Fre'dd's lofty steps. The two men were soon close enough for Enri to see them through his own eyes, so he put down his terminal and looked forward, noting how bright Fre'dd's blue, yellow, and red necklaces shone around his neck.

"Where've you been?" Enri asked Fre'dd. "You were gone forever!"

"We had a little chat," the TurTek representative on Fre'dd's shoulder explained.

Fre'dd lowered the smaller man graciously and gently placed him down on the ground. The large man noticed the trail of blood coming out from the land-pod and began to follow it along the ground, finding Ranke's body lying dead in the dirt. He howled out in unimaginable pain, shaking the ground around him with the force of his powerful voice.

# 6 : desire :

**"The tools brought matter less than the skills learned through adaptation."**
-Transcripts of William

### <29:22:04 a.s.t.><day 1><Anok>

"We're clones!?" Fenna yelled at the TurTek Rep, perhaps a bit too passionately for Enri to believe the authenticity of her surprise.

"No, technically not clones, but rather perfect duplicates," the company representative explained as he sat on top of his land-pod's plastic cubby and put up a hand to hold his hat steady. "Biological clones are born in the same way as are natural humans—developing from an egg to an embryo, through childbirth and infancy to adolescence and adulthood—while we, on the other hand were not *born* at all. We were all *made*. The four of us were *created* as exact copies of original human beings, constructed in replica of their true bodies, minds, muscular compositions, cellular structures, neural connections, feedback loops, even down to the electrical flow through their brains and the memories of their pasts."

"So we're not even real human beings anymore, right?" Fenna posed with fire in her tone. "You're saying we're all *fake*, just like little tukking manmade *toys?*"

"No—of course not—we are nothing like toys!" the TurTek representative exclaimed, as if the analogy caught him by surprise. "Everything about us is perfectly human, just artificially reconstructed from the sub-atomic level up. Other than the man-made technology that created us, we are all four completely identical to our organic original selves and, thus, just as identifiably human."

"Pshh," Fenna smirked. "So says a TurTukking liar! For all we know, we could all be hooked up to some godsdamn machine network right now, being fed images up the virtual wazoo. TurTechnicks could have injected me with tukking pazz and left my body sitting in some corner somewhere, rotting from the inside out!"

"I am here, and I am Fre'dd. That is no illusion!" the former Martian gladiator insisted from behind her. "How I got here matters not."

"Exactly—no illusion there, indeed!" the Rep agreed with gusto, spreading a porcelain smile wide across his face. He fiddled with the hat on his head, making himself comfortable on his cubby. "Our bodies are exactly as we remember them, as are the minds in which our thoughts are assembled. This planet, this landscape, and everything else we see around us is as real as we perceive it to be. Rest assured that our mission here is far more important than some heedless simulation!"

"So this people-duplication process you say we went through…" Enri interjected, tired of the workaround but fascinated by the possibilities. "Seems kinda far-fetched, no? How would something like that work?"

"Oh yes, far-fetched indeed," the TurTek Rep admitted with pride. "And the technology involved spans far wider than solely duplicating the human form. It has the potential to remake anything at all, given the right blueprints. If you had only lived through the long decades of strife in which the goal of base atomic recomposition had seemed to conflict with the known laws of elementary physics, this would all seem ever-the-more impossible... But it has nonetheless come to develop and pass, and, thus, we are all here."

"Ok, ok," Fenna cut him off. "Wouldn't it have been much easier to just ship us over here, wherever this dreadful tukking place is, exactly?"

"At the level it took to get us where we are, there was surely no such thing as easy," the representative explained. "But the idea of using molecular reconstruction to bridge the gap of space and time had always appeared the most reasonable option when it came to matching a desired end-result predictably."

"What the tuk does that mean?" Fenna barked back, unsatisfied with the explanation.

"Well, it's just like printing something out from a terminal record, just on the atomic scale," the Rep proclaimed. "Throw the right amount of protons, electrons, and neutrons in the right direction at the right speed, energy, and degree of fluctuation, and you can make anything down to its exact specifications, barring substances above a certain level of instability or too large a unified size. Given the digital records from the quark-scans that each of our original selves took back home, TurTek can recreate our exact forms perfectly every single time, no matter how far away they need us or how long it takes to get there."

"Now you're saying we're printouts?" Fenna laughed sarcastically. "Yay, great...I've always wanted to be compared to a scrap of paper!"

"You say that TurTek *created* us, that it printed us out specifically to come here..." Enri extrapolated. "But how did we get onto this planet, really?" He couldn't yet understand the feelings in his heart, but, as long as he got the right information, perhaps he could clarify the endless confusion in his mind. "Did TurTek mass-manufacture us on a space-station or something and shoot us down here to thaw out?"

"Oh no, not at all." The Rep laughed. "Although I wouldn't dare say that such methods hadn't been experimented with in TurTek's past. But no, we ourselves were alchemized on the spot—so to speak—as our land-pods captured energy from breaching this planet's ozone."

"Zeus, what does that even mean?" Enri asked with increasing curiosity. "We simply materialized straight into our tanks? How is that even possible?"

"Yes indeed!" the Rep exclaimed. "Each patented TurTek land-pod is equipped with an inception tank and a set of duplicator cubbies!" He tapped happily on the plastic seating of the cubby beneath him. "This ensures that, given enough energy, matter, and molecular blueprints from the TurTek databanks, those who wake up on the planet have access to recreate anything needed."

"Holy wow!" Enri exclaimed. "You mean we can materialize anything on record from out of these cubbies?" He turned around and looked up at the ring in the ceiling where the bio-tank had retracted. "What about people? Can we still make more of them?"

"Theoretically, yes," the Rep explained. "The land-pods tanks are still able to perform their functions exactly as designed, but that does not mean their internal batteries have enough energy to power a complex recreation like a live human body. For that, it would most likely require a chain of active nuclear reactions and a heavy flow of gaseous matter. However, our solar-charging batteries certainly do have enough power to spark up the cubbies and duplicate any supplies we need, given that we wait for the recharges."

"That is amazing!" Enri almost felt overwhelmed. "Although, you know, doesn't this all mean that there is some copy of each of us—err…some original self— somewhere out there, walking and talking and living out their lives as per usual, as if we never even existed?"

"Very astute," the TurTek Rep admitted, "but no, not necessarily. As you may have realized by now, this planet is nowhere near Earth—in fact, it is far, far away. The Deep Space vessel that would have had to bring our blueprint information through the galaxy to get here must have taken nearly a millennium to cross the stars… So no, our original selves are probably no longer living out their lives as per usual."

"Tuk, ok…" Enri muttered under his breath, thinking the consequences of this notion through. He sat down on the rubber-bristled ground, allowing himself time to take it all in. "So our original selves would be dead and gone by now, along with everyone else any of us has ever known."

"Yes," the Rep agreed. "We are far removed from any old life remembered."

"Excuse me, officium," Fre'dd asked gently. "If we are no longer near our own Sol, can you tell us where we are?"

"Why yes, Mr. Invictus, yes indeed," the TurTek representative replied eagerly. "We are on a planet called Anok, at least 50 light years further down the Orion spur of the Milky Way than Sol."

"Yeah well, wherever we are, we're stuck on this Taur-hole for good," Fenna complained. "There's no return trip for us in the books… unless we all want to die out in space."

"Correct—there is only going forward for us now," the TurTek Rep admitted. "Of course, this was always to be the expense of such a large exploratory effort, which is why our original selves would have all had to sign off on such a category of expedition following their molecular bio-scans. Rest assured they received full compensation for their services—and that once we culminate our preliminary efforts in our own mission, we will have full matching compensation and access to the TurTek credits in their personal long-range accounts."

"What the *TUK*!?" Fenna barked. She grabbed the TurTek Rep by his collar, pulling him up against the curved metal wall. His bulking top hat fell down onto the rubber-ridged floor.

*"COMPENSATION!?"* she yelled in anger. "Our entire lives are over—don't you get that already!? Who gives a *SIREN'S CALL* about our gods-damn compensation!? We're never going back home, no matter what we do! We're stuck here for life, and it's all thanks to your precious tukking, self-righteous TurTechnicks!"

The TurTek representative kept his porcelain smile locked across his face as he answered. "No, that presumption is simply not true. It's based entirely on misinterpretation. How can our lives be over when in truth they have only just begun? Yesterday, our bodies were nothing more than particles of dust scattered in the wind—they simply did not yet exist. Without the mission that we have been assigned, none of us would have ever come into being in the first place. Discounting that fact discounts your own existence and, incidentally, discounts the very thought which thinks it."

Fenna eased off and backed away, allowing the TurTek Rep to straighten his suit and pick his hefty Pandora's hat up off the ground. "You expect us to be grateful for being reanimated straight into a desert wasteland?" she asked. "Psh, as if!"

"Alright." Enri stood back up to face the company representative. "So can you tell us why we are here? If we do believe everything you have said—and that is a *big* if—that still leaves the issue of what exactly TurTek expects us to do once we get here."

"Well, Mr. Riatu, phase one is easy, so to speak. Our preliminary assignment is to explore the local environment and find what we can, establishing a baseline assessment of how friendly this planet would be for human life."

"What makes you think that any of *us* would follow *you* anywhere, *hat-head?*" Fenna demanded, still irate over the situation. Enri put a hand on her shoulder to calm her down.

"Let's hear him out," he said. "I mean, we're already here, right? What else are we going to do?"

"Yes, indeed," the TurTek Rep replied. "The truth is that at this point of our endeavor, regardless of anyone's intention for the continuing future, exploration of the Nokkian environment remains in everybody's best interest."

"Yeah sure, but exploration of what?" Enri asked. "I assume TurTek didn't expend such an extravagant effort to molecularly reassemble us for just anything... There had to be something specific that they wanted us to find."

"It is not about the search, Mr. Riatu. It is about the result!" the TurTek Rep explained. "At least for now, during phase one."

"And phase two?" Enri insisted. "What will that be about?"

"Well, depending on the results of our assessment, phase two of TurTek's itinerary will be to continue efforts towards small-scale colonization."

"Colonization!?" Fenna demanded disapprovingly. "You're conspiring to trap even more people down here?"

"That is a possibility, yes—but not the only one out there," the Rep clarified. "It is, however, the favorable goal. We're here to establish whether or not colonization of this planet would be a viable option and, if not, whether it would be worth involving ourselves with at all, be it for mining operations, material salvage, cellular scanning of local wildlife, technological augmentation, or any range of possibilities."

"Am I missing something here?" Fenna asked. "We are to get the lay of the land and decide what's up and down, and then choose how else to waste the rest of our lives? No matter what we find here, the result for us will always be the same—staying stuck on this oven of a planet and helping continue your company's godsdamn agenda!"

"That much will be up to you," the TurTek Rep explained. "Those of us who have been duplicated for phase one have technically only been chosen to serve in an exploratory capacity. Phase two will include its own set of duplicated specialists meant for whatever need our assessment deems necessary. Whether you choose to personally aid them in these efforts will be completely up to you."

"Hold on a minute," Enri jumped in. "Didn't you just say that we don't have the power needed to recreate more people? Something about an endless line of nuclear explosions…"

"Yes, exactly," the Rep chimed happily. "Our own available means for duplication are only meant for phase one of the colonization effort. However, the Deep Space station currently orbiting around the planet is powerful enough to initiate a large-scale duplication. Once we send word up to the TurTek system and confirm viability for continual efforts, the station will start recreating whatever new supplies and people are needed and send them down to greet us."

"Wait!" Fenna jumped in. "There is a ship in orbit? Why in Hades didn't you tell us we still have an active ship up there, a Deep Space, no less?

"How else would we have gotten all the way to this planet?" the TurTek Rep replied flatly.

"Are you trying to hide something from us, you corporate monkey!?" she spat back.

"I am perfectly happy to answer any further questions you have," the TurTek Rep said with practiced enthusiasm. "Just ask."

"TAURSHIT! Who can order a meal without knowing the menu? Tell the orbital station to send a shuttle and come get us this instant!" Fenna insisted. "Tuk your godsdamn mission!"

"I am afraid that would be rather impossible, even if it were advisable before rudimentary exploration—which it certainly is not," the TurTek Rep replied, never dropping his porcelain smile. "None of our terminals have yet been able to send any wave off-planet—the signal keeps bouncing back. We might eventually have to build a more comprehensive radio transmitter from replicated parts if we do not find a way through."

"Yeah, I've been thinking about that," Enri admitted. "I think the wave-spires outside have a canopy above them. We could be layers underneath the planet's true surface. That's why the sun disappears around midday and reappears hours later on the other side of the spires."

The Rep nodded. "We shall have to investigate that matter further. If we find a way up the spires, perhaps we can learn more about this planet and communicate with the station above."

"Hey, shut up. I'm still talking here," Fenna complained. "If we need to climb that beast of a mountain out there to get me a shuttle off this heap, so be it. Just tell me one thing, and be honest for once in your godsdamn life!"

"Yes, what is it?" the Rep asked innocently.

"Let's say that we 'explore' this planet, just like you said, but discover in the process that it is simply an absolute shithole and a complete waste for TurTechnicks to send down any more stuff. What then?"

The Rep frowned. "I believe you have already answered your own question, Ms. Caae. If we deem the planet a waste, then that is exactly what we tell the Deep Space station."

"So it can run off on its own and leave us stranded here forever!?" she demanded.

"Yes, indeed," he admitted, never dropping his smile.


<4:15:39><day 2>

Based on the sun's recorded movements in the sky, Enri's terminal determined the planet of Anok to be on an approximate 32 hour day cycle—a span one third longer than that of Earth. The party had spent the last few hours of the night busily alternating shifts of duplication duty, recreating in the TurTek cubbies everything they could think of, from food to hiking gear to an inflatable, electro-Kevlar tent to provide shelter along their way.

Rationing out power before the land-pod's energy supply ran out, the group managed to crank out several simpler strains of nano-bot healing creams, digestion modulators, pressure equalizers, heat regulators, and immune-system boosters. They even managed to create tiny inflatable robo-alleviators meant for reducing lung difficulties in higher altitudes. They duplicated heat lamps for the cold and head-lamps for the dark, outer protection for the unknown and internal monitors for the unseen, all the while making sure to keep the stock relatively light with no more than they could all carry comfortably. Everything the group could think to create seemed to already exist and be available for duplication within the TurTek databanks, including many instances of strange foreign tech that Enri had never even seen or heard of—which was certainly strange for such an avid adventurer.

The hours of the night were growing deep, dawn was soon approaching, and a restless Enri could not bring himself to close his eyes for even a second, let alone allow himself to drift away into the comfort of a well-earned sleep. With more questions to ask than he had the time to understand, the explorer's mind felt abuzz with the possibilities of the new day, leaving him no chance of claiming a moment's rest amidst the turmoil of both depression and simultaneous excitement.

Enri cast his gaze across the rubber-ridged land-pod floor to where the TurTek Rep lay fidgeting in his freshly duplicated sleeping bag. *There is still more to the larger story than meets the eye,* he knew. While the representative had answered every direct question earnestly, Enri could not help but feel every explanation was somewhat evasive and sparse. *There has to be something here yet unrevealed, but for now it'd be best to play along… until I have a reason not to.*

Enri looked at Fenna, who was asleep in a seated position with her back against the wall. He could see that she was still clutching her oval turtle-shell backpack protectively, despite being asleep. He wondered why she still felt the need to keep her defenses so high up. *Does she think one of us is a pickpocket or a thief? Wasn't it she who just murdered one of the troop? If anything, we should be suspicious of her, not her of us.*

Moving onwards, Enri noticed that Fre'dd was also wide-awake. The large man was grinning like a kid in a candy shop with his eyes darting back and forth as he played with the flashing lights of Enri's handheld terminal. Witnessing the glee in the gladiator's eyes, he chuckled at the fact that it had taken a trip to such a wondrously alien land for the large man to gain exposure to such a common human technology. *Not that Fre'dd is all that common himself,* Enri realized, remembering the multiple times he had noted the gladiator's foreign peculiarity. Fre'dd was bigger and stronger than any other human Enri had ever seen, seemed to heal faster than even best nano-bot healing creams could ever manage, and donned clothing and ornamentation of a completely unknown origin and technology. Like with the TurTek Rep, much had yet to be discovered about the large man. *Perhaps more about him will make sense once a certain familiarity had been reached.*

Enri grabbed his knapsack and stood up, walking gingerly over to the gladiator. The large man's necklaces shone brightly around his neck and shoulders, visibly bubbling with brightly colored liquid and emanating heat through the air.

"Hey," he said. "Can't sleep either?"

"Sleep?" Fre'dd asked, looking up.

"Yeah, you know… like rest from the day."

"I only rest when weary."

"You don't sleep at night?"

"Sometimes," Fre'dd admitted. "But we have not exerted any energy in hours, so there is no reason to feel weary right now."

"I've never been too keen on sleeping at night either. I always feel like I miss out on so much during the hours it incapacitates me."

"Hours?" Fre'dd asked in audible concern. "How often does this happen?"

"Sleep, sleep, sleep, sleep—Enri loves to dream and hates to sleep," the explorer's terminal chirped out from within Fre'dd's hands. "But he should know, and you should too, that to dream without sleep is to cut yourself short and to sleep without dreams feels as if you have died!"

"Speak for yourself." Enri chuckled. "What would a computer know about dreams?"

"A touch of nonsense out from the streams of truth!" the terminal chimed back whimsically. "Truth, ruth, proof, poof!"

"What is it saying?" Fre'dd asked, confused. He handed the clear device back to Enri.

"I don't even know half the time." Enri laughed. "Sometimes it's best just to ignore it and move on. I don't even know why I leave its personality so active."

"Hey, that's mean!" the terminal protested. It flashed a bright light into Enri's eyes, blinding him momentarily.

"Okay, okay, I'm sorry!" he apologized, holding the light away from him. "I'm just kidding!"

"Such an odd thing, this... What did you call it? A terminus?" Fre'dd mused

"Terminal," Enri replied. "Like a network hub or something." He paused, remembering Ranke's wristband terminal in his knapsack. "Hey, you want one of your own?" He pulled the device out of his bag and handed it to Fre'dd. "Maybe this one won't have as *explosive* a personality as mine!" he joked.

"Explosive?" Fre'dd asked.

*WhOoOo!* A fluctuating whistle strung through the air, breaking the silence of the room. Enri looked up in surprise as the noise thickened into the sound of a detonating blast. *Faa-BOOM!*

The room lit up radiantly with strings of wavering flame. In the brief moment following the explosion's catalyst, a metal object, twisting like a DNA helix and paneled in a way resembling human-made technology, flashed into sight just above Fre'dd's head. Before Enri could identify what it was, its core burst apart violently with flames wisping out colored mixtures blazing yellow and red. The golden threads of silken fire curled before him fast, leaving him no time to cover up from its exploding core.

Fenna sprang up from sleep, jumping straight from unconsciousness into a standing stance with both her pneumatic pickaxes held up defensively like shields before her. The quick-reflexed woman saw the shimmering fire approach and reflexively turned away, covering herself with her turtle-shell backpack to minimize exposure.

*Wow, that was fast!* Enri thought as he failed to move nearly as quick. Feeling his pupils shrink from the intensity of incoming light, he shut his eyes tight and simply waited for the end to come. But it never came.

Enri opened his eyes cautiously and blinked in disbelief at the sight of a solid flame frozen in the air. The blazing inferno of orange and red spiraling fire had somehow stopped moving completely, although only for several seconds before mysteriously beginning to reverse. The entire explosion shrunk inward in puffs and bounds and then popped completely out of existence above Fre'dd where it had formed, leaving behind a three-dimensional image of the helical metal craft Enri had been previously unable to identify as it exploded. Written upon it in very small print was the name Olympia.

"Was that a joke!?" Fenna yelled out, rising straight to anger. "What in the godsdamn river Styx is wrong with you? Who does that in the middle of the wretched night? SHAME!"

"Me deprecan," Fre'dd apologized quickly. "I didn't mean to do that!" He held Ranke's wristband terminal before him like a delicate glass egg, fearing its unpredictable power. "This thing est novum ad me."

"Well, make sure it never happens again," Fenna said, unimpressed. She sheathed her dual pickaxe blades into her ovoid backpack and sat back down on the ground.

"Holy...woah!" Enri exclaimed in gleeful surprise. "That was a hologram? I've never seen something like *that* before!" He took Ranke's device from out of the Fre'dd's extended fingertips, pondering with wonder at the implications of such marvelous technology. He had never even *heard* of an honest hologram that could successfully project light and sound out of thin air. *Technology like that was unheard of!*

"Yeah, good sir Earthborn, a freakin hologram!" Fenna chortled sarcastically. "Jeez man, sometimes I forget you're from the *dark* ages!"

"Sometimes..?" Enri muttered softly, wondering about Fenna's wording. He flattened the wristband terminal in his palms and inspected it up close, marveling at the minutia of its wear and tear. It was far more worn-in than he would he suspected.

Under his breath, Fre'dd began to recite a verse to calm down.

*"Up and down, left and right, fear and loathing through the night.*

*Can you stand with power to fight, when in your bones you rock with fright?*

*Yes you can, push forth your might, for the Aren order, it must burn bright!"*

"Transcripts of the Emperor, 2232," Enri's handheld terminal squeaked out. "More a poet than a leader, really!"

"Quiet, you!" Enri whispered.

"No, speak up!" Fre'dd insisted, towering over the much smaller man. "Your terminus, what did it just say? Did it recognize my words?"

"Yes, of course. A terminal always knows best!" the terminal chimed. "Chords of the Aren'A, unrevised preamble, part one of seven, Ares Prime."

"Can the terminus find me other passages of the Aren?"

"Yup, the terminus can!" the device replied happily.

"Here, keep it for now," Enri said, tossing it over to Fre'dd. "I've got this other terminal to figure out anyway."

"You're giving me up that easily?" the terminal whined in mock complaint. "Replacing me for a shiny new toy?"

"Yeah, sure. Why not? Treat the big guy well, okay?"

"Okee-dokey!" the terminal chimed back.

"Gratias," the gladiator thanked Enri. He clipped the device onto his belt. "Read to me of the empress," he requested. "From the beginning, please."

Enri sat back down near his sleeping bag and played with the physical form of Ranke's wristband terminal, finding its material to be far more malleable than he had initially realized, almost like soft molding clay unable to break or tear. Unlike his own terminal, which could change its basic shape upon pressure and readjustment, Ranke FourtySeven's wristband device seemed able to stretch wide as he could pull it, responding semi-intelligently to Enri's twists and pulls with anticipatory density fluctuating underneath his fingertips. On Ranke's wrist, the clear band had seemed thin as a ribbon, but now it somehow seemed much thicker, having had stretched further than its light mass should have allowed.

The terminal lit up in response to Enri's thoughts, flashing its digital interface straight into his eyes. *WOW!* Enri gaped, understanding the implications of it all. This was not simply an unknown brand of terminal. It was *future* freaking tech—something which *should* not yet exist!

For the first since waking up on this alien world, Enri truly understood what it all meant. So many questions asked along the way could suddenly be explained under the same branching context, such as the group's widespread cultural dispersion. Although they had all been duplicated upon this planet together, the survivors' original selves back home could have taken their quark-scans years or even decades apart from one another. *After all,* Enri realized, *the TurTek Rep had admitted that nearly a millennium had come and passed since our Deep Space ship departed from Earth's system. The others could have come from literally any era between the inception of TurTek's quark-scans and today—which statistically means that most of them were likely born in my own future!*

# 7 : pursuit :

"Grande obsessions damage likewise a healthy mind as does a fiery blaze to a house of timber. They both feel comfortable and warm just before they begin to nip and burn, and by then it is far too late to stop them"
-Transcripts of the Empress

### <2113 C.E. - the age of illusion><Earth Orbit>

Fenna's first kill occurred at age 18, after months of following every single lead she could find. It was the rush of a new era as the civilizations of man became hooked on pazz, drifting further and further from the realm of reality. With nothing solid to go off, Fenna had been grasping at straws for years, feeling the pressure build before her hunt for answers went completely cold. It had been half a decade years since the young huntress' former life had ended, and, in all the time henceforth, she had found nothing but more pain. Leads were thinning and answers always came up short. If anything of significance ever popped up in relation to the Olympic Station disaster, Fenna made sure to pursue it with full fervor.

Lately, the young huntress had been left following leads as far-flung as they came. First, she went off chasing direct associations. Then, she moved on to second-degree connections, then rumors, then mere inferences, after which she was left with no option but to make inferences of her own. She chased any loose leads dealing with independent crews of manufacturing distributors who dealt in explosives during the days of the Olympia station's construction. The list was surprisingly varied, and, after months of research, Fenna ended up vetting most of the crews she could find as being completely legitimate. At this point, the only crew left for her to investigate was the one gang she had always hoped to avoid: the Hands.

This gang did not acknowledge any government based on the surface of Earth. They spent the majority of their time in an orbit so deep that the planet around which they revolved appeared to the naked eye as no more than a blip in space—not that any true Spacer would ever dare rely on only their naked eyes. The crew ran less like the typical corporate computer and more like an organized religion or cult, with outcrops and reformists attempting to sway the public with independent coalitions over an ever-spreading network connected to the same web. Their tool of conduct was the neurochemical/nano-bot known as pazz, and their influence created widespread usage through the general population of interplanetary humankind.

Although Fenna's trail of the Hands' operations began with their presence in the Olympia station's initial development, the crew's proliferation far after the Olympic Station tragedy caught her interest to a greater degree. In the aftermath of the disaster, the Hands shifted to the exclusive production and distribution of pazz. Over the years, Fenna heard various third-person accounts of the gang's escalation and increased tendency towards criminal behavior, clashing with local governments here and there in pursuit of pushing the pazz free-market everywhere at once. Soon after their rise to popularity, the Hands declared themselves completely independent, outside the purview of any law but their own.

Although she quickly discovered that, even at their peak, the Hands had never pulled off a job quite as big as the Olympic Station explosion, their subsequent change of direction and extreme commercial success gave her enough suspicion to search deeper. *If I can find the reason for their change of pace, perhaps I can discover someone who had motive to destroy the Olympic station.*

Fenna's 18th birthday had come and gone with little progress on her quest for truth, so the young huntress made the conscious decision to face these nano-drug peddlers head-on. The best way she knew to find these criminals would be to work from the bottom up, starting off with a simple drug deal and chasing its path back up the chain of distribution. The Hands had fought hard to extend their monopoly over the realm of pazz, so, by all rationality, following its exclusivity would lead to finding their base of operations.

On the eve of the Olympic Station disaster's fifth anniversary, Fenna found herself flying through the urban spacer neighborhoods of the high-populous township of epiChicago, which consisted mostly of high-rise space-stations adjoined to Turian flower-esque parking outlets with shuttles crossing to and fro, carrying people this way and that. Her rented craft passed under miles of glimmering railways, and, for a moment, she felt invisible. *Surely anything I do in a neighborhood this large will go mostly unnoticed.*

Scanning out through the city with her terminal-lensed eyes, Fenna searched for the loosest form of pazz marketeering—someone friendly enough to not pose a threat, yet shady enough to guarantee distance from any local government authorities.

The state of decay throughout the zero-gee community astounded Fenna. Through cracked windows patched with rubber filament and taped up structures preventing the escape of air, homeless citizens and junkies wandered the inner stations' streets in a semi-comatose state with eyes as white as pearls. Often decrepit, sometimes missing limbs, these junkies huddled alone anywhere there was power flow, with eyes white as pearls and a blank look across all faces. Although upsetting, this last detail reassured Fenna that this district did in fact have an active pazz trade. *If I keep looking, I will surely find someone who can lead me in the right direction. Such is the nature of the hunt.*

After half an hour of making rounds without aim, Fenna's terminal eyed a group of likely candidates walking through an overhead airtight strip of a grass-filled park. They were three college students with pazz cartridges bulging out from underneath their sleeves, all young and friendly enough for her to approach without too much concern. However, she soon realized with frustration, as long as she circled around in her ship, she would never be able to reach them anyway. *By the time I actually find a place to land, these pazz leads will already be long gone…*

"Tuk!" she swore out loud.

The closest place Fenna could find to park was a gas station hub, and although her craft's tank was more than half full, she had nowhere else to go. She descended through a cluster of traffic and suited pedestrians and docked inside the comfort of the hub's airtight chambers to begin the procedure for pumping fuel. Her terminal lenses flicked this way and that, jumping from person to person and scanning for pazz in their systems. In reality, it helped very little, so she shut off the display. With the rip and roar of air chambers opening for the entry and exit of shuttle craft, this place was chaotic enough without her eyes going spastic. She searched through the station now with clear eyes, seeing if she could find someone or something which stood out from the rest of the hustle.

A man with a cluttered sweatshirt and scraggly beard stood in the cross-section between the enclosed gas station and a tube-bridge walkway leading across to an adjoined building, asking people here and there for money. Most people disregarded his presence while others handed him morsels of change, but, nonetheless, he kept on trying, unfazed by his lack of success.

After a minute, he noticed Fenna's stares from across the platform and smiled wide, motioning her over. She shrugged and motioned him back at her.

"I can't come to you!" the man yelled across the platform.

"What?" she yelled back, not understanding.

"I'm not allowed in! He doesn't let me cross!" The man's cupped hands projected his reply across the station.

"Who?" Fenna shouted over the noise of the pumps.

"The station manager!" The scraggly man motioned her over again with wide waving arms.

She nodded and held up a hand, telling the man to wait. His eyes flickered white for a brief moment before he nodded back. Fenna walked over to her rented ship and reached inside to grab several scattered coins, pocketed them, picked up one of two pneumatic pickaxes and hung it on the back of her belt. She headed across the platform to meet with the scraggly haired man, hoping he could help her in the pursuit of the local pazz distribution chain. *Who knew where a simple conversation could lead?*

Half an hour later, Fenna was hot on the trail, passing through street lanes and alleyways as she followed her unwitting lead to and through a donut-shaped, lazily revolving space-station that looked and functioned as a hotel, a restaurant, and a mall. She made sure to stay far enough back so as to not be noticed, watching from around corners as the scraggly man disappeared into the bends of the station, and eventually tracking him all the way across it and behind its main residential towers to the back-alleys where the average crowds dare not go.

This space-station was one of relatively primitive design, with a centrifugal spin pushing its inhabitants outward and simulating gravity in the most rudimentary way possible. This station reeked of rust and ozone and squeaked like broken wreckage, with back-alleys rustling with the roar of vacuum chutes sucking trash out of the air and the ground wobbling about as the donut frame spun. She was no landlubber herself, but Fenna scoffed at the squalor. *How can there still be people ok with living like this? This place is just another tragedy waiting to happen!*

Behind the final abbey of her chase, Fenna's scraggly haired target stopped moving, and another man who looked far more like a gangster than she would have liked joined him. The new man had a cipher cast over his system's pazz to hide the frequency of its waves.

The young huntress snuck up a rattling staircase as quietly as possible, positioning herself behind a wall on a second-floor balcony with an overhead viewpoint of the men below. She instructed her terminal lenses to decrypt the gangster's outgoing waves and her earring headphones to whisper an amplification of the men's conversation into her ears but was disappointed when the cipher blocked it. The two men brushed past each other and a supply of pazz passed from one hand to another, with Fenna's credits presumably cast straight into the gangster's pockets. The very interaction she had chased came and went before she had even gotten a whiff of the information she needed.

*Shit!* This was completely unacceptable. Fenna felt compelled to gain some extra time in her hunt. *If I don't tag this pazz gangster now, there will be no way whatsoever to follow him up the Hands food chain!*

Before the opportunity was gone forever, Fenna did something completely unexpected: she sent a direct wave to her initial contact, knowing full well it could give away her position.

"Hey!" she projected towards the pazz in the scraggly man's system. "Have you gotten the stuff?"

"Huh!?" he shouted, stopping fast in his tracks. The gangster whom he had traded with stopped as well, turning around to look over at the scraggly man in confusion.

"The pix, pixels, pazz!" Fenna announced to her contact. "You got it or not?"

"Who is this!? How did you reach my wave?" the scraggly man asked suspiciously.

"You sent it to me, remember?" Fenna lied. Before her contact had time to think, she continued talking, hoping to gain a few more seconds to allow her time to catch the other man's wave. "Listen, make sure the pazz is Technicolor brand, 24 hour degradation!"

"Everything is cool, sister. I already gots what'ch you needed!"

"Your visual feed is on," Fenna lied again. "You're clearly holding a 48hr degenerator!"

"Hey! Who are you talking to?" the pazz gangster barked at the scraggly haired man.

Fenna's contact immediately hung up on her. She smiled to herself and began to reposition her stance over the balcony. *At least I bought myself another few seconds!*

However, the pazz gangster himself seemed to have other objectives in mind. He and the scraggly haired man began to argue, elevating their pitches to shouts of rage. Yelling turned into pushing, then diving into an all-out brawl. The gangster wasted no time at all in pulling out a concealed blade, and then gave Fenna's contact an undercut straight to gut. He grimaced in disgust as the scraggly haired man's innards gurgled forward. He released his blade like a disposable tool, letting it drop to the ground with his opponent.

Fenna gasped aloud, feeling the guilt build in her stomach. She covered her mouth with her hands, forcefully keeping herself from either retching or screaming. Pressing herself far out of view, the young huntress began to hyperventilate, feeling the pressure inside her build. She gave herself a long moment to build up a mental wall and will the strength back into her body. She peeked out and watched as the gangster dragged his victim away in the opposite direction. Either nobody noticed or nobody else cared, but for Fenna, it was a trauma that wouldn't stop. *I caused his death!*

Fenna immediately realized the gangster was heading to the closest vacuum chute ejecting trash out of the station. *He's dumping the body.* She nearly choked up in tears. *This is all my fault!* She promised herself that no matter what, this Hand gangster would not get away with murder. *He will pay!*

She launched her body expertly from window ledge to window ledge straight up the alley wall, ascending rapidly as she vaulted from handhold to handhold in lower and lower gee. This made it easier for her to climb the higher she rose. Never pausing long enough for her momentum to stutter, Fenna marked a thin window balcony a hundred feet above as her target destination and instructed her terminal lenses to lead her there ledge by ledge.

By the time she reached the peak of her climb, the pseudo gravity pulling upon the young huntress was so low the idea of slipping and falling never even came to mind. Instead, all she could think of were the logistics of her imminent dive and the vile man far below who deserved what was coming.

Fenna looked down the alley and spotted the Hand dealer still dragging the body of her dead former contact, trailing a long line of blood and unraveled guts behind him. She recalled years of elite athletic low-gee holoplay action, never knowing that she would ever face a real-life situation such as this. Her life echoed through her mind, from her brother's atmospheric diving lessons to the years of hardship following the Olympic Station disaster, all the way up to her frustrating quest with no answers. This particular lead might be the last one she would ever find, and she felt the pure guilt of what had happened to the scraggly haired man. *It's now or never!*

Fenna jumped off the window ledge with no fear in her heart, expertly aiming herself in the air and diving with arms extended as her brother had taught her once upon a time. Like an arrow, she shot downward, crossing clotheslines and balcony rails, dodging between beams and open windows, and gaining overall momentum the further down she dropped. She turned herself around in the air, aimed both feet down, and, within seconds, reached the man below with force enough to pommel a wildebeest.

Just as the Hand thug dumped the scraggly man's body outside the roaring vacuum hatch, Fenna slammed straight into the back of his shoulders with her boots, smashing him down into the ground and cushioning her own impact through his crumpled body. She sprung off him into the air, landing poised and ready with both pneumatic axes out of her belt and held threateningly before her. This last measure of defense, however, turned out to be completely unnecessary, as her initial impact with the Hand thug had knocked him straight out of consciousness.

She sheathed her blades and looked down at the man, assessing the damage she had wrought upon him. After confirming he was still alive, the young huntress pulled out a smart-rope and tied him up, leaving one end slack to secure around the vacuum hatch's metal grate. Once done, she signaled the rope to stiffen and lock him in, allowing no wiggle room for him to try and break free.

Beneath the starry black cloak that was traditional of ranked members of the Hands organization, the gangster wore a shirt even less flattering, presenting a simple message with two words made of letters big, bold, and extremely distracting: **TUK YOU!** Beneath the words was the hand-shaped insignia of the **Hands** with its middle finger pointed up, further exacerbating the message.

"Charming," she said out loud, frowning down at the body. She sat down on the curb and took a sip of water from out the turtle-shell pack on her back. *This man is a complete scumbag! Getting information out of him won't be easy...*

Minutes later, as the Hand gangster was waking up and opening his eyes, Fenna walked up to him and pulled back his hair, snapping his head backwards and forcing him to look at her upside-down. She brought up a pneumatic pickaxe and held it out in front of his eyes, making sure his pupils dilated and focused upon it before she eased it down and let the cold steel brush against his neck.

"*Ex-plo-sives,*" she said, enunciating the word slowly as if he were a child. "Tell me everything you know."

His mouth widened from shock to amusement. "See my shirt, bitch?" he asked, chuckling as he spurted foaming blood from out his mouth. "TUK YOU!"

Fenna froze, shocked at his boorish resolve. She had assumed that the threat of death would be enough to get this man talking, even if just to spout out lies. The young huntress had prepared an interrogation in her head, hoping to gradually trick him into the truth from among the tons of taurshit that he was bound to spout. However, she quickly realized this method would not work. Instead, she would have to throw him straight into the deep end, hoping for the love of Olympus that this scum would be willing to swim.

"Are you sure you want to go this way?" Fenna asked politely, stepping around him and facing him head on. "It will lead to you through a world of agony."

"Tuk you!" He laughed, attempting to spit a blob of mucus-filled blood at her face but instead only managing to drool.

"Really?" she shouted in disgust. "So you choose the option of *pain*!?"

She lifted her foot up high, placing it on the villainous Hand's shoulder and forcing herself to smile at the confounded expression on his face. She waited until the confusion led to the horror of realization and then kicked him hard, pushing him backwards into the open vacuum duct behind him. The resilient Hand fell into the open hole, screaming bloody murder, pulling behind him the slack of rope until it ran out of length and snapped taut. His earsplitting bawls tore back up through the narrow hatch, revealing his breaking point through the heavy roar of wind. Fenna pulled out her dandy spinner and attached it to the rope, instructing it to pull the man back up and out of the hatch.

"Tuk, tuk, tuk," the gangster whimpered through his shivers as his frostbitten body dragged across the ground. "You bitch! You psycho bitch!"

Fenna kicked him in the gut and pressed her heel across his throat. "Why do you do it?" she asked. "Why are you such a dick?"

He gurgled in response.

Fenna removed her foot from his neck and leaned in closer. "What?"

"Ttttt...TUK YOU!"

She pushed him back into the hole, sidestepping the uncoiling rope trailing behind him as he fell. It snapped taut, leaving him dangling in pain.

"Shit!" he screamed. "Shit, lady, shit, shit, shit!"

She brought him back up, even more frostbitten than before.

"Explosives," Fenna repeated. "What do you know?"

"What explosives, lady? I'm a godsdamn pazz dealer!"

"Before the disaster," she explained calmly. "The Hands used to deal with explosives."

"The station Olympia!? That what you talking about? That was a long time ago..." he said between shivers. "You're living in the past, missus. Those days are long gone."

"Not for me," she whispered. "Those days will never go away."

"Explosives—tell me everything," she reiterated.

"You want a list or something, lady?" he asked. "We dealt in lotsa things before the big Olympia bang!"

"The godsdamn tukking *explosives*!" Fenna shouted, kicking him in his ribcage. "Tell me what blew up the tukking Olympic space-station! NOW!"

"WHAT IN THE HELLS!?" the Hand yelled back in defiance. "You think we had something to do with blowing it up? That was the worst day of my life! In all of our lives!"

Fenna grunted in anger and kicked him again, pushing him closer to the open vacuum chute. "LIAR!" she screamed, and then embedded a pickaxe in his knee.

"TUK! BITCH! TUK!" the Hand yelled into the air. "YOU TUKKING LITTLE WHORE!"

Fenna pulled out her axe and pushed the man back over the edge, gasping for breath as she tried to gain control of her emotions. The thug fell into the chute and was left hanging yet again. This time, his voice was so weak she could scarcely hear his screams over the roaring torrent of air.

Once Fenna regained her composure, she signaled her spinner to bring the man back up. He was nearly frozen stiff, barely able to open his eyes as he desperately gasped for breath. His skin looked crackled and blue, his wounds no longer dripping. All the blood off his leg and chin hung solid as icicles, breaking away as Fenna's spinner dragged him unceremoniously across the ground.

"Well?" she asked him. "Explosives?"

"It wasn't us..." he croaked out. "The Hands love tourists. Olympia brought us more business than we'd ever had before!"

"Then how did your profits go so far up in the following years?" Fenna asked skeptically. "Why switch all the Hands' focus to the sole distribution of pazz?"

"People grew tired of the physical world... you know," the pazz dealer explained. "Reality is just a big tukking pile of stinking taurshit and broken rubble."

"And so you cast society into a great big lie instead!?"

"Dreams and illusions, lady," the Hand insisted. "Dreams and illusions. We give people visions of what they have always wanted to see. We give their lives new meaning!"

"So you're great big humanitarians now, are you?" Fenna smirked. "Great big, murderous humanitarians?"

"Hey, it's supply and demand," he replied earnestly. "Profits don't lie!"

Fenna was starting to believe the frostbitten man, which was a problem. *If the Hands weren't tied to the disaster that had ended my family, then who was? If my last lead into the matter that defined my life fizzled away with nothing to show for itself, where would I go now? Where will I seek the hidden truths I am so desperate to find?*

As Fenna took her time contemplating what to do next, the frozen thug stayed silent. Unbeknownst to the young huntress, he had been whittling away at his own hands behind his back, cracking the frostbitten skin off his thumbs and palms and gaining leeway underneath the smart-rope. Without betraying as much as a grunt, the gangster freed himself from his entanglement and stretched his stiff joints to warm himself up. Fenna looked away for a moment and the Hand stood up, casting away the rope and posing to pounce straight at her.

Hearing the crunch of icy clothing, Fenna turned back around and gasped in surprise. The Hand charged at her clumsily but found her gone as he fell on the ground. The nimble girl had instantly slid herself forward and snapped at his legs, making the gangster tumble forward and trip. She unsheathed her pneumatic axes as he turned to face her, and, before reconsidering, embedded them both into the soft skin on either side of the Hand's neck. She pulled backwards violently and he died instantly, slumping down on top of her and soaking the young huntress in a red mass of ooze.

"GAH!" Fenna shouted, panting heavily as she pulled herself out of the carnage. She backed away, watching the body twitch on the ground in its final throes of death. Once he stopped moving, she stepped forward and kicked the body hard, pushing the Hand thug back out through the open vacuum hatch to fall free into the frozen waste balloon outside.

She turned away and began to cry, but then stopped herself short and forced away the tears. *No more dreams!* she promised herself. *No more illusions!*

# 8 : forest :

**"A new set of queries can be readily worth more than the answering of a single question."**
-Transcripts of William

<10:53:24 a.s.t.><**day 4**><Anok>

Fenna gazed out at an open world of nothingness, mulling over thoughts of a reflective nature. The steep cliffs and wide views beneath soothed her mind like a fresh breeze in an arid room, reminding her of the times when she felt the most free. Never a girl to stay on solid ground for longer than it took to resupply, Fenna had found voyaging the dry wasteland below a dizzying experience.

Now, though, having the chance to see the land from so far above felt comfortably familiar to the zero-gee native's mind. With a distant horizon easing her frustration over her feelings of confinement and a swirling breeze blowing through her hair, she finally felt at peace, albeit nostalgic towards a life that had been long gone years before her quark-scan. Although the distant view of ethereal wave-spires crossing land and sky felt wholly unfamiliar, the endless heights they represented made Fenna feel right at home. When she squinted, the lot of them sort of resembled a magnificent array of Turian flower stems bringing down lines of traffic from the border of space.

The sound of distant echoes and fluttering wings erupted from out a nearby alcove, followed by the burst of a flying creature shaped like a blue lizard with heads on both sides, eyes on each end. Hummingbird wings shimmered and buzzed as they bobbed its mass up and down through the air. Fenna's terminal lens quickly began to scan and to try to identify the beast, falling short of its goals as it had never seen anything like it before.

"Leave me be, gekkon!" the large man, Fre'dd, cursed unhappily. He stood wavering in a perilous stance upon a smooth, gray-striped stone ledge, swatting at the bobbing Nokkian lizard with barely a foothold to keep himself upright. "Decrepitus buzzard!"

"Gekkon, smekkon, alabekkon!" The handheld terminal Enri had given Fre'dd squawked out from its roost on his belt. "That's not a word, just a noise that sounds absurd!"

"Hey, you ok over there?" Fenna asked in concern. "Need some help?"

"Non," the gladiator replied. "I am fine." He watched as the creature fluttered before him.

Using his practiced battle senses to wait for the opportune moment, Fre'dd darted out his hand and caught the flying alien midair, leaving it unharmed between his fingers. He tossed the Nokkian lizard out into the open air away from the cliff, watching fearfully for a moment as it fell like a stone.

He exhaled in relief once it opened up its wings a couple of dozen feet below him and fluttered out of sight. However, he soon realized he was now staring out over a dizzying height of nothing but air. Fre'dd breathed in slowly and out fast, beginning to hyperventilate. He backed up as far as he could and hugged the wall behind him.

"How bad has it hit you, big man Herc'?" Fenna asked the Martian gladiator, hoping to distract him. "You know, that feeling in your gut that tickles and burns, sinks your body like quicksand, and keeps your breath underwater?"

"Are your words for me?" he demanded, bellowing out his discomfort.

"You have the look of a man gripped dismal," she replied in an upbeat tone that offset the gravity of her words. "This is not a good mindset. Believe me, warrior. I understand—I know the pull of a churning fear."

The gladiator looked up reluctantly and nodded back at Fenna. "It is true what you say," he admitted. "The murmurs of Phobos rustle through my mind."

"By day they fall, by night they plunder," Enri's terminal decided to add to the conversation. "Your thoughts of fear…? Guffaw! They are only illusion."

"Shut it, computer!" Fenna commanded. "Keep looking at me, Fre'dd. Away from the cliff!" She stepped towards him, showing no apparent concern over her own safety. "It's nearly impossible to turn off your emotions completely, you know," she said, gesturing wildly to draw his attention. "But that certainly does not mean they can't be redirected."

"I think not." Paranoia rattled through Fre'dd's bones. "As long as these heights remain, so will the fear in my blood." He pressed himself closer to the wall.

"Nonsense!" Fenna exclaimed. "Yeah, sometimes our bodies and minds can get overwhelmed, jumbled, and confused with the amount of data they are fed simultaneously. Far from a weakness, this limitation can actually be used to an advantage, allowing us to steer our thoughts and passions as we see fit and focus on what matters."

"How would that help?" Fre'dd's eyes drifted towards the open cliff. "If I fall over, will I not be thrown into Hades all the same?"

"Prioritize your thoughts, big guy. Prioritize," Fenna urged. "Find a way to push your concerns to mean something entirely different."

"Quid dicis? I don't understand."

"Visualize your thoughts, visualize your fears," Fenna instructed. "Start by focusing tight and holding your nightmare strong, making everything but your present fear go away. Exaggerate the pain in your mind until nothing else exists, casting you into the deepest paranoia you have ever felt. And then, once the fear is all you have left and your nightmare is the only truth you can see, let it all go. You will only then gain the power to do with it as you will."

"That is absurd!" Fre'dd bellowed, doubting the validity of Fenna's advice. "If fear is the only thing left, how could it possibly go away!?"

"Oh no, it does not go away," Fenna admitted. "But it will never feel quite as strong again. Once you have pushed your fear past its natural boundary, its eventual reoccurrence will seem muted at best, like the dithered remains of a city that once stood strong. After the direct intensity of your worst-case thoughts, the fear needs not ever overcome you again."

"I understand… I think. But forgive me if I disagree. Some battles should never be fought."

"Don't sweat it, Herc'." Fenna nodded, holding out her arm to help guide him along the cliff wall.

"Hey, what're you guys doing down there?" Enri called down from above the curled purple rocks beside Fenna. He extended down an arm, offering help to pull her up. His wristband terminal projected out a hologram animating a series of comic arrows pointing upward and bidding Fenna take notice. She ignored the gesture.

"You gonna be okay?" she asked Fre'dd, worried her advice had only caused him further panic.

"I'll manage." He nodded curtly, resuming his slow trek across the rocks.

"Come on, you dozing or what?" Enri's voice echoed through the rocks. "It's amazing up here!"

Fenna grabbed the dangling arm and pulled herself above the dry stone into a forest of blue. Nokkian plants big and small grew in masses, sprouting from ground much softer than the rocky cliff edge only a dozen feet or so away. Countless twisted aquamarine, palm-like trees with striped spines and cotton-ball canopies cast the area into shade, covering the landscape with gray and blue fuzz like fur on the back of some gigantic beast.

Fenna walked forward in awe, and the foreign beauty of the alien woods filled her periphery in blue. The sharp, sweet smell of citrus intensified around her. Her terminal lenses zoomed in on a blue tree trunk, determining that it was not just striped but segmented like spinal bone. Cerulean shades of dark and light blue alternated up their twisty heights, each ending in a fluffy gray orb.

"Fre'dd, how're you doing down there?" Enri's voice echoed through the trees. "Here, sling this around your waist. Maybe it'll help!"

Fenna looked back. He was leaning over the cliff, handing down some sort of chain from out his knapsack to the large man out of sight below. Her terminal lenses identified the object as a TurTek mobility belt. *Shit!*

Beneath the cliff ledge, Fre'dd magnetically strapped Dirk Fairwinter's mobility belt just above his own rumble belt but began slipping immediately once it turned on. With his back pressed against a crackling stone slab and a mere sliver of rock left beneath his feet, the bursts of rosy air pushing out from around his waist did nothing to help his stability. Thus, when the large man began to topple over backwards, there was nothing he could do to stop it.

"Fre'dd!" Enri yelled from above, watching his new friend fall away beneath his feet. "Turn it off!"

A rush of wind blew past the explorer as a figure leaped recklessly off the cliff beside him and into the open. It took him a moment for him to recognize it as Fenna. A pair of ropes trailed out from her turtle-shell backpack, connecting her to safety. Arcing downward with her smart-lines in tow, she fell past an out-of-control Fre'dd and looped a length of rope beneath him before he had the chance to plummet. As he stumbled off the ledge, her net stopped the toppling gladiator, pinning him between the legs and torso and slowing down his momentum. The large man's chest was pulled back tight, leaving him gasping for air but alive, nonetheless.

"Hang on, Fre'dd," Fenna called out as she passed him again on the way up. "Keep yourself fastened to the line!"

Fre'dd's leveraged weight pulled her straight up the cliff wall towards the lip of the stone overhang until she signaled the smart rope looped around him to snap tight and disconnect from herself. She bound up her own rope and flipped nimbly over the ledge to land alongside a baffled Enri, returning to safety less than a minute after her initial dive.

"Woah!" Enri exclaimed, feeling awestruck by her athletics. Fre'dd groaned like a steam engine below, which snapped Enri right out of his daze. Springing straight into action, he pulled on the rope holding the large man suspended in the air below. Despite the explorer's most earnest efforts, Fre'dd's weight was far too massive to budge, like an anchor holding down a ship at harbor.

"Expending efforts on an impossibility remains redundant," the TurTek Rep declared. "Our strengths combined come nowhere near the amount of force needed to pull Mr. Invictus up and over the ledge."

"Have you got another idea?" Enri asked, letting go of the rope beneath his grip.

"Don't worry, Earthboy, I've got it covered!" Fenna said, passing him as she followed the taut rope supporting Fre'dd's weight towards the alien tree to which she had tied it. She knelt down, unfastening the line supporting her own weight, and snapped it back into her turtle-shell backpack. Taking the oval pack off her back, she split it in half down its axis, off-centered it across Fre'dd's taut rope, and snapped it shut across the stretched line.

"Woah, what the hells?" Enri asked in wonder as she tinkered with her contraption. "Why does your backpack split in half?"

Fenna looked up and smiled. "It's not just a backpack. It's a multi-form spinner." She pulled out several thin buckles from the spinner's edge fastened to sturdy straps from within, threading them out and weaving them around the tree to latch together upon its opposite end.

"Wait a moment," Enri insisted. "We've gotta warn Fre'dd first!"

"Yeah, no shit." She stared at him. "Well...?"

"Understood," the TurTek representative nodded from beside them, catching his top hat as it slid off his head. He walked off towards the cliff ledge.

The large man below was in severe pain, hanging rather agonizingly due in part to the thinness of the rope. Harnessed crudely in a loop around his body, the smart-line had saved Fre'dd from a certain death but, in doing so, may have stopped all circulation to his legs and arms. Although he was thankful for the quick save, the Martian gladiator found himself losing consciousness fast. No matter what genetically-enhanced effort had gone into his creation back in the Aren'A of Mars, under this pressure, not even he could last much longer.

"Ready Hercules?" Fenna's voice echoed out from above the salted cliffs.

"Mr. Invictus, get ready to move," the TurTek representative called down to him.

Above the cliff rocks and inside the forest of blue, Fenna's turtle-shell pack began to spin, coiling Fre'dd's line around it and groaning under his massive hanging weight. The cable began to move inch by inch, pulling the gladiator straight up the cliff. The striped tree on which the cable was tied creaked like a rusty hinge and released a scent like a ripened orange into the air. The alien flora jolted through its trunk, sending a slender layer of grey dust into the air. The entire thing began to twist and stretch like the spinal column of an acrobat in motion. The fuzzy cotton ball atop the tree shook off a cloud of purple, making it rain bits of dirt upon Enri and Fenna below. They both coughed.

"Tartarus deep!" Fenna exclaimed. "It's squirming like a snake!"

The striped Nokkian tree bent down into a skeletal arch—oddly full of purpose and surprisingly graceful in its movement—before suddenly changing direction and spreading up tall as it could get, far away from the taut rope weighing it down. In a sudden jolt of kinetic energy, its fuzzy canopy slammed down into the soil below and punctured the purple dirt, sending out another spray of gray dust into the air. Enri and Fenna jumped backwards, nearly colliding with the TurTek representative approaching from behind.

The Nokkian tree did not stay silent long. Moments after embedding itself down into an arch, the blue tree began to pull up its opposite end with Fre'dd's recoiling rope still attached, rising from the gravel in an explosion of gray grit and uprooting a second dusty purple ball of fluffy cotton in an instant. The second canopy flipped up high into the air above, dragging with it Fenna's turtle-shell spinner and the Martian gladiator Fre'dd, who propelled over the stone cliff in one swift movement, lunging right past Enri, Fenna, and the Rep.

"Mi deus!" he shouted as he swung out of control. "Why have I been forsaken!?"

"Keep strong, Herc'!" Fenna yelled. "Don't give in!"

The tree continued its flurry of activity, swinging its canopy forward in an arc and smashing it back down into the ground before it, whipping Fre'dd along with its actions. His rumble belt's magnetic tethers separated with the heavy blow, and Dirk's thruster-blowing mobility belt hung free.

"Gods of Olympus, spare me my torment!" Fre'dd's echoing bellows shook the forest as the cotton-ball sphere beside him erupted from the ground, swung him up into the air, and then struck itself back down into the soil further ahead. The Martian gladiator slammed straight into the ground like the load of a misfired trebuchet.

Each swing of the tree placed it dozens of feet deeper into the aquamarine forest, flipping up, over and down, up, over and down, up, over, and down, until it disappeared from sight among the chaotic squirming of countless others of its kind. Every arc brought Fre'dd into the air and then straight back into the ground, haplessly struck upon other trees and anything else in his path, until he, too, faded out of view in the forest of blue.

"FRE'DD!" Enri yelled as he began running. "We're coming!"

The Nokkian jungle twisted and turned, animated with ever-shifting plant-life unlike any forest Enri had ever seen before, real or virtual. A variety of lush, rubbery flora greeted the path before him, dense with shades of translucent blue. Trees in every direction flipped, walked, swayed, and readjusted before Enri's frantic footpath, some moving calmly and some distancing themselves with fierce determination. The gray soil underfoot gave way to a soft layer of turquoise moss, punctured in places with imprints like small craters marking the wakes of the numerous moving plants that had crossed over it.

Deep in the forest of plants, Enri encountered his first batch of wild Nokkian animals, most of which ignored him in his stumbles. He held up his wristband terminal, recording everything he saw with three-dimensional moving scans and building up a virtual map in representation of everything it recorded, complete with topological detail he could not discern on his own. He gaped with awe whenever a new species of creature crossed his path, pointing his wrist forward to try and get quality footage while continuing to run fast as he could after Fre'dd. There was a purple, three-orbed blob that stuck itself from tree to tree like a hitchhiker catching a ride, a glowing yellow band of frog-like balloons that bobbed up and down in the air, flat crawling armadillos shaped like four-pronged starfish, large caterpillars that bounced as they walked, and coral-like tumble-weed that rolled slowly from place to place and up moving trees alike.

Most numerous of all, though, were the four-winged gekkons—as Fre'dd had called them—flying every which way between moving branches, sometimes in schools and sometimes solitary. As a whole, they seemed far more curious with Enri's presence than any other life form, often lingering to circle him in the air and flash at him a varied palette of colors.

Despite the distractions, he trekked onward through the unfamiliar jungle, swerving left and right as he pulled himself through its increasingly packed, constantly writhing trees. Fenna and the TurTek Rep had disappeared within the thicket of blue around him, leaving Enri completely directionless. He found a high vantage point and held up his wristband terminal, recording a detailed panoramic shot and scanning for the likeness of another human being. However, instead of humans, the software returned to him the locations of numerous other species.

One result looked unlike the rest, inorganic and unnatural to the alien blue forest. The terminal identified it as a TurTek-made mobility belt, commissioned for customization by professor Dirk Fairwinter, now sitting lifeless upon a patch of blue moss.

The sun faded away in the sky, setting the land into perpetual midday dawn. Enri allowed the terminal to guide him through the forest towards the belt on the ground. A school of gekkons circled around it, dipping themselves down and across the inactive thruster vents where the smell of blue roses masked the heavy citrus of the woods. As soon as he neared them, the gekkons fluttered away like butterflies, leaving the mobility belt untouched. Enri lifted up the device and strung it around his waist, harnessing it to himself with form-fitting latches and threads.

"Hey, what about me? I thought we were buddies!" a high-pitched voice squeaked nearby. Enri found his old handheld terminal sticking out of the dirt. He picked it up and brushed it off, then placed it in his knapsack.

"Gee, thanks," the device murmured through the bag.

Turning on the mobility belt around his waist, Enri grimaced at the pressure it took to lift him in the air. He withstood a heavy current of blue-rose smelling air and floated up high, drifting above the forest of aquamarine. His terminal quickly identified the freshly disturbed path that Fre'dd's Nokkian tree had made in the forest below. He leaned forward, carefully urging his thrusters to carry him onward.

Over, under, through, and around, Enri's visibility decreased as he navigated across the branches of wildly swinging trees. Their shadows misled him, confusing shades of light and dark over the perilous obstacles in his way. Between flora so dense he occasionally had to physically push his way through narrow passages of tight blue vegetation, Enri wrestled his way through the forest, seeking open patches of unhindered light to its plausible end.

A perfectly circular purple clearing, no more than fifty feet across, lay smack dab in the middle of the lush, raging jungle. Outside its ring, blue plants and walking trees wandered free and unhindered, wild and bustling with constant activity. Within it lay nothing but flat gray and purple, like an oasis in reverse sucking the life out of an otherwise flourishing ecosystem. The circle was dead as dirt, contrasting the lively forest with a grim hint of artificial impediment.

Enri leaned forward and approached the patch of dry land from above, spotting Fenna standing across it with her hands upon her hips. Next to her, the TurTek Rep looked straight up a Nokkian tree that had stopped dead in its tracks upon the barren circle's outer edge. Fre'dd dangled above him with his harnessing rope completely retracted and his chest pressed firmly into the turtle-shell spinner above.

"Ho, Fre'dd! How's it hanging?" Enri glided in, greeting his entrapped companion with an upbeat attitude. His companion merely answered with a grimace of pain.

The TurTek Rep straightened up to address him. "Mr. Riatu, we have a dilemma. This whole area seems impervious to our wireless signals; we haven't even been able to signal Ms. Caae's appliance to release Mr. Invictus from above!"

"No dilemma there." Fenna brushed past him, crackling her knuckles with a sly smile on her face. She jumped on Fre'dd's tree and bound up without a harness, reaching him within moments and fiddling with her turtle-shell spinner that was holding him in. She tossed an object that looked like a bottle and hissed like a snake onto the dusty ground below Without even waiting to see the device spring open like a cushion, she signaled her spinner and smart rope to snap open, releasing the large gladiator from his torment and dropping him down onto padded safety below.

<14:01:12 a.s.t.> **<day 4>**

The group of travelers decided to rest and allow Fre'dd as much time as he needed to recover, despite the fact that he insisted he needed only a few minutes. After a turmoil-filled thrashing that should have killed off any mortal man, the Martian gladiator was clearly in no condition to walk. Although his muscles were bashed and his bones had been rattled about, he still turned down both Enri and the TurTek Rep's offers to help wrap up his wounds and apply healing solutions as needed.

After a quick x-ray wave scan told Enri that none of Fre'dd's bones were sprained or broken, he relented and left him alone, handing Fre'dd several food bars to chew on as he prepared lunch.

Enri took out a cooker from his knapsack and placed it on the dusty purple ground of the barren circle. He peeled open a food bar labeled "Beef - Dinner" and plopped it into his heating pan, squinting as it fizzled, melted down, and began to pop, arranging itself in strands and solidifying into small strips of meat. The mouthwatering, chemo-biologically engineered tastes of TurTek's master science-chefs soon overpowered the citrus smell of the forest.

Enri separated the food into individual meal portions, giving Fre'dd a substantial amount more than the rest. He looked up, spotting the TurTek Rep nearby placing bulbous alien fruits into his bulking Pandora's hat.

"Say, what's your name?" Enri asked out of the blue. "I'm sorry, but I can't for the life of me remember."

"Name?" the porcelain-smiled man replied without looking away from his curiously diligent task. "I am but a representation. My name is irrelevant."

"Yeah, but you've gotta have a name, right?" Fenna joined in.

"Whatever name my original source had once been called no longer matters."

"Oh gimme a break, hat-head!" Fenna insisted. "Why not just tell us?"

"Whoever I used to be is simply no longer who I am. Even if my memories tell me otherwise, the physical entity that is me is not the same person who I remember—not the cells in my body and not the impulses in my brain. We are all but copies, not the originals who possessed the names we may remember ever so clearly."

"You reject your old identity completely?" Enri mused.

"Yes indeed," the Rep agreed, showing no quiver through his porcelain smile. "That old identity is no more me than a man can be his own father or a woman her mother."

"New leaf, new color, eh?" Enri asked. "I can respect that. So... what do you want us to call you?"

"If you wish to know, my specific duplication title is: TurTek representative, senior first class, number eight, version R. MMDCCXLII."

"What do those numbers mean?" Enri asked.

"It's roman numerals!" his handheld terminal squeaked out from in his knapsack. "2,742!"

"That is the date of the last quark-scan from which I have been duplicated."

"Ok, so *rep* it is!" Enri decided. "Who needs a name? Anyway, food's ready!"

"Food! Food food food food!" his handheld terminal piped up.

"Esurio multum—I am starving," Fre'dd looked up eagerly and accepted a plate of food, scowling at how small and unappetizing it looked. He took a bite of the beef-like substance and was immediately surprised to find it to taste better than it looked, with a multitude of compressed tastes that the Martian gladiator had never encountered before. Every strand struck his tongue with the weight of individuality, boasting flavors matching grilled, roasted, stewed, fried, boiled, dried, salted, smoked, and spiced beef.

Fre'dd finished his food so fast he felt pangs of sadness at the sight of his empty plate. Surprisingly, though, he found himself no longer hungry. He gazed up to take in the environment with refreshed eyes. He took notice of his companions around him talking philosophy.

"Are we human?" Enri was asking. "What do you guys think?"

"What?" Fenna said through a mouth full of food.

"If we are no longer the people we used to be, are we really even people at all?"

"Yes, of course," the TurTek Rep replied matter-of-factly. "We are Homo sapiens one hundred percent—every single cell and strand of DNA which makes us."

"We're only *impersonations* of human beings, not the real thing, man. If I get what you're saying about the duplication process itself, not even a molecule of the elements that make us has ever made contact with an actual human being."

"Incorrect," the Rep disagreed. "The materials of which we are composed may not be of Earth, but the patterns in which they are arranged come from blueprints only possible by the evolution of mankind. If our originals hadn't existed, neither would we."

"I agree with the hat-head," Fenna declared. "What's the difference between a perfect copy and the real thing? If our originals were human and we are exactly the same as them, what else can we be but human as well?"

"You know, I guess it doesn't really matter anyway," Enri admitted. "We are here, and we are who we are. So in the end, what does it really matter what we call ourselves?"

"Cogito ergo sum—I think therefore I am," Fre'dd stated. "I feel as me, and, therefore, I am as me."

"Descartes, 1637!" Enri's handheld terminal piped out.

Fre'dd placed a hand behind him to lean upon a blue tree trunk and pulled himself off the soft, springy moss. "All right, enough is enough! Where to next?"

"Wait, Fre'dd, You took quite a bruising back there; why don't we just take it easy for now?" Enri asked. "We should camp here until the sun returns, and then we'll still have a few hours of hiking before the long night."

"Satis!" Fre'dd demanded. "Let us set off already—enough talk!" He turned his attention towards the TurTek Rep. "Where to next?"

"We enter the face of the mountain." The TurTek representative pointed out above the forest to the all-encompassing, gigantic wave-spire looming closer than ever before. He gestured towards the closest stone cliffs several hundred yards away where a deep fissure led into darkness. "There must be a source of water flowing through the spire to support such abundant life. The best way to find it would be to go inside."

"A cave!?" Fenna complained. "Tuk no, I did *not* sign up for that!"

"Gratias." Fre'dd thanked the Rep for his direction. He raced onwards through the forest of walking trees, disappearing out of sight a couple dozen steps in. The TurTek Rep followed close behind, eager not to lose Fre'dd again.

"Godsdamnit! I hate caves!" Fenna grunted. Enri patted her sympathetically on the back as he passed by her, trailing the path of broken moss left behind by Fre'dd. She harrumphed to herself and followed along.

# 9 : caves :

"The uncontrollable fear of impending doom lurking out from every hidden shadow can force one's sense of self to whither and fall within a moment's notice. However, there notably exist those outlying few whose sheer willpower and perseverance deters the pull of existential breakdown. These people we commonly name as our *leaders*."

-Transcripts of William

<16:34:52 a.s.t.><day 7><Anok>

Marble caverns of dark maroon greeted the travelers with extravagant variation upon every forward step. Fantastic pearl-white veins wove through them like strands of stray hair, marking each and every surface with its own fingerprint of stone. Above the humans at random heights hung endless lines of rounded stalactites stretching up impossible distances, ranging in presence from barely visible in the shadows to almost blocking the travelers' paths as they dipped down low to the ground. Although sometimes a challenge to circumnavigate, these natural pillars provided the hikers much fascination, giving them an often-needed break in routine to simply get around and the occasional platform on which to spend several seconds of rest.

The four travelers had individually equipped lamps upon their heads several days before, casting away the black as they transitioned from the rustle-bustle of frantically dodging blue, walking trees outside to the dead chill of trekking through series upon series of echoing chambers. They had bid the crazy cerulean forest and its citrusy atmosphere a swift farewell, and the subterranean stage of the humans' journey began with nary an acknowledged word. Nearly half a week had passed— according solely to the digital readouts from the humans' terminal screens—and nothing of much interest had happened. The caves seemed simply too dark, too cold, and too isolated from sunlight to have anything interesting exist within other than perhaps the occasional flurry of flying gekkons.

Enri led the team blindly through many a passage and tunnel using nothing but instinct to guide them forward. His wristband terminal established a fairly competent auto-updating three-dimensional map of the plethora of variable cavern sizes, lengths, and convoluted passageway angles they passed by. In his past life, the avid explorer had travelled underground numerous times and, as a result had long since developed one basic rule: leave a physical trail. Despite all of his digital data-gathering methods, Enri remained resolute in marking up each and every cavern intersection with a simple arrow denoting direction, using his old handheld terminal's spray-paint feature to leave behind a visible breadcrumb path of where he had come from and where he had gone. However, as the days grew long and access to sunlight remained scarce, Enri's old handheld began to run out of juice, leaving him no option but to dither down usage and conserve its power. Although the terminal vocally complained at its own continued disuse, eventually even its squawks began to wind down, saving energy.

"When I was young, my brother used to recite these whimsical jokes to make me laugh," Fenna spoke up. The further underground the group trekked, the worse her inner rumblings became, intensifying down her spine into ice-cold shivers of a mostly psychological nature. Instead of allowing her own mind to drive herself crazy, she consciously diverted herself from this line of thought, choosing to cast herself out of her claustrophobic loop.

"You have a brother?" Enri asked, intrigued.

"Jessie Caae, traversal expert first class!" the TurTek Rep announced knowingly.

Fenna continued, ignoring the implications of the Rep's reservoir of intimate knowledge. "Back then, I never truly understood how completely idealistic his jokes were—not until it was far too late to ask him about it."

"May we hear one?" Fre'dd requested gently through the short, blue rose-smelling blasts of Dirk's mobility belt automatically shifting pressure around him to assist with the verticality of these cavern heights. "I am unfamiliar with jokes of whimsy."

"Yeah, okay. Here's a little brainteaser I always found completely ridic: 'So a peacock, a dog, a tiger, a mosquito, a jungle otter, and white-backed rhino wake up on the moon. Which of these does not belong?'"

"What is a jungle?" Fre'dd asked.

"None of those species belong," the TurTek representative answered factually.

"Wrong!" Fenna exclaimed. "It's a low-gee lunar zoo; they're all sideshow attractions!"

Fre'dd muddled his brow. "So which one does not belong?"

"The mosquito, *obvio*! They're extinct!" Fenna explained enthusiastically. "Who would ever resurrect the godsdamn mosquito to put it in a zoo?"

"Resurrect?" Fre'dd asked. "Resurrectio?"

"Like recreate from DNA scans?" Enri suggested.

"Well yeah, you know... that's the joke, Earth-boy. Who would ever pay to have them recreated them on Luna? They used to suck your blood and made you itch, you know—grody, man, grody. Tiny freakin' *vampires*, the lot of them!"

"You never know, space-girl," Enri retorted back with a snort. "Maybe if you tried you could do a lot with a mosquito on the moon... Ever hear of plain old unbiased *research*? The unexpected benefits of scientific discovery, maybe?"

"Fine, yeah, sure, that's great and all," Fenna agreed tentatively. "But really now, what possible benefit could ever come from recreating a species of flying biters? Useless, really."

"Non. I heard rumors of them once being used through the Aren'A circuits," Fre'dd responded.

"What, mosquitos?"

"Yes. Banned usage of modified mosquitos as weapons."

"Weapons!? For what? Pest control?"

"Entire battle zones were brought down to their knees overnight with a single tube of altered mosquitos. By the time morning broke, the sabotage could go so far as to alter a combatant's genetic structure and forever destroy an army's ability to fight in combat."

"Holy Zeus, that's vicious." Fenna whistled. "Wouldn't it be easier to just infect their opponents with something fatal, simply killing them instead of disabling them for life?"

Fre'dd paused unhappily. "That would be... unforgivable. Murder is the worst of sins—a slap in the face of the gods."

Fenna shut herself up, feeling the weight behind the large man's words and the hypocrisy of her own. "Unforgivable" was not a term to take lightly, especially around new and future company.

The TurTek Rep broke the awkward silence, oblivious to the unpleasant emotions hanging in the air. "You know, Ms. Caae, Mr. Riatu is absolutely correct," he said. "Many avenues of close examination end up having far greater significance than we could ever initially expect. For example, did you know the common 21st century solution for curing leukemia required a genetic delivery system created from a modified HIV viral agent? Also, don't forget the relatively unpopular 22nd century pursuit pertaining to the advent of fungus under the influence of a precise electro-magnetic field. Although seemingly unrelated, it eventually revealed absolute wonders towards the understanding of slowing and potentially preventing the cancerous degeneration of all types of organic cells."

"I have no idea what you're talking about," Fenna replied dismissively.

"Just that the most significant answers can often come from sources unknown, despite all preconceptions into the matter," the Rep explained. "That is all."

"Yeah ok, whatever," she said, pushing forward into the dark. "Let's just get moving already; these godsdamn caves are making me sick!"

A fluttering school of yellow-green gekkons dipped down into view, weaving through the stalactites overhead and disappearing through the shadows of an upcoming three-way junction. Enri pulled up his old handheld terminal to activate its electric paintbrush. He quickly checked its power level, noting that it would surely run out of energy by the day's end. Deciding to use it anyway, he sprayed out a neon green, glow-in-the-dark arrow on the wall, curving it leftward from the floor up in indication that the travelers had come from the cavern behind and chosen to go onwards in the left direction.

"Why left?" Fenna asked, unhappily eyeing how narrow the walls drew in the passage but completely unwilling to admit this fact aloud.

"Why not?" Enri shrugged, looking back to the top-hatted TurTek representative as if to gain some confirmation. He got nothing more than an empty stare. "You have any reason to choose the other way?"

Fenna frowned. "Fine, whatev," she relented, making a show of entering the narrow passage before any of the others.

The stone ceiling hung lower than ever, with rows of stunted stalactites ending less than ten feet above the floor and tightening considerably within the length of several dozen steps. Only a few hundred feet away from the junction, the cave finished abruptly at a jagged dead-end.

"Why not, he asks!" Fenna laughed to herself as she reached the cracked maroon wall at the end of the passage. She smirked as Enri reached her with a disappointed look upon his face.

"Oh well, no biggie. Let's just turn back and try the other direction," he replied. "No, wait." He gazed past Fenna and ducked down by her feet, nudging her out of the way. "The search ain't over till it's over!" he exclaimed. "At least, that's what my old mentor, Dirk, used to say."

The crack in the red marble turned out to be no mere cleft, but rather a hole cut deep into the ruby veins of the wall's stone. Its edges curled down through the floor and onwards, presenting a narrow passage the width of a single human. With Enri's headlamp shining directly into the crevice, the pitch-black shadows within lit up to reveal another room behind it—a substantial cavern dropping down deep into a grand chamber below. Sounds of dripping echoes stirred faintly through the shadows, hinting at flowing water yet unseen.

Enri stuck his head through the crack and shone his headlamp into the chamber, illuminating a large artificial looking room dripping with reflections. Far down below was a perfectly straight white marble floor with several dozen spotted pools of clear water connected through a circular network of liquid passages. A grid of descending glass pillars and hanging ledges between him and the water added to the straight-cut feel of the watery chamber, all sparkling bright with the heavenly-white light cast out by the explorer's headlamp.

Enri held his arm forward, allowing his wristband terminal to capture the chamber in full. Once satisfied with his recording, he backed out of the crack in the wall and looked up to find Fenna, Fre'dd and the TurTek Rep staring down at him. He held up his wristband terminal and projected out a hologram of what he had just seen. They gaped at it for several long moments.

"This verifies the fact that there is indeed water flowing through the spire," the TurTek representative announced. "That is one big advantage towards the prospect of colonization."

"Coming through, Earthboy!" Fenna reached back and pulled one of her pneumatic pickaxes out of its sheath in her turtle-shell pack. Without waiting for a response, she smashed it down into the ground, embedding its blade into solid rock before looping a smart-rope around it and signaling her turtle-shell spinner to ready itself for an assisted descent. She threw the length of rope down the hole in the wall, pushing her legs through the fissure opening and wasting no time entering. She looked back at Enri with a wink.

"You coming?" she asked and then was gone.

Enri monitored the cable holding onto Fenna's impacted pickaxe, making sure it did not slip and cast her down into oblivion. Only once he heard the light *thump* of her safe landing on marble floor and saw her axe had stopped bearing weight did Enri turn around to acknowledge Fre'dd and the TurTek representative behind him. He noticed the nervous trepidation that had taken grip of them both. Neither of the two looked pleased with the prospect of following Fenna's example and pushing out through the wall.

"Nullo modo am I fitting through that crack," Fre'dd announced straightforward.

"Wooo-wee!" Fenna's voice echoed up like a wavering ghost from the chamber below, followed by a splash and a stream of childlike giggling. "Wow, you've gotta come see this!"

Enri pulled up Fenna's rope and braced himself for descent. "I'm going down. You guys can stay up and explore some of the other paths that wind around and into that room. I saw many wall openings in there."

"Please report back via terminal as soon as you can," the TurTek Rep told him. "Your device's shortwave should have enough bounce to reach us through these tunnels. Keep your geographical map syncing with ours."

"Will do," Enri replied. He signaled to Fre'dd and pulled his old handheld terminal out of his knapsack. He handed it up to the large man.

"Hey? What? Oh! Tired!" the device squeaked out, displeased with its low battery life.

"Mark your way across the cavern intersections as I did," Enri instructed Fre'dd "It wouldn't do to have us all lost and apart."

"Aye." Fre'dd nodded. "It shall be done."

Without further hesitation, Enri jumped down after Fenna, descending quickly with both hands upon the cable before him. His gaze centered upon the red marble wall rushing up past him. A splash of water beneath made the explorer look down mid-descent, twisting him around and breaking his concentration.

Enri's rope suddenly went slack and his stomach lurched up into his gut as he plummeted down through the air. He splashed unceremoniously into the cold water below with no chance to take a gasping breath and prepare himself for complete submersion. As Enri sunk down to the bottom of the clear pool, his wristband terminal flashed him a quick message: $H_2O$ *mixture safe, non-hazardous levels of $CO_2$, $Na$, $Ca$, $Mn$, and $Si$ detected.* He kicked up off the ground and shot up through the water gasping for air.

Fenna burst out laughing as soon as she caught his eyes. She pulled herself out of the water as he swam across the glowing pool to reach her.

"What happened up there?" Enri asked. "Why'd the line go slack?"

"You let go," she replied with a smirk. "That's what happened."

"Wait," Enri paused, pointing a finger at Fenna to quiet her down. "Hold that thought."

He handed her his drenched knapsack and kicked off the pool wall, taking a deep breath of air before diving back down into the water. He grabbed an object off the pool floor just as his lungs began screaming for air and then kicked back up to make a quick ascent. After splashing back up to the water's surface, Enri swam back over to Fenna. He handed her a pneumatic pickaxe out of the water.

"You were saying?" he asked.

"Huh, my bad, Eartho. I guess you really didn't pull that tuk-up on your own." Fenna sheathed her weapon back into her turtle-shell backpack were it belonged. She helped Enri pull himself out of the water. "What are Herc and the Hat doing up there?"

"Good question. There's no way they'd have detached me intentionally, right?"

"Probably not," Fenna admitted. "Those guys have no humor."

Enri looked up the wall from where he had come and, finding it spackled with numerous dark cracks, fissures and crevices, could not make out which exact hole he had emerged out of. He cupped his hands over his mouth.

"Fre'dd! Rep! You guys up there?" Enri shouted as loud as he could, hearing his voice echo out through the caves lining the chamber walls. He held up his wristband terminal and began to amplify his voice fourfold. He also sent out a wave of data, hoping to ping it off the other men's terminals and determine their current locations. "**FREDD! REP!** What's going on!?"

After receiving no response, Enri spun around and looked beyond Fenna into the cavernous water-chamber room. It appeared roughly rectangular over about an acre-wide span, with a white floor and four crimson walls. Flowing rivers of sparkling clear water crisscrossed the room, connecting stagnant pools through an unnaturally clean-cut network. It seemed to glow of its own accord. Above the pools hung a grid of sharp rock formations that looked far too oddly uniform, with edges cut sharply as if fashioned by tools and a structure arranged like a wireframe building.

Enri looked up through the lattice of hanging rocks, noting horizontal pathways, vertical stacks, junctions, rivets, and so forth, all of which simply should not exist in a natural setting. *What could have made this?*

"What is this place?" Fenna wondered aloud, following Enri's example and looking around the room. "Seems kinda out of place after so many days of nothing but caves, huh?"

"Yeah... There's definitely something unnatural going on here," he agreed. "Something must have carved this chamber out."

"You mean like a Nokkian creature? One of those walking trees? Or a little flying guy?"

"Well, I dunno," Enri admitted. "Anyway, something that liked having water around."

"You think maybe this room could be manmade?" Fenna speculated. "Like, maybe there were humans here long before us?"

"Hmm." Enri looked back at her with a puzzled look on his face. "I hadn't really thought of that. I guess I just assumed we were the first ones here."

Enri caught a glimpse of an indentation carved out of crimson marble on the chamber's outer wall. He held up his wristband terminal and zoomed in on an intricately carved depiction of a Nokkian creature of some sort. It looked like a cross between a two-sided snake and the walking blue trees from the writhing jungle outside—long, with an exoskeletal spine and symmetrical from end to end. Unlike the walking trees outside the spire, this creature was thick in the middle. Instead of a puffy cotton ball on either end, it had an articulated claw with a bulbous orb-like eyeball within. Its pupils spiraled inwards into ink-black whirlwinds like galaxies spinning into supermassive black holes. *This carving is a masterpiece!*

"Hey, you see that?" He pulled Fenna along as he moved to get a better view. Hopping over glowing white channels of water, he pointed out the extraterrestrial artwork above. With shadows dancing at the light of their moving headlamps, the sculpture looked alive, complemented by its amazingly crafted form.

"What in Hades is it?" Fenna murmured.

A rustle from above caused them both to look up. They stood silent for a long moment.

"HeeeEEeeLLppp," the Rep's voice echoed down through the stonework lattice grid near the chamber's ceiling, and then a solid object promptly smashed down into the ground beside them. Enri and Fenna immediately recognized the object as the TurTek representative's bulking top hat.

"AHHHH! Let go, let go!" the TurTek Rep yelled out from somewhere else above. He dipped down into view, hanging upside-down far up the lattice of stone. They could not see his legs, as a force of spastic motion pulled him up and dipped him ferociously back down in another location. He popped in and out of view though several separate sections of the sharp stalactite grid above.

"HELP!" the Rep screamed as he zigzagged through a lower section of the hanging rock wireframe, moving in short, violent jerks. "Help, help, help, help!"

"Rep!" Enri yelled up. "Hang on tight!" His wristband terminal caught sight of a swaying object within a set of brilliantly reflecting green gems above. Zooming into the image, the terminal holographically displayed a large man rocking back and forth on a balcony edge, donning a mobility belt blowing at full blast. *Wait! Could it possibly be...? What was Fre'dd doing up there?*

He zoomed in further on the wristband terminal's hologram and had the device positively confirm the fact that it was, indeed, the Martian gladiator Fre'dd Invictus standing in the rafters far, far above. The large man's three liquid tube necklaces were glowing bright around his neck, illuminating him from the dark and cascading long shadows beneath. His eyes were shut tight.

"HeEeEeLp!" the TurTek Rep shouted as he passed unseen somewhere beneath Fre'dd.

The Martian gladiator jumped out into the air despite his evident fear of heights, flying forward with his arms spread wide. Timing his plummet perfectly, he collided head-on with the screaming TurTek Rep below and grappled onto him for dear life. The Rep screamed out in pain as the weight of Fre'dd's body added to his own, and the hidden creature holding them up began stuttering and groaning under the added effort, struggling to keep them all afloat. It lost strength with every swing, groaning out deep bellows as it eventually released its hold completely and dropped its human payload. Fre'dd and the TurTek representative fell down in the air towards Enri and Fenna.

Fenna cast down a can that rattled like a snake and puffed up instantaneously into a cushion. The two men dove straight into it, owing their subsequent lack of broken bones entirely to the huntress's remarkable reaction speed. Enri looked back up to try and spot the creature that had dragged them but found nothing but empty grid-work left behind.

"What happened up there?" Enri helped the Rep up and handed him back his Pandora's hat. Fre'dd's glowing necklaces faded, soon left inert upon the large man's neck. He took a bite into the blue one, drinking the liquid inside and draining its contents. Enri hand him a fruit chew. Fre'dd smiled.

"I made a mistake," the Rep admitted. "It was my fault."

"What do you mean?" Enri asked.

"I tried to communicate."

"With what?"

Fre'dd's smile turned into a look of absolute horror as he caught a glimpse of the strange snake-like artwork carved into the crimson marble above. He gestured wildly and wheezed.

"It was *that!*" He proclaimed. "That is the CREATURA which attacked us!"

"Tuk, I knew it! Those things are monsters!" Fenna cursed. "Let's take them all down before they get us!"

"Woah woah there," Enri cautioned. "Don't rush to any conclusions."

"Yes indeed, you don't yet have all the information," the Rep replied. "The truth, I am sorry to say, is that the encounter that caused all this was entirely my fault."

"Okay... so?" Fenna looked back to him with suspicion. "What did you do?"

"Well... I stuck a hand in its eye. Turns out it wasn't a terminal interface after all."

"The tuk is wrong with you, idiot?" Fenna chastised. "Are you trying to start a species war due to pure stupidity?"

"I need to sleep," Fre'dd announced, acting uncharacteristically forward. "I will not last much longer." He went limp, sinking down into Fenna's cushion behind him.

# 10 : flavors :

"We run, we play, we seek, we hide—humanity at its core is nothing but simple."
– Transcripts of the Empress

### <2118 C.E. - the age of illusion><Earth>

A grueling decade after Fenna had begun her search for the true answers of the Olympic Station disaster, tales of her pseudonym had become infamous among hushed whispers of the Zeun over-ground and in the wild legends of her redemptions abound. The stories told of the hidden assassin Artemis seeking revenge for the fall of the station Olympia and warned all third parties involved of a coming echo in the night and the unforgiving ferocity that would follow. Her rumored reputation rose through the shadows, depicting her as an unseen hunter goddess ready for any big game, a hired hitwoman blessed with a touch for the spinning of fates, striking hard through the zero-gee dark.

In truth, Fenna took little pleasure in the admiration she received through ill-gained snippets of praise. She felt merely a girl forsaken and forlorn, without friends, confidants, or any knowledge of a life with companionship. Therefore, she filled her lonesome days with the mere chance of tracking down all her far-fetched leads anywhere they would take her, donning the alias of the huntress Artemis primarily as the means for Fenna to make a living. Every year her leads spread ever thinner, and her life began to require more expenses than her devoted pursuit for truth alone could fulfill.

Luckily, finding lucrative jobs had never really been all too hard for someone with Fenna's degree of skill, as there always seemed to be someone out there on the Zeun net willing to pay exclusive sums for access to her destructive wake. Most job requests sent Artemis' way turned out to be no more than ramblings of nonsense, completely unworthy of her time. Every once in a while, though, Fenna got a message on the public web that intrigued her enough to instigate a background check on the contact and schedule an indirect exchange of information. She was picky about the contracts she chose, always leaning with bias towards low Earth-orbital Zeun missions and all farfetched jobs with any relation to the Olympic space-station. Although the majority of these missions led nowhere interesting, every so often, Fenna would divert onto an unexpected path and receive unpredictable fountains of information.

Such unforeseen discoveries included a black market station posing as a floating science lab and a structural development site that she discovered to have an unusual tendency towards commissioning an unnecessarily large security force—both of which turned out to be wholly unrelated to the Olympic station disaster. Some jobs required finesse and others required a bang, while a rare few required a touch that was substantially less straightforward, like the rescue and babysit of a VIP zero-gee native. Nowadays most missions turned out to be more lethal in nature, contracting Artemis to bring a person or institution to an end.

Fenna's vigilante mission to expose the truths of all things Orbital and all matters Olympic had initially begun as a consequence of necessity. At first, her trail had seemed rather simple. After all, a tragedy had occurred on a scale previously unknown on the fringes of Earth-space, so one would have expected commissions and governments worldwide to have pushed for redemption—or at least for some sense of unaugmented truth. But this notion had turned out to be vastly optimistic. Yes, there was an outcry—there had to be, with over 25,000 internationally affiliated men, women, and children blown out of the Olympic station and only 8,700 subsequently rescued and revived from the vacuum of space—but it was not the outcry Fenna was looking for. No, this was but a whimper where she had wished for a hurricane of noise!

Every answer given freely to the public had been so incredibly shallow, so close to the surface of expectation, that it boiled Fenna's blood to the core—but nobody else seemed to care. The public didn't want answers, just a scapegoat to blame. They didn't need redemption, just a spectacle to see. The world had mourned all right, projecting their grief through multi-billion viewer broadcast television with corporate celebrities here and there donating money to supposedly help support the desperate cause.

Monuments were erected, space vessels were dedicated in name to those who had lost their lives, and a whole new set of safety regulations were added on top of the old to double, triple, and quadruple the screenings and protocols before allowing an increased number of people aboard a space-borne craft. Multimedia movies were emblazoned as new-age memorial events, expressing deep concern through broadcasts and terminal waves alike, bringing stories of the Olympic Station disaster to the minds of all but, in the end, doing nothing to find the real truth behind why it had happened.

Fenna had searched and searched and searched, until her eyes felt heavy and dry and her void of loss numb under a festering impatience. After all was said and done, she still had no solid explanation of what had gone wrong to make the Olympic station explode in the first place. After years of research and exploratory infiltration, she had found no particular cover-up explaining the truth, just a complete lack of data. Conjectures left and right had been made as to why the Olympic Station had spontaneously torn open and shatteringly decompressed, but the options were all fabricated and statistical, containing no weight of reality. Far too early in her short life, the lonely young girl was forced into skepticism and disillusionment, realizing not everyone's opinion was as helpful as they made it out to be. Sometimes people were just spouting taurshit!

By the age of 15, the teenage girl Fenna Caae had become more defiant than complacent, more subversive than publically inclined, more the huntress Artemis than anything resembling who she had been before. As her alias gained the status of celebrity throughout the Zeun net, she soon found out that she was not quite alone searching for the answers. Someone else was out there too, a master enigma who was yet to be seen. And he seemed intent on keeping her in the dark.

The first time this person had stumped the legendary Artemis was during an intelligence-gathering mission off the coast of a restructured geothermal nu-Pompeii magma extractor. Fenna had arrived on scene from the sky above, diving down from orbit several minutes too late. She found not only all local terminals and data nets wiped clean, but the entire volcano emptied of its heavy machinery. Over two tons of welded metal and infused polycarbon had been scooped clean, along with half the mountain, leaving nary a sign of who or what was responsible and not a footprint left behind, just a whole lot of lava.

Over the following months and years, tales of peculiarities and unexplained eventualities began to surface in Fenna's circles, telling of shuttles hijacked mid atmospheric-transit, of abandoned warehouses filled to the brim with a flood of molecularly identical diamonds, of mock ghost-towns built overnight on the flatlands, mountains, and oceans of Earth, and of space-stations repositioned in orbit, sometimes reappearing hundreds of thousands of miles away from their previous trajectories and sometimes never reappearing at all.

At first, Fenna suspected no correlation between the varied mysteries, simply marking them as proof that everybody was always lying. But after a while and a few rounds around the professional block, Fenna started to pay heed to the incidents that stood out above the rest, categorizing them as noticeably more enigmatic than any other on the circuits. Whoever the enigma was, he was a true master of deceit—a harbinger of oblivious chaos who felt no need to leave a self-righteous message for the public to decipher. Instead, he kept all his affairs perfectly silent. As with the legends behind Artemis herself, the mysterious infiltrator's tales spread through indirect stories of vague recollection and contemporary mythology gathered over time. As such, he was labeled with a pseudonym similar to her own: Apollo, god of light and brother of the goddess Artemis. As the mysterious infiltrator kept striking, the corporate damage he dealt rose higher and higher, and soon there seemed no option but for Artemis to pay full attention to his full repertoire of trickery. Her clients nearly demanded it.

By 24, Fenna, as Artemis, was an expert at her game and had the pick of the litter when it came to clientele. Her current mission had come from multiple sources in many different anonymous postings all over the waves of the Zeun web, but each one had been clearly meant specifically for her eyes only. Even though the postings had given her no details of names, dates, or locations, Fenna's data bots had noted her high statistical chance of being interested in whatever this mission would turn out to be and of the immediate emphasis for haste. They had urged her to pursue it and hinted that it had something to do with the mysterious Apollo. Ever the sucker of a good pursuit, she picked one of the many posted requests and accepted the contract. It held the geographical coordinates and imminent timeframe for a single reentry event through the atmosphere of Earth… scheduled to be performed by the enigmatic Apollo himself. *Tuk yes!*

Four hours after initial contact with her anonymous client, Fenna found herself on an inward path towards Earth, rendezvousing with a ship with a channeled underbelly soft as rubber and an upturned tail like a whale's. She recognized it as an old cargo ship like the one her mother used to pilot but repurposed with weapons and fortified with defensive capabilities.

Fenna's contact lens terminal classified the vessel as a militarized cargo runner originally meant for transport to and from the mining belt, routing supplies to those around and beyond Mars and transporting back raw mined materials. It instructed her to dock in the ship's underbelly and elaborated that, due to the unpredictable sizes involved in asteroid mining, the flexible hull opened up in channeled strips and allowed the padded entry of oblong shapes and sizes. This made it perfect for the delivery of fragile goods and building materials and for the ferrying of small-to-medium ships over long distances.

After a thorough debriefing over an indirect contact lens terminal message from her client, Fenna donned a heavy-duty flight suit and pressed herself up against the vessel's underbelly, watching the view of planet Earth expand beneath her. Her terminal lenses kept her up to date on the current location of a high-priority cargo container inside the ship in anticipation of capture by the phantom thief Apollo. She was ready to launch at a moment's notice and catch him in the act if and when he came.

Finally given the chance to catch her long-awaited prey head-on, the young huntress was prepared to do anything to see it all through, waiting like a tiger in the brush. Using her lens terminal's overlaid virtual map to see the soon-to-be targeted cargo capsule's spatial coordinates in relation to her, Fenna was ready to leap as soon as it began to stir. And sure enough, half an hour later and exactly on schedule, it stirred.

She wasted no time detaching from the ship's hull and immediately shot forward along the channeled underbelly. As fast as she was, though, Apollo was faster. The cargo capsule picked up speed and erupted out of the whale's mouth, accelerating towards Earth as if attracted by a magnetic pull. Luckily, this was exactly what Fenna had anticipated. Having kept a constant eye on the capsule's tracking beacon, Fenna had already reached a good approach when the javelin shot past her—quicker than her own eyes could see but replayable in slow-motion as overlaid within her lenses. It accelerated fast as it raced towards the looming blue planet below, ever further from Fenna on its tail but still trackable by her lenses. By the time Fenna managed to twist and align herself in the right angle to follow the careening, stolen capsule towards the atmosphere of Earth, its beacon told her it was already half a mile away and shrinking out of magnified sight into the brightness of the brilliant, half-crested planet. Fenna propelled after it, accelerating at peak suit-power towards the path set by Apollo—100 mph, 200, 400, 800, 1.5k— but found herself unable to move at a fraction of enigmatic thief's speed.

As the crescent of Earth expanded into a full night sky with Fenna continuing to accelerate at it, the cargo capsule's indicator dropped down past the officially recognized border of planetary reentry and soared right through the upper atmosphere. Although it was too far away for Fenna to see even with magnified sight, as the capsule entered the sky of Earth, she knew it had begun blazing in a hellfire of ozone.

An empty silence of space and mind reflected the heavenly external view as Fenna approached the darkening planet below. Night crept over the globe as she broke orbit against its spin, looking down with zoomed vision to see the night lights of the great cities of Africa crackle into view below, highlighting the heavy presence of humanity with vein-like formations and brightly-lit speckles. Fenna knew the torrents of flames would soon overtake her, impeding her vision of Earth and sky in a maelstrom of white fire and noise. She turned up the volume of music streaming through her earrings to drown out the noise and darkened her helmet to block the view of the upcoming hellfires. The map layered over her terminal vision showed current satellite images of the night above Africa as Apollo's beacon blinked over its Eastern tip—by now several miles ahead of her in descent.

Outside Fenna's line of sight and past the flight suit's helmet, the frenzy of fire came fast and strong. Wisps of heat and combustion from the atmospheric gas around it crept out and expanded behind her into a long trailing wake of flames. Fenna's flight suit easily shielded the immense heat generated and the monumental pressure building but rattled something awful, keeping her ever aware of the awesome energy exploding around her in the ozone.

Even before the flames cleared over the fringes of her visor and she turned off her displays, Fenna already knew which region of the world she would have to land—or rather, which island: Madagascar. She adjusted her trajectory minutely to point herself in the right direction, aiming towards the Western side of the island in question, closely matching the pinging cargo capsule's coordinates lest she were to miss her target by hundreds of miles. As the inferno around her helmet cleared away along with the darkened filter, a night-cast Madagascar came into actual view, lit in clusters and patches of electric-fed illumination.

Within a minute of her sight returning, Fenna dropped low enough through the atmosphere to see the metropolitan lights below dim to a distinguishable articulation, with lines and grids of fields alight between large dark areas of pitch black. The lights stretched around her, the coast grew in size, and Madagascar itself expanded through the flattening horizon from the planet's globular form. A vast network of human cities and towns below spread out and elaborated in detail with many conglomerated blots of separate disjointed villages.

Beneath the atmospheric diver's plunging path, a single city came up faster than the rest, spreading its lights through multiple layers rising up at different paces. Her terminal lenses labeled the region as Tsingy Heights, elaborating that the city itself floated far above the ground, hanging high in the air through many different levels of tethered bands. Beneath the city lay the infamous stone forest of Tsingy, hosting row upon row of tall, natural pinnacle rocks standing side by side, far and wide.

The high-floating city above the stone forest was composed of rings like ancient garden towers in Babylon. Disjointed city clusters spread wide over gradating heights, each tethered separately to the tall rocks below with mile-long, grand cloth canopies. City bands bobbed in the sky like rings of balloons in a parade, independently swaying under the varying wind speeds at different heights. Shuttles buzzed about them like flies in the air, zipping back and forth from cluster to cluster.

Fenna could not help but be impressed as she continued to plummet, noting the mystical contrasted beauty of the natural landmark technologically repurposed with the sky-city swaying high above it. She could also not help but wonder why Apollo had chosen here of all places to bring his prize plunder down from space. *Does he know I'm on his tail? Is he leading me straight into a trap?*

Night turned to dusk as Artemis dove between floating city clusters and crossed through a network of cloth tethers, hovering buildings, and inner-city railed vehicles, dodging structures and slowing herself down in the air by easing on her flight-suit's thrusters. The spire-filled stone forest below the city was rather well lit despite the early dusk, illuminated under the metropolitan canopies and open-air city avenues projecting light downwards. Waterfalling streams of filtered liquid sewage poured down from above in wavering thicknesses, filling the deep-cut passages of the stone forest below with a constantly self-draining flow of temporary rivulets and brooks. They shifted around as the floating structures above them swayed in the air, providing little continuity as to the location of their downpours.

Pretty as the sights were, Fenna was not here for sightseeing—no, she was still Artemis on a hunt. Instead of watching the lights flow around her, the young huntress focused downwards upon the tracking beacon of Apollo's stolen cargo capsule. She identified it as it landed half a mile beneath her within the spiky natural abyss of the Tsingy stone forest, somewhere far below the floating heights of the brilliantly lit Madagascan city. Fenna dove onward, mostly unnoticed by anyone of any note and wholly ignored by those who did happen to see her. The farther she dropped, the brighter the omnidirectional spotlights above her lit her up, until soon she and her flight suit were completely cast in white.

The Tsingy stone forest of Madagascar below came up fast at her with its hundreds upon hundreds of jagged grid-lined pinnacles. Thin strips of green trees and vivid plant life peeked out from within deep welts between the rock spires, growing happily bright despite the tall, impassible stone walls all around them, aided in large part by the abundant intake of resources falling from the city above. The unnaturally high amount of water and light had done much to make the forest flourish with more life than it had ever seen before. Plants and animals took advantage of the endless stock and supply coming down from above and, in the process, began to crumble the rock forest that held it all up.

Fenna passed through a plane of wispy white steam and adjusted her thrust towards the thief Apollo's indicator beacon on the ground, decelerating herself quickly to prepare for landing. A series of tall, gray spikes protruded up from the unseen depths of the forest below and gave Fenna a bit of a challenge to dodge on her way down into the lower green forest's ground level. She would be far enough away from Apollo's location to remain unnoticed but close enough to allow an approach on foot.

She landed with a thud and a splat in a puddle of muddy water, breaking the silence of the forest ravine and setting animals fleeing every which way. Her flight suit sunk down to waist level, sticking through layers of wet soil, so Fenna popped out of it and pounced into the jungle on her own. She went spelunking through the warm water and did a quick scan of the green forest locale to search for any nearby threats. A flock of birds erupted above, a group of lemurs approached in avid curiosity, but nothing of danger stood out.

Twenty minutes and a vertical rock-climb later, Fenna discovered the source of the stolen capsule's tracker beacon within a suspended, cylindrical wooden hut braced to a pinnacle of rock, harnessed with roots of rubber, cloth, and wire vining. Fenna's terminal lenses reaffirmed that Apollo's signal emanated somewhere within it, so, without delay, the eager huntress climbed up the circular cabin's artificial vines and sought to find an indiscernible way in. She braced the roof's paneling and melted out several metal bolts to pry open a glass skylight panel. She then slipped into the house from above, landing catlike within its one and only room, which turned out to be void of all but a silver post mid-center and a spectacular view from out its large singular window. Apollo was nowhere to be found.

Fenna almost gasped aloud in frustration, but the Artemis inside her did not allow her to make a peep. She approached the silver post and swiped it with her hand. It lit up at the touch and displayed out of its circumference multiple holographic terminal interfaces containing the images of newspaper clippings, article printouts, spreadsheets of recurrent search algorithms, and so forth.

"The tuk?" Fenna muttered under her breath, truly confounded at what she saw.

She singled out several terminal interfaces of interest to focus upon and stretched them away from the silver post like wads of gum pulled apart. They puffed up and stabilized in the air, giving the curious huntress a detailed look at a range of content varying from TurTechnicks shuttle blueprints to redistribution-factory openings to the founding of a marketing hub outside of the perimeter of Mars. Countless virtual documents covering a variety of subjects loosely related to the company of TurTechnicks filled the entirety of the terminal post, all laid out cleanly for her to see and record. *What exactly is going on here?* she wondered. *What have I been led into?*

One article in particular drew Fenna's attention. It read:

**Four conditions related to the onslaught of the Olympic Station Tragedy—Number 1:** The boom of industry preceding the possibility of a changing extra-global market promised hope but brought with it an unsettled fear of local abandonment and a deficit in governmental involvement. **Number 2:** Lucrative efforts without central monopolization promoted the mismatched creation of ragtag developments, lacking any source of standardization. **Number 3:** Fast expansion and loose safety standards allowed undocumented oversights in zero-gee construction efforts, including but not limited to the overly vast production of large, linked, single-space corridors. **Number 4:** Where the influx of supply and demand brought an overflow of unregulated physical development in zero-gee space, it brought also the ability and desire to manipulate such a system for personal gain.

Underneath the article were several notes hastily written by someone with an angry hand, presumably Apollo himself. They read:

TAURSHIT INCARNATE!!! **NUMBER 5:** Plans made consciously are due for changes without bidding. **NUMBER 6:** Those who make plans resent changes to those plans. **NUMBER 7:** Centuries of development dull not the lofty pain of singular greed. **NUMBER 8:** Gestures of power must match the scale of the example being made. **NUMBER 9:** AN EXAMPLE WAS MADE LOUD AND CLEAR—but then blamed on third-party error—WHY, TurTechnicks, WHY!?

Fenna stepped back and breathed deeply. She swiped aside the article, noticing something textured upon the actual surface of the terminal pole. An intriguing red handprint rippled like a physical crease of paint on the otherwise smooth pillar. The eye-like emblem of TurTechnicks was printed cleanly within, donning the words: "**Seeking Turia through the hands of Man.**"

Out of pure impulse, Fenna placed her palm upon the red handprint. It fit perfectly within the paint and the acrylic rubber under her fingertips began to hum. The silver-white post outlined her hand with a stroke of neon green.

The message: "**Handprint accepted—access granted,**" appeared in sharp green letters as a circular panel looped around Fenna's hand. A flood of pixels, images, and videos projected themselves into her line of sight, instantly making her very angry, very fast. The images were of her!

The young huntress took back control of her lens imagery and swept through the virtual folders in disgust, grazing through details of her own life that she had always held secret. Within the files Fenna found not only mission specifics that she had never even told her clients but also a fair amount of handwritten speculations about her own process, meticulously detailed down to the very tools and methods she had used to get her jobs done.

Fenna nearly retched at this personal invasion of her privacy. *How had Apollo obtained this information? Why would he possibly need it, anyway?* The whole of Fenna's Artemis identity, considered elite in the underground circuits of the Zeun, looked but a joke in the face of Apollo's investigations into her. *This is repulsive!*

Fenna passionately tossed aside mission account after mission account until she went through each and every virtual folder. Only one image remained—a personally hand-written note that sent shivers down her spine:

The world grows restless as humanity bases its levels of content on parameters set by disagreeing observers. I want you to know the truth, Fenna—I really do. Keeping hidden these long years has torn me asunder, Fi, and watching the pain you wore in the dark was truly the hardest of all. If you feel you must fight, then fight—but know that although the shadows may hold the truth, the answers are not necessarily those you seek.

Things dither from life to life, sweet Fi, from century to century. Make no mistake of assuming uniformity, Artemis. Following any single path as a true guiding light is a sure means of eventual destruction. Avoid these.

She stepped backwards, feeling the wrath burn inside her, matched in intensity only by the roaring sound of water splashing down upon the wooden cabin from a swaying waterfall outside. Her heart flustered and her mind choked at the possibilities laid before her by her own enigma of the chase. *Why did Apollo bring me here? Who is he?*

# 11 : alone :

"Watch out for the perpetrators of irrational thought—a shot in the dark is not the calling of prophesy. However, this being said, it has been noted that several unyielding occasions in the past may have called for exactly such an unpredictability."

-Transcripts of William

<0:39:25 a.s.t.><day 8><Anok>

Enri felt dreadfully bored and could not for the life of him sleep despite the ridiculous comfort of the TurTek sleeping bag that the Rep had duplicated for him nearly a week before. Cool air circulated through the ventilation slits in the group's fold-up electro-kevlar tent, but Enri still found himself sweating profusely. The explorer's mind was restless beyond thought and fluttered chaotically between decompression and analysis of the information acquired in the last few hours. There were so many new leads to follow that his brain raced with possibilities, none of which involved any desire to go to sleep. Questions begged for answers that he just didn't have. *Nothing here makes sense!*

**—HuMmMmMmMm—** ting, **ting,** ting, **ting —** **HuMmMmMmMm—** ting, **ting,** ting, **ting —**

The interplanetary explorer took a moment to pause and think of the three others who had come with him far and long over the past week of adventure. Although he had been on many TurTek expeditions before, he had never been on one with no prospect return, stranded with teammates who would be there to last. Every voyage Enri had ever been on had always been under the presumption that those he had been placed with would be mere flashes in his life. Now there were three—the huntress, the gladiator, and the representative—that were here to stay.

Enri had no idea which qualifications caused TurTek to choose these people to accompany him on this trip, but he knew that it no longer mattered. They were all stuck together now, whether they liked it or not. He and his current teammates would have their fates intertwined for the rest of the foreseeable future, regardless of any specifics of why they were here in the first place.

"…mi dea…" Fre'dd mumbled in his sleep. "Where are you, my empress?" He was half sitting, half leaning against a hardened section of tent propped up against a corner edge of a red marble wall outside. His necklaces glowed ever so slightly.

The last few days had been rather rough for Fre'dd, but the gladiator had taken it so calmly that a casual observer might not have even noticed his distress. The tough man had gotten so many bumps and bruises from the walking trees, gekkons, and mysterious Nokkian snakes alike that Enri was surprised he could even walk. He was flabbergasted at how the Martian seemingly healed within hours every time after taking damage, gaining much respect for the man over the last week as he saw him deal with the cards he had been dealt.

Beside Fre'dd lay the TurTek representative, fidgeting in his sleep with his arm wrapped in a protective embrace around his bulking top hat. This was a man who Enri could not understand—a question mark under a porcelain façade.

Last but not least, Fenna the huntress was gently nibbling on her thumb with her sleeping-bag blanket up to her face, looking innocently relaxed in contrast to her normal ferocity when awake. Enri had no doubt she would be ready to jump up at any moment given the need. From what he had seen, this was a woman clearly unafraid to bring her lethal talents up to the surface. After everything, Enri was glad that she was on his side, although he knew he would always need to keep a cautious eye open when dealing with her. He had witnessed firsthand how quickly her violent nature could rise but was certainly relieved to have such a steely-tempered protector nearby.

Enri made the final decision to give up on sleep and go explore the water chamber instead. He arose from his sleeping bag and began navigating his way through the electro-Kevlar tent. It had propped itself into a niche in the chamber's corner, hardening and softening along its edges for optimal size utilization, providing the four travelers shelter and a slight ease of paranoia against the unpredictable, lurking dangers outside. And, yet, nothing could truly ease their minds against such an unknown fear—nothing but the gathering of enough information to make it no longer unknown. Enri zipped open the tent and stuck his head outside into the glowing Nokkian water chamber. His skull pounded, his mind raced, and each accentuated thump of his heart rattled his ribs like an energetic bird far too large for its tiny cage. Enri's throat felt dry enough that he felt like dipping his head straight into the glowing water, so he cupped his hands and approached the nearest pool.

Luckily, the TurTek representative had done a molecular sweep and cleared the water for drinking hours before, noting it was purer than much of the recirculated tap water regularly accepted as usable upon any common TurTek Deep Space vessel travelling isolated from its planet.

**—HuMmMmMmMm—** ting, **ting,** ting, **ting —** **HuMmMmMmMm—** ting, **ting,** ting, **ting —**

Enri's desire to take a drink disappeared immediately. He stared out through the voluminous water chamber and saw the shadowy figure of a heavyset man, barely lit by the room's sparkling light and silhouetted before a set of dark cave entrances. Enri's heart jumped into his chest. Before the explorer could think of what to do, the man in the distance glided backwards into the dark, disappearing like a phantom of the mind. *Who the hell…!?*

"Hey, wait!" Enri yelled out. His curiosity piqued like a scourge of rockets in the air and his mind raced to understand what was going on. *Did I just imagine that, or is there truly another survivor out there? Maybe it's someone unrelated… Someone who was waiting here before we even arrived.*

Without even noticing that his feet had started to move, Enri began to run as fast as he could muster, forgetting his sleeping companions behind him and losing power over his conscious desires. Channels of glowing blue-white water passed beneath as he moved, barely registering as obstructions in the overzealous explorer's mind. He made quick passage through the chamber and vaulted into the cave corridor beyond, finding himself immediately enveloped in darkness. A jittery buzz rushed up his spine.

**—HuMmMmMmMm–** ting, **ting,** ting, **ting –** **HuMmMmMmMm–** ting, **ting,** ting, **ting —**

The world rumbled and, with it, Enri's mind. The man of mystery came into view, lit by stripes of green. Although the stranger's face was completely hidden from sight, Enri found his stare glaring, waiting passively for some reason yet unknown. After a few moments of silence, the mysterious man yet again disappeared, vanishing through a backwards glide into pitch-black darkness. The confused explorer followed along.

The world flashed green for a solitary moment of time.

*Drink your wine 'cause you deem it divine, and yet still all your demons will spread, and yet still all your demons will spread. The world I know has stopped all its flow, but here I remain ever fighting, but here I remain ever fighting.*

**—HuMmMmMmMm–** ting, **ting,** ting, **ting –** **HuMmMmMmMm–** ting, **ting,** ting, **ting —**

The walls darkened as Enri ran, but his mind lit up like city streetlamps after dusk. Barely conscious of his own movements, his head began to spin as the world around him twisted in a completely irrational way. Soft orange lines emerged from the floor and ceiling and probed the air like fragile tendrils of light, coming together in a spiral that made no sense.

Enri stumbled on his own confusion. Up was down, down was sideways, and upside down was a yellow balloon on Jupiter. Although the avid explorer knew not what was going on, he could recognize the feeling of trepidation washing through him. He flushed with inexplicable nostalgia. A shape like a manta ray flew through the air far above him, casting a shadow down through the orange haze. Enri was scared and happy and angry and hungry; , he was proud and out of control. These emotions were not his own—Enri was being manipulated. *But how? And why?*

Enri's memories, past and future, flowed through snippets of his mind. He saw his friends, his acquaintances, and all of those that he could not quite remember. Some memories felt fresh, some distorted by time, and some, he was rather sure, had never even happened, despite feeling uniquely his in vision.

**—HuMmMmMmMm—** Enri saw Fenna Caae use her pneumatic pickaxe as a blade of judgment and slice deep into the throat of Ranke FourtySeven, tearing it open like splayed meat and revealing tender flesh never before exposed to open air. Blood rushed at Enri and curded beyond recognition—**HuMmMmMmMm—** Enri saw the cold snows of Antarctica with his mentor Dirk Fairwinter. **—HuMmMmMmMm—** He slingshotted over Mars in a spaceship, enjoying the view along the way. — **HuMmMmMmMm—** Enri's emotions turned bleak and his memory shot forward into the future, past anything he could even remember. A nexus of metal the size of a continent rose up around him from a sea of sand. —ting, **ting,** ting, **ting—**

A hollow bulb of light swirled in the air, and an ink-black whirlwind flared open like an iris. Enri's head pounded and his eyes made no sense of what they saw, but, surprisingly, nothing here struck him as wholly unfamiliar. It was a meandering echo of a voice heard long ago, completely lost in origin. The avid explorer could not think it all through at the speed it came, so he simply kept stumbling forward, flowing through visions like a pebble skipping over water. His mind began to deny its own reality, seeking comfort in an unstoppable tide of deductions and formulated answers. *Questions, answers, questions, answers; which are which and what is what?*

—**HuMmMmMmMm–** Enri lost sight of who he perceived himself to be.—**HuMmMmMmMm–** *Nothing is true, reality is a blur.* —**HuMmMmMmMm–** *Is my name even Enri, or is that fake too? Am I even a real person, or am I just somebody conceived by an author's mind, by the recollection of a narrator long past? Are my memories really the truth of my life, or are they truly no more than images of a bygone dream in an age forgotten?* —**HuMmMmMmMm–** *Can a cloned duplication of a man even consider himself human, or would he always feel as but an approximation of a true living being, a sophisticated computer sent on a task of impersonation?* —**HuMmMmMmMm–** *Am I no more than some toy, recreated over and over for children to play with? Will I be doomed to feel lost forever, left to wander the voids of meaninglessness?* —**HuMmMmMmMm–** *Do I even deserve to live? Am I not merely the result of TurTek playing a god, sending duplicates of real human beings to scout out the stars? What right do I even have to walk upon this alien planet? Am I not the invader here?* –**ting**, ting, **ting**, ting–

The questions were tough, and Enri's mind was a blur, no more equipped to straighten his answers than a star could escape the pull of a black hole. He felt lost inside and out, unable to discern fact from fiction. Obscure memories passed through him and seemingly physically manifested themselves in the air amid bright flashes of green.

Enri rubbed his eyes as his skull thumped like a drum. He walked with eyes closed, trying to shut the visions out and allow his outstretched arms to be his sole source of guidance along the tunnel walls. The neurochemical urge in Enri's brain to go forward was as strong as ever despite all logical reasoning against it, so he simply continued onward, ignoring the confusion and muddled thoughts emitted within.

Eventually, the landscape beneath Enri's feet began to dip, and he was left with no choice but to open up his eyes and reappropriate the situation he had brought himself into. He ended up gasping at a completely new sight to behold. A windstorm tornado of red, orange, and yellow swirled all around him like billows in a breeze, encompassing all that was, is, and was yet to be. He had wished it would not come to this. *Not again!* Enri would have preferred any other memory than this to come to light. *Anything at all but Jupiter!*

**—HuMmMmMmMm–** ting, **ting,** ting, **ting –** **HuMmMmMmMm–** ting, **ting,** ting, **ting —**

"No!" Enri yelled out loud. "Show me anything but Jupiter! These illusions do not fool me. Damn you all straight to Hades!"

He lunged headfirst into a well-lit room of bright green, void of any shadows or angles. The mysterious man appeared before him, hosting a mobility belt around his waist. It was Enri's former mentor Dirk Fairwinter, live and in the flesh, despite the fact that he had been dead in his land-pod not a week before. He seemed completely unperturbed by Enri's sudden presence.

"Why hi-yah there, Enri!" Dirk exclaimed with both hands waving enthusiastically. His mobility belt rocked him in the air as it adjusted to his various motions, blowing gusts at Enri as he stood nearby. "Long time no see, eh? What has it been, like a thousand years? Heh-heh!"

At first, Enri made no attempt to react. His sense of nostalgia overwhelmed him, but his skepticism was also at an all-time high. The curious explorer may have been in a complete daze, but he was not stupid enough to believe anything he saw. He simply stood dumbstruck and shut his eyes, waiting and wishing and wishing and waiting for the heartwarming vision to pass. He could not let his emotions get the best of him or allow himself to crave what simply could not be true. *Dirk is dead. This isn't him. Dirk is dead. This isn't him!*

"Oh come on, m'boy!" Dirk sounded offended. "You giving me the silent treatment? Have you completely lost your manners, Enri? Can you not still act like a civilized man when placed outside of your element?"

Enri opened his eyes in shame and looked upon his former mentor. "Dr. Fairwinter, you're not really here... you don't actually exist."

"What are you talking about, m'boy!?" Dirk floated forward in the air and held a questioning finger up to Enri's face.

"You're dead, Dirk, I saw it myself!" Enri coughed, taking a step backwards. "Your body was torn apart on landing."

"Am I not here?" Dirk poked him on the forehead. "What would that mean? Are you poking yourself in the head?"

"Yeah, I guess. I'm probably hallucinating this whole thing. Maybe I'm asleep in the tent, dreaming this whole thing up..."

"That doesn't matter!" Dirk insisted. "It doesn't matter at all."

"How does it not matter? You're just a delusion!"

"Why are you here, m'boy? Why are you actually here? That's what matters. That's the question you should be addressing."

"I'm here because…" Enri looked around the impossibly green room. "Well, I'm not here at all, am I? This is all fake as shit! Had I fallen asleep eating ham, it would look like a giant room filled with bacon."

"NO!" Dirk barked back, floating backwards in his mobility mount. "Why have you come *here*? "Remember, remember! What brought you to chase me? Whether it's real matters not! Are you not still you? Are the decisions you make not still enacted of your own volition?"

"Ok…" he replied, unsure of himself. "I followed you because I was curious. I wanted to know why I had been awakened on this alien planet with nothing but a loose narrative to follow. In fact, I still wanna know!"

"I've already told you, m'boy! It is all about the Numeri—it has always been about the Numeri! The numbers come and the numbers go, but the cycles remain the same."

"What in the hells are you talking about? This is no time for old philosophy! Those days are no longer relevant."

"Then or now, why would that make a difference?" Dirk replied questioningly. "Don't the truths still hold true? The flow of time cannot be set aside for a concealed sense of *purpose*."

"No Dirk, it's all too late. For all we know, humanity itself is already extinct!"

"Nonsense!" dream Dirk exclaimed. "Existence does not just disappear, and neither does your sense of meaning! Matter cannot be created nor destroyed, and neither can the natural truths around us. One plus one equals two, no matter when or where you look at it."

"Stop it. You're mixing subjects!" Enri was tired of being lied to.

"You know what you have to do, m'boy. Choppety chop, there's no time to dawdle!" Dirk replied. "Or wear pajamas," he added in jest.

Enri looked down and realized Dirk was right—he was still wearing pajamas, having had stepped out of the electro-Kevlar tent ill-prepared for trekking. He hadn't put on shoes or socks, not even his wristband terminal. Now his bare feet were already starting to bruise. *Rookie mistake!* he admonished himself internally. Then he realized he had just made another equally embarrassing blunder—*never take your eyes off the target!*

"Reach for the nexus, m'boy! Never accept singular defeat!" Dirk's voice echoed through the chamber, gradually fading into nothingness.

**—HuMmMmMmMmMm–** ting, **ting,** ting, **ting –** **HuMmMmMmMmMm–** ting, **ting,** ting, **ting** —

Enri knew Dirk would be gone from sight even before he looked back up. He wasn't surprised when the entire room of green disappeared around him and confronted him instead with another riddle. Four separate pitch-black tunnels branched out before him, each of which could potentially lead to either a dead end or a perilous drop. As soon as he attempted to gaze directly at any one of them, it began to fade away like a bright shine in a poorly rendered dream, fluctuating and shifting in view. Try as he might, his eyes simply couldn't focus upon any single tunnel, and, the more he tried, the more everything in view seemed to twist and spin. *What is the right path?* he wondered. *Would it be foolish to simply make a random choice and bargain everything on an impulse?*

His old handheld terminal appeared in his hands. "Oh darn, that's quite a choice, isn't it?" it squeaked. "Sometimes life gives you too many options to know what's right, huh? You've just gotta clear out the confusion and make a choice!"

"What in the hells?" Enri bought the device up to see. "I didn't bring you along... you're not here."

"Oh yes, you traded me out for a shinier model, didn't you?" the high-pitched voice asked.

The terminal disappeared from his hands, along with three of the four tunnels before him, leaving him but one possible path. The befuddled man clutched his thrumming head, quenching his feelings of hopelessness. His sanity was slipping and his mind was rife with hallucinations— either that or someone was directly messing with him. *Is Dirk really alive? Is he responsible for all this? Or, is it something altogether different? Could it be something alien attempting to sabotage my mind?*

Enri walked onward, accepting that his fate was no longer in his own hands. The walls of the corridor melted away in ripples of orange and white mist, leaving nothing before him but a narrow path with steep drops on either side. Gale force winds started in, threatening to push him right off the edge of reality. His nostrils flared with the burning smell of ozone, making him grimace in distaste.

"No, not again!" Enri cursed aloud. He recognized the orange mist and feared what was to come. It seemed any action he took would be futile against whatever was going on in his mind. If his memories from the past were determined to embrace him—whether by external influence or the twisting of his own mind—it seemed it would all come tumbling at him one way or another. The only way to know exactly what was going on was to follow it through to the end. Fighting the notion would do nothing but slow him down.

"Who writes your fate?" an ambiguous voice whispered in the air, almost in direct response to Enri's thoughts. "Must there be an author to the tales you have spun?"

**—HuMmMmMmMm–** ting, **ting,** ting, **ting –** **HuMmMmMmMm–** ting, **ting,** ting, **ting —**

Enri stood alone in a field of peach-colored clouds swirling, twirling, and curling around him like ribbons in a breeze. He felt wet and vulnerable as the air chilled down past freezing and the narrow path before him all but disappeared under active gusts of red and white spinning through the golden vapor.

A sudden drop in the path almost tripped Enri off balance. All of a sudden, his body felt heavy, and he knew exactly what was coming. He was no longer in a cavern on Anok, no longer in pajamas, and no longer walking along a path. Instead, he was wearing a heavy-duty spacesuit with full protective gear and gee-alleviators and operating a mechanical flying beast in the shape of a manta ray. *I'm back on Jupiter... Tuk!*

Enri's vacuum-balloon carriage rattled violently under the force of the epic planet's peach-colored storms. It was barely able to geo-locate itself within the endless sky as the wind threatened to tear it apart. This vivid memory was dire as could be.

"DROP IT!" Dirk Fairwinter's voice echoed through the manta ray's cabin speakers. "DROP THE PAYLOAD NOW OR WE'RE ALL GONNA BURST!!!"

*Oh well, might as well get on with it.* Enri pulled the closest lever to his left and released his vacuum-balloon's lofty payload—a large, multi-billion dollar partition of the TurTek Jupiter lab below—just as he remembered doing. It plummeted down through the heavy air.

Enri remembered what was to follow, be it hallucination or not. In several minutes, a cascade of nuclear explosions would vaporize the very mist that swirled around him, propelling a grandiose shockwave across thousands of miles of Jupiter sky. Ragnarok, Apocalypse, Armageddon, and the like, would dominate the skyscape an instant hell of fire and flame, all at once and all together, and all of it completely his fault.

Enri's manta ray shaped craft docked with the remaining TurTek lab just as the shockwave commenced, and his vision went dark as his guilt. He began to cry.

"Always think before you leap in the dark," Dirk's voice echoed. "Is your mind in your head or are your impulses driving you?"

"What do you mean!?" Enri shouted through a stream of tears. "I don't understand any of this!"

"The future is coming, Enri m'boy, and mere acts of faith are no proper tools for a scientist!" The voice changed to become that of Walter Watterton, Dirk's former partner and director of TurTek.

"The tides of Chronos will not be appeased by the random acts of a mortal," he said. "One must be a god to successfully negate the unforeseen."

"What are you talking about?" Enri cried. "What do you want from me?"

"Who are you, really?" the voice asked. "For whose motivations do you exist? Are you just the culmination of somebody else's imagination?"

—**HuMmMmMmMmMm**– ting, **ting,** ting, **ting** – **HuMmMmMmMmMm**– ting, **ting,** ting, **ting** —

Enri was back in the Nokkian cavern, stumbling through the dark. His feet were mangled, and his pajamas were stained with his own blood. A light blinked before him, illuminating a wide pit the size of a crater.

He sat down and laid his head down in his hands. *Who am I? Why am I here?*

# 12 : priorities :

**"Of their depth, they shall rise—from their wealth, they shall try—for their death, they shall fry. Illogical thoughts at best, but pointed enough to deliver a message to the masses."**
-Transcripts of William

<4:12:24 a.s.t.><**day 8**><Anok>

"What is a palm tree?" Fre'dd asked Fenna through a nibble of strawberry chew. "Ubi est? Do they live on water?"

"Water...?" Fenna repeated absentmindedly. "Uh, not really, Herc'. They grow on the sand. Usually along a shoreline, though, so near enough by water. Why'du ask?"

"My eyes have never seen one," Fre'dd explained. "Enri said the Nokkian trees looked like Seussian palm trees, but I do not know what that means."

"Haha, yeah, I can see that." Fenna giggled, turning her focus towards the large man sitting beside her. She treaded her feet in the glowing pool of water below and sent ripples across its surface. "You've never been to a beach before?"

"Nescio—I don't know," Fre'dd replied. "Maybe, once... in a dream long ago."

"You know what? Hold out your terminal," Fenna instructed. "Earthboy gave you his old piece of junk, right?"

"Yes." Fre'dd took out the clear, stretchable device.

"Morning!" the handheld terminal piped up as it lit in his hands. "Aww, no sunlight!" it moaned. "Battery's dying."

"Voice off," Fenna instructed. She sent an image from her terminal lenses to display holographically through the handheld's screen. It opened up a 3D rotatable photograph of an ocean shore, displaying row upon row of pristine green palm trees. She held up her fingers and flicked the terminal screen in Fre'dd's hands. The projected image zoomed into a solitary palm tree with a thick canopy of brilliant fanned leaves and a nest of coconuts drooping down like cocoons.

"This is from before the Caribbean went full-Atlantis," she explained.

Fre'dd stared at the brilliant image in awe, glad to have something to keep his mind occupied. The glimmering liquid of the water chamber's pools flowed passively beneath, not providing much of a distraction to drown out the fears growing in his head. The constant flutter of gekkons overhead only added to his growing list of concerns. Fre'dd could not help but ruminate in fear on Enri's sudden disappearance. For all the Martian gladiator knew, his small companion's life was in risk.

"What do you think happened to him?" Fre'dd asked, unable to keep his worries silent. "To Enri."

"He sounded pretty crazed, you know" Fenna said, hiding her own concern through skepticism. "Maybe Earthboy just had a nervous breakdown and took off. Methinks he simply went mad!"

"Where would he go? Will he come back?"

"I really dunno, ya know? I almost wouldn't blame him if he decided to ditch us and get out of these taurshit caves without us."

"He would not do that!" Fre'dd insisted. "Well, I don't think he would..." He lowered the handheld terminal screen and looked over at her, noting that her face betrayed a hint of hidden anxiety. "Anyway, he went out solus without any of his belongings. Enri would never intentionally do that."

"Well, it sounded like he was chasing after someone," Fenna speculated, "but I'm willing to bet that was just a figment of his imagination. It's understandable, you know; these caves are likely to make anyone go insane."

"I am afraid I would have to agree with you on that," a voice admitted behind them. The TurTek representative stepped out of the electro-Kevlar tent. "Although we did find a bountiful source of fresh water, these sunless chambers would certainly not be conducive to any true attempt at colonization."

"Oh shut up, you!" Fenna exploded, popping her feet out of the glowing water and jumping up to stand. "Why are you even here, corporate monkey!? "To be a godsdamn worthless leader!?" she accused. "You're just here to boss us around!"

"No," the Rep replied without any hint of offense. "Any hierarchical structure sanctioned towards an initial assessment mission would be counter-intuitive, given the highly unpredictable circumstances involved. We are each units of a whole, collectively meant to analyze the prospects of this environment before any more effort is expended upon it. Each of us is meant to benefit from each other's progress, and any one of us can be removed from the equation without compromising the mission itself."

"Great. So we're not even a well-built team, just a flock of human guinea pigs! Our lives were created merely to be thrown away for the sake of experimentation."

"Yes indeed," the TurTek Rep admitted. "That is why we are here."

Fre'dd got up and gazed around the room. "What if Enri does not return?" he asked. "Will we go out and search for him?"

"Yes," the Rep replied, "but only as much as supplies will allow. We have a limited amount of food, and it would be futile to comb these caves too long."

"Asshole," Fenna scoffed. "I shouldn't have expected you to stick your own ass out for someone else."

"My priorities lie in the long-term. Otherwise, this whole journey would have been for waste."

"Enri!" Fre'dd suddenly yelled aloud, projecting his voice across the chamber. "Enri!"

"Hey, what the hells!" Fenna barked, immediately annoyed.

"ENRI!" Fre'dd bellowed even louder. "Ego te vidi, Enri!"

"For the love of Zeus, why are you shouting?" she demanded.

Fre'dd pointed and waved his hands in the air. "Enri!"

Enri limped out of a cavern passage across the chamber wearing torn pajamas, bleeding and dripping onto the marble floor. He did not look up as he walked, slowly making his way across the chamber in silent contemplation. Once he reached the tent, the explorer stopped and finally acknowledged his companions' presence.

"What happened?" Fenna asked without any hostility in her voice, dropping her usual emotional barrier for a genuine sense of worry. "You ok?"

Enri looked up, choosing his words carefully. "I know where to go next." He tried to step around Fenna to enter the electro-Kevlar tent, but she blocked him with her arm.

"Uh, uh, buddy. We need a little more than that."

"No more aimless wandering..." Enri gestured with his hands. "I found a way out of the caverns."

"Sold!" Fenna exclaimed. "Tuk these caves already." She moved out of Enri's way to allow passage, but the TurTek representative took his turn to move and block him.

"Please elaborate," the Rep requested. "What exactly did you find?"

"Alien tech. A whole tukking lot of alien technology."

"You mean like electric?" Fenna asked.

"At the very least," Enri replied. "But I'm pretty sure it goes further than that. I'm not even sure how far. I just need to get my stuff together and get back there to find out."

"Back where?"

"Up." Enri pointed. "There's a whole city up there."

"Yes, yes, that is indeed noteworthy," the Rep replied cautiously. "That would certainly change our ultimate endgame. I will mark it down as a location of high interest."

"Location of interest? Didn't you just hear me? After I get my shit together, I'm going straight back there!"

"Yes, I understand," the Rep said. "We will certainly go back to whatever it was you found and record it in full. However, if you are suggesting an imminent complete ascent of the wave-spire, I am afraid we cannot afford to traverse that far on this stretch of our journey. The land-pod outside the wave-spire is our only constant known source of resupply, so we have to go back relatively soon."

"Isn't this exactly why TurTek sent us here?" Enri asked, annoyed. "Didn't they want us to determine the lay of the land and figure out what's what?"

"Well, yes, for now," the Rep admitted. "But that doesn't mean breaking standard protocol to do so."


<5:23:17 a.s.t.> **<day 8>**

Enri led the others down a darkened passage he had travelled twice before—once following an illusion and once on the painful way back. This time, though, he had on his shoes, a headlamp, and his wristband terminal, which automatically established a virtual map along his way, making sure that he never gets lost here again.

A fork in the tunnels ahead posed him the first real decision on the path, teasing him with flashes of distorted memory and recollection of a room lit entirely in green.

"Hey Earthboy, you even know where you're going?" Fenna sped up to walk beside him. "It must have been pitch-black the last time you came through here."

The explorer slowed his pace. He held up his wristband terminal and gazed through its hologram.

"Enri?" Fenna asked, stopping him with a hand upon his shoulder.

Yet again, he offered no real response, simply looking up with an enigmatic smile and gesturing at the terminal across his wrist. He held his other arm behind it and displayed a cross-section of his own skin where his gash had just started healing thanks to the TurTek nano healing cream she had helped him apply several minutes before. Through the terminal screen, Enri's blood glowed red, displaying as a trace element.

"Impressive!" the TurTek representative exclaimed, coming up beside them. "Fairwinter was right about your resourcefulness, Mr. Riatu, that much is evident."

"What?" Fenna asked. "I don't get it."

Enri lowered his wounded arm and pointed the other wrist with its terminal at the tunnel floor. He began scanning the ground. A red glowing footstep displayed through the holographic screen, tracing Enri's blood imprinted in the dirt. He traced up a jagged path of his own prints leading backwards into the tunnels, step by step indicating the limping struggle he underwent on his lengthy trek back to the tent.

"Gnarly," Fenna admitted.

Enri's hazy, disturbed memories flooded back with the sight of his bloody footsteps. Through the truth of the light, his degraded mental status shone bright as the path of his own blood on the ground. However, now was not the time for such thoughts, so he simply walked onwards, following his footsteps through the correct tunnel past the junction and thinking no more of the room that had been completely green.

After less than a dozen minutes and a travelled distance of no more than a quarter mile, the travelers entered a short, straight corridor that Enri only vaguely remembered and the entrance to the final room where they were to go. He clicked off his headlamp before entering it, signaling to the others to do the same. Although they did not understand why, they complied anyway, leaving the entrance completely dark save for a blinking scarlet-red strobe light coming from somewhere inside. Upon every flash, the chamber and its convoluted contents illuminated with brilliant light, bracing the travelers for whatever oddity they may find inside.

The chamber inside was large and shaped like a tall pie wedge, filled entirely with a confounding assortment of crisscrossed glass branches and complex metal barbs coming off the curved outer wall. The red light inside came from somewhere near the entrance, leaving the rest of the room mostly wrought in shadow despite the brilliance of every flash. Who knew how far in it could go?

Before anyone could question him as to where they had arrived, Enri walked straight into the room and veered towards the source of the light. Going around flashing glass spikes, the eager explorer reached a metallic pedestal like a harpoon lodged into the outer wall. He climbed atop it and tipped it down with his weight, activating a process within.

The Nokkian pedestal clicked and began to wobble in place, humming and then lighting up with a stripe of bright green. It displayed a physical control panel of pliable push nobs and colorful indicators. The entire room turned on, lighting up through fifty foot vertical columns of sharp, sparkling white. Connecting ceiling to floor, these revealed the partial-cylindrical chamber in whole. Mechanical walkways wove together in intricate patterns, flaunting an astounding variety of hooks, dips, passages, and complex lines. A gigantic vertical shaft stretched out beyond the room itself, intersecting the pie-wedged chamber with many others like it over countless levels and heights. A sleek golden frame of flawlessly round, immaculately equidistant horizontal rings supported its perimeter, repeating above and below further than the eye could see.

"Olympus almighty!" Fre'dd exclaimed. He ducked through and around the room's chaotic metal-glass overhangs and approached Enri at the pedestal by the wall.

"Take a look at this central shaft!" Fenna whistled, feeling right at home with the immense chute's heights.

After being nauseous and tired of traversing through claustrophobic tunnels, she had immediately pepped up upon seeing the grand open space.

She leaned over the shaft ledge and listened for the echoes of her voice, allowing her terminal lenses to calculate the depths pinged by the interval of time the sound waves took to bounce back.

"Who made all this?" Fre'dd asked, truly shocked. "Was it the Nokkian snake creaturas?"

"It does appear that way," the TurTek representative said. "The distance between these pillars matches quite closely the length of the specimen we encountered. They would be able to cross this room in seconds flat." He took off his bulking top hat and knelt down on the ground to pick up a loose glass rock from the floor. He placed it in his hat and put the cap back on his head.

The vertical shaft began to rumble, shaking everything in sight with an earthquake of force. The humans nearly tumbled over, adjusting to the heavy vibrations.

"Whoa!" Fenna called out. She hung off a large golden perimeter ring, holding herself over the open air of the shaking vertical shaft as she looked straight down its depths. The rumbling quickly intensified, showing no sign of dithering.

"Get out of there!" Enri exclaimed.

"You said there was a lift?" Fenna yelled back, gawking down into the distance. "What kinda lift?"

A glowing ring of light grew from the depths, coming up fast from far below until it filled the space of the shaft entirety. Fenna pulled herself back up into the pie-wedged room for her own safety.

The shaft's golden frame rattled, intensifying into an abominable shriek like a plague of locusts. The wide ring of light charged past ground level and burst high into the air. Behind it came a golden-frilled, multi-tiered elevator capsule, rising into view like a vertical subway train of impossible length.

"Valde stupenda!" Fre'dd yelled over the heavy grinding. "Just like Ares Prime of home!"

"Very interesting!" the Rep agreed.

"Is that right!?" Fenna shouted incredulously. "Man, how far does this thing stretch?"

"Just wait," Enri said, coming up behind her. "A few more seconds now."

Soon enough, the rising lift tube began to slow, along with the screeching of grinding brakes straining hard to slow down its massive upward momentum. Several dozen seconds passed and then *KATHUMP;* the golden lift stopped completely, shaking the world with a thud like a meteor strike and leaving a two-hundred foot golden wall over the space that had just been a wide open hole. Horizontal golden-yellow rings subdivided the wide tube's height in the same style as the immaculate perimeter frame of the shaft itself. Tall twin doors hissed open, revealing the lift's interior chamber.

The travelers backed up and looked upon the gigantic lift with awe, gaping at its sudden appearance before them. Its rounded surface looked aged with eons of ingrained purple dust, yet it was still as exquisitely detailed as the day it was made. Its open entrance was over a dozen feet up, further solidifying the fact that its intended occupants had been much different than themselves.

Before anyone could say a word, Fenna bounded forward, determined to climb this new obstacle as fast as she could muster. She crouched down in full stride and pounced several feet up to grab hold of a golden rung above, pulling herself up without a hitch and, from there, proceeding to climb. She jumped, caught, shimmied, and heaved herself over the golden doorframe in seconds flat, sitting herself down with a leg on either side of its narrow girth. A draft of warm, steamy air blew out the golden lift tube, and she realized how truly cold the cave below had been.

"Whoa!" Fenna yelled down. "It reeks of old in here—really tukking old!"

Fenna allowed her terminal lenses to record and label everything she saw, sending the data streaming over to Enri to allow him to watch along as she searched. She spotted a series of long, octagonal marble poles coming down from above, each fitted with a puffy golden orb upon its bottom end, presumably meant as a claw-hold for a Nokkian snake. The lift's curved inner wall was lined with tall vertical windows between each set of doors. Embroidered on the wall were banners of formerly glamorous red silk coated with dust from eons of neglect.

Everything made of metal and gold was ripe with chips and dents, and the brass floors below looked to have undergone the impact of many heavy objects dropped down from above. Multiple golden orbs that had, over untold years, detached from the hanging marble poles above lingered where they had fallen, scattered upon the dented ground like ghostly remnants of a rowdy past.

Only after recording all that she could see through the lift tube's inner chamber did Fenna turn around to address her fellow companions. "So guys," she posed innocently enough with a wide smile spread across her face, "we're getting on, I assume?"

"Hells yeah we are!" Enri exclaimed.

"Negative!" the TurTek Rep declared. "The risk is far too high for us to embark on this vehicle and go wherever it may take us. As I explained before, we will mark down these coordinates as a high-priority avenue for future exploration once we go restock back at the land-pod and reassess our situation."

"Are you freakin' kidding me?" Fenna shot back. "We're here now!"

"No kidding involved. I must admit Mr. Riatu was correct that the existence of Nokkian high-technology changes our endgame entirely, but that also makes our reports back to TurTek all the more valuable."

"What does that have to do with anything?" Fenna asked.

"Our mission is over. That's what he means," Enri explained. "We're done with our 'initial assessment,' and our answer is a resounding yes."

"Our mission is over? How can that possibly be true? We don't even know where this lift goes!"

"Well, the mere presence of this Nokkian tech means that this planet is worth TurTek's continual efforts. The raw potential of this discovery means that Anok have been pushed straight past phase one of our TurTek invasion."

"TurTek does not perform invasions!" the TurTek representative insisted without humor. "Colonization is very much reliant on sustainable cohabitation!"

"Relax, I'm only joking. I'm just saying that this technology proves the planet is both ripe for life and conducive for the highly-evolved advent of intellectual life. The moment we saw these lights turn on, our TurTek representative's doubts towards the value of setting up a colony in this spire blew straight out of the water."

"Yes, that is correct," the Rep confirmed. "This new information is of vital importance. It alone means that we are ready to send our positive confirmations back up to the station, which is now to become our utmost priority. You have to understand that we must establish contact with TurTek over everything else now, especially anything that could compromise our ability to do so. Otherwise, our mission here could still be deemed a failure and our lives will automatically have been considered lost in the preliminary pursuit. If the TurTek vessel above feels like it has no reason to stay in this planet's orbit, it will decide to move on."

"You're saying that if we don't rush back to send word to your damn company, the Deep Space station will just leave us stranded here for good? What was the point of even dropping us down here if it was just going to abandon us?" The pit in Fenna's stomach sunk down deep.

"No, it would not leave right away," the TurTek Rep admitted. "The vessel is set to orbit for at least two complete solar cycles before assuming the worst of our conditions. That is not the point, though. The real danger lies with the potential threat to our lives. If we take an ascent up this extraterrestrial lift, we may never come back down it with our lives. If that happens, nobody will be left to contact TurTek with our results, and our whole duplicated existence will have been in vain. We cannot risk such a hazard."

"You're such a corporate puppet—not to mention a total coward!"

"Risky behavior is nothing to be lauded."

"Live a little, man. Face it—you wanna go up too! How could you not?"

"Yes, I admit that the idea of gaining exposure to a completely foreign civilization that we could study and ultimately scan into the TurTek databanks is a rather tempting proposition. And, once we return to the land-pod and figure out a way to send our signal up to the station, we can come back and explore whatever is up there to our hearts' content. We just have to take this all one phase at a time."

"You know what? Screw it!" Enri announced. "Fenna, toss down a rope. I'm coming up!"

# 13 : blinders :

**"Far too often do the impacts of our past affect the foundations of our future."**
—Transcripts of the Empress

### <2128 C.E. - the age of illusion><Jupiter Orbit>

"Is that you, Artemis? Have you finally come?" An old voice creaked through the dark, offering Fenna no hint of where it originated. The station's interior was darkhosting no more than faint orange reflections from the magnificent planet outside its grand open windows. For all she knew, there could be thousands of night-vision lenses recording her every movement. She held her ground, trying her damnedest not to show any fear for those who may be looking.

The orbiting Jupiter station Fenna had entered had been astoundingly hard to locate around the enormous size of the planet, despite its actively pinging signal. Flying her craft manually, she had had to overcome the immense gravity below and aim her trajectory perfectly in an intersect path with the TurTechnicks lab, pulling full counter-brakes to prevent vaulting right past it and necessitating another entire circuit around the massive planet. Fortunately, highly skilled as she was, the infamous

Artemis made contact with her target on her first try around, insta-docking her speeding vessel into the magnetic tethers of the orbital lab and entering it amid an automated system eager to let her in.

"Please come forward, my dear. Let me have a look at you," the old voice requested lightly, echoing from somewhere unseen.

"Who's there?" Fenna demanded, holding up her pneumatic pickaxes defensively as her terminal lenses began to artificially illuminate the room for her to see. She hid her rising trepidation through a sheer force of intent, unwilling to betray any weakness. "Who are you?" she snipped. "Why did you send for me?"

"I've been waiting for you a long time, my dear." The voice chuckled aloud. "I feared you wouldn't make it in time for me to greet you face-to-face."

"What are you talking about?" Fenna asked. Her lenses finally spotted the source of the voice: a seated, floating human figure. A large, glowing window with an astounding view of Jupiter below backlit him. "What do you want from me?"

"Oh, just fulfilling an old promise," the shadowy figure replied. "A promise made long ago to a mutual friend of ours."

"Apollo…" Fenna whispered under her breath. "Is that who you mean? Is he the reason you signaled me from half the godsdamn system away?"

"Apollo?" the old voice repeated. "Yes, that is right. I recall that title having had been used. I was never really one for polytheistic symbolism myself—or for names in the first place. But, then again, the speculating public never really cared about me a fraction as much as they did our friend."

Fenna stepped closer, now seeing the figure clear as day but still unwilling to let her guard down. The floating man looked ancient and wore a bulking top hat far too large to be at all comfortable. He was clearly not Apollo himself but was, quite possibly, just as mysterious.

"Who are you, old man?" Fenna asked. "What do you know of Apollo?"

"Oh," the old man replied through a porcelain smile, "I'm just an ordinary caretaker stuck in a single assignment far too long. As I said before, I've never really been much for names."

"You'll have to do better than that!" she growled, stepping towards the old man with both her weapons held threateningly before her. "I better not have come all the way to Jupiter for nothing!"

"Now, now there… pneumatic pickaxes?" the old man chuckled at the hot-headed girl. "What are you planning on doing with those, young lady?"

"Don't test me, old man," Fenna warned. "I'll do what I have to do."

"Oh really? Is that a promise!?" The caretaker laughed enthusiastically. "Could you truly grant a stranger that much kindness?"

Fenna backed down, softening her expression. "What do you want from me?"

"Never mind that…" the old man responded. "That is not why you have come this far. Think hard…What glimmer of light drove you so far through the long dusk?"

"This is not about me!" Fenna insisted. "You've been pinging me with cross-system waves for over a month!"

"Yes, that may be," the elderly caretaker admitted. "But one would think that the infamous Artemis would be used to such fan-service by now."

"Yeah," Fenna shot back, "but your wave was different—sent with a freakin' antiquated TurTechnicks brand originating well outside their usual corporate system. Seemed suspicious enough to investigate…"

"Hmm, yes," the caretaker agreed. "I suppose it *has* been quite a while since I've contacted anyone outside of my own little bubble. Nonetheless, I can well assure you that I am still a qualified representative of the company."

"So this *is* a TurTechnicks station after all?" Fenna asked doubtfully. "Why is it all the way out here?"

"Yes, yes, young lady. That is certainly a good place to start!" The elderly caretaker waved his arms wildly. Every light in the orbital station came on at once, revealing a pristinely white set of floors and ceilings, identically smooth and completely void of shadows. The old man sat grinning in his floating chair, now fully illuminated but for the thick slice of shade cast down from the large hat on his head.

"What kind of place is this, anyway?"

"This, my dear, is my home, as I have been its sole caretaker since conception. Years ago, this station was established as a research lab, set upon the task by the company formerly known as TurTek. It was made to be strong and hardy, fitted with extravagant gravity-alleviating solutions to allow deep submergence into the turbulent gaseous clouds of Jupiter."

"You see, we had always been interested in the idea of artificial atomic recomposition, so having a dedicated lab located directly within the solar system's largest resource of hydrogen seemed like a worthy investment to make. The planet of Jupiter has so many layers of hydrogen that its density varies greatly from the top of its gaseous skies to the oceans of liquid metal that surround its core, giving us the ability to analyze in detail the base structure of the universe's simplest chemical element. And so, for the first several years of this lab's life, it operated as nothing more than a base of atomic experimentation."

"Ok, ok, stop," Fenna complained. "First off, I have no idea what you're talking about, and secondly, I don't see what any of this has to do with me!"

The elderly caretaker blinked. "Well, it doesn't," he admitted. "Not really. But it begins to explain why we're here."

"Why? Because of some old science?" Fenna asked incredulously.

"Initially, yes. That was the preliminary foundation for this laboratory's existence. It was only years later, once the research proved fruitful and we realized the far-branching potential of our findings, that we decided to convert it into a permanent orbital fixture, far above the constant degeneration unavoidable within Jupiter's gaseous clouds. Formerly a station of atomic experimentation, this lab eventually became more of a database hub, far isolated from the raucous inner-system goings-on of the company at large."

"All right, so what?" Fenna demanded. "Did you bring me here for a history lesson?"

"My dear, I thought we had already agreed that you brought yourself here. Oh well, never mind that. My story is only to satiate your curiosity. The truth is that my wave for you to come was only because I feared I would not long be able to complete a promise made to your benefactor—our mutual acquaintance of mystery."

"Promise?" Fenna asked. "What promise?"

"To fulfill my main responsibility as the keeper of the gate!" the old man declared proudly. "The very reason this growing databank needs a constant caretaker."

"Which is?"

"Well, that's what I've been getting at, my dear—the culmination of this lab's research and the promise of custom molecular recomposition. You see, compiling atoms is one thing but having the blueprints with which to reconfigure complex matter is a separate challenge entirely. That is an issue that requires infinitely precise measurements and a gigantic database to keep all results contained, you understand? If we were ever to dream of breaking down atoms and recreating anything more than basic molecules from the ground up, we would need the exact knowledge of what it was we were trying to create, be they raw resources or the foundations of life itself."

"Wait, what? What does breaking down and building up atoms have to do with life? And again... What the tuk does this have to do with me?"

"Well, we weren't simply trying to make atoms out of atoms... We were aiming much higher than that," the elderly TurTechnicks representative clarified. "We meant to give ourselves the ability to recreate anything out of everything—taking pure elements of any kind and reconfiguring them into apples and oranges, shovels and terminal screens, into human beings and fluffy dogs and space ships the size of cities. We meant to give ourselves the ability to recreate the whole of human civilization on a whim, you see. But such a lofty dream required quite a lot of groundwork and meticulous documentation, which is exactly what this orbital lab's databank became: a molecular-blueprint catalog for the ground-up atomic reconstruction of anything ever recorded."

"Uh, ok... So you're here to do what, sit on this data? Doesn't that get old?"

"There are new scans coming in every day, detailing everything from newly founded technology to custom-designed furniture to fresh new breeds of genetically-modified crops. Someone needs to stay here and monitor the feeds—a gatekeeper, if you will. Otherwise, it might all get scrambled!"

"All right already, I get it. You guys have a god complex..."

"This has nothing to do with gods! Actually, quite the opposite!" the caretaker insisted. "This is simply the demystification of a previous unknown—with no assumptions involved. Which now brings us right back to the point at hand: why you are here!"

Fenna was caught off-guard. She had no idea how this all connected. "Ok, why?" she asked. "For the love of tukking Zeus, why am I here?"

"Our mutual friend has long been a trusted scout of talent, seeking out people and items to benefit the blueprint databanks with their inclusion. And he, my dear, chose you personally, making me promise to scan and enter you into said database myself."

"Chose me?" Fenna repeated absentmindedly. "Why me?"

"Don't be afraid now. It will only take a second."

"Afraid of..."

The elderly caretaker waved his arms in the air, gesturing for the lab around him to start up a whole new chain of events. The ceiling flashed bright, momentarily stunning Fenna in a daze. Before she could react, a circular crease formed in the ceiling panel above her and a set of spiraling rings came down to wrap her up in heavenly light.

"What the tuk!?" She jumped backwards and attempted to roll out of the way, but the rings followed her every movement, intersecting her path easily and bathing her body in light. She ran in desperate circles, hoping to escape the spirals. Backed into a wall, she held out her pickaxes in vain and failed to make any contact as she swiped the air.

The rings followed her unperturbed, spiraling through and around the wall as if it was not there. Several moments after beginning their frenzy of motion, they slowed down to a stop, lingering a second before they rose back up through the ceiling above.

"Fiery Styx of Hades!" Fenna shouted in surprise, demanding an answer from the elderly caretaker. "What in the name of the gods was that!?"

"That, my dear, was your personal entry into the far future," he explained with a porcelain smile spread wide across his face. "Your sub-atomic data has been entered into the databank cloud."

"Listen, grandpa, I came a long-ass way to get here, and I'm in no mood for games!"

"Now, now, young one, immortality is no gift to be taken lightly," the elder caretaker insisted, floating forward on his levitating chair and bringing himself to height with her eyes. "Entire civilizations have risen and fallen for more minor a bounty."

"Whatever," Fenna replied disappointedly. "Is that the only reason I'm even here? Apollo sent me all the way to Jupiter for a tukking quark-scan? I thought it was going to be... something else."

"Yes." The old man nodded. "However, that does not mean the questions you sought in coming here will not be answered."

"What questions?" Fenna asked.

"Do not forget where we are," the caretaker reminded her. "This is the biggest database of answers in human history! Ask and you shall receive." He gestured with his palm in the air and brought up a holographic display projecting Fenna's newly acquired scan data before him.

Fenna stepped closer, looking upon the projected data with a wary grimace. A simplified representation of her DNA double-helix swirled slowly in the air, supplemented beside a preliminary summary of her amino-acid footprint and a basic mental analysis of her recorded cognitive functions. Her anger at the invasion of privacy this represented laid just a nudge below her imminent curiosity.

"Wait!" the elderly caretaker called out suddenly. He blinked and stared at her, waving away the hologram and floating closer to look upon her in greater detail. He grabbed her face and squinted, analyzing her complexion in momentary disbelief. "Oh, this makes perfect sense now—I should have guessed!"

"Get off me!" Fenna wrenched herself from the old man's grasp. "What in Hades is wrong with you now?"

The elderly caretaker backed down. "Ms. Fenna Caae, you sure are a lucky girl."

"Hey! Who told you my name?" Fenna coughed out in surprise. It had been many years since she had heard it out loud. "Was it Apollo?"

"Don't be ridiculous, my dear. You just saw me pull up your biological data right now. The databank simply crosschecked your DNA with all on public and private record and quickly identified who you were. Don't worry. Your guardian angel Apollo has never spilled as much as a word of your identity, although he surely knew it."

"Yeah? Why is that?" Fenna barked back.

"Perhaps he supposed that if I knew who you were, I would never have agreed to let you past the gate. And perhaps he was right…"

"You better start spilling now, geezer. I'm getting really annoyed!"

"Please sit down, Ms. Caae. I did not mean to scare you," the elderly caretaker responded calmly. He signaled the lab to bring up a floating chair like his own from the ground below and gestured for her to sit down and rest easy. "Our mutual friend's secrets are now yours by right; no longer does this information need to stay hidden."

Fenna sat down on the hovering chair warily. Her heart beat faster in her chest than she would have liked. "All right, so tell me already—what does Apollo want from me? What am I to him?"

"You are his only living relative," the old man revealed. "His precious little sister."

"Sister…?" Fenna's eyes filled up with unbidden tears. "What do you mean? That's impossible!"

"It's actually rather probable, now that I think about it," the caretaker admitted. "Your brother Jessie has carried this burden alone for far too long… I should have realized it much sooner. However, this does put the authenticity of your qualification into the TurTechnicks resurrection pool in doubt, you see, knowing that no matter what you did all along, Apollo would have remained biased unto your recruitment."

"I don't care about that! Fenna said through heavy tears. "Where is he? Where is Jessie now!?"

"I'm sorry, but I cannot answer that," the old man replied regretfully. "I simply do not know."

"But you said you knew him personally, right?" Fenna demanded. "Was that a lie?"

"Indeed I do know your brother, but the last time I saw him was long ago, my dear girl—half a decade at least. I'm willing to share with you every relevant communiqué I have, but I am afraid that it will not do you much good."

"No matter what you have, it's infinitely better than what I have now. When was the last you heard from him?"

"Very well," the caretaker acquiesced. "Last I heard—about eight years ago—Jessie Caae was heading up a spacial-research development somewhere within the great expanse of the Solar System's inner asteroid belt. However, as you well know—having flown through it on your way here—the volume that that region encompasses happens to be vastly larger than the entire space between the four central planets combined. There is no telling where exactly he could have gone—and I stress that this information is eight years old. He could be anywhere, really."

"And there's no way to track him? Is there anyone else who would know more?" Fenna asked readily. "Anyone Jessie would have trusted?"

"Unfortunately, no. I'm afraid not…but that is entirely by his own design. Mr. Caae worked hard to distance himself from his old aliases—you know how he can be. It seems your brother never quite learned to trust anybody but himself."

Fenna contemplated this notion without betraying a hint of how she really felt. "Thank you," she finally replied. "I will find him, no matter how long it takes. At least now I know where to start."

"Really?" the caretaker asked in genuine surprise. "You'd turn your life completely around on drop of a dime, based on nothing more than hearsay?"

"Why wouldn't I?" Fenna asked back. "He's my only brother—nothing else matters!"

"Do you really think so low of the rest of your life's pursuits, my dear?" the old man probed. "Have you already forgotten what brought you here?"

"What are you talking about, grandpa? I thought you said that *this* was why I came here."

"Yes, but what brought *you* here? What answers were *you* hoping to find?"

"Well, I thought it might have something to do with..." Fenna gulped. "The Olympic Station disaster..." Her eyes filled back up with tears.

"What does your databank know about it?" she asked.

"Everything," the old man replied glumly. "It knows exactly what happened."

"Why would... Son of a Taur!" Fenna jumped straight into anger. "Was it you all along? Did TurTechnicks blow up the station?"

"No, of course not. That is ridiculous!" the caretaker vowed. He waved his hands in the air and brought up a hologram of the gigantic, single-helix structure that had been the Olympic station, pre-tragedy. "But we do have full access to the wealth of information scanning in this station's databanks, including every technical spec involved in the creation of the station Olympia."

"What does that mean?" Fenna demanded. "Are you saying that it was sabotaged from the inside? Did TurTechnicks rig it to explode?"

"Well, no, it's not as simple as that," the TurTechnicks caretaker explained. "You see, the station Olympia— originally called project Pegasus—had been in development by the former TurTek for over half a century before it ever got attached to the idea of a zero-gee Olympic venue. It was only over the long years of its construction process that other companies and private entities alike joined in to capitalize on the growing market of its expanding breadth, hoping to gain a foothold in the orbital settlement bloom which was to come. And that popularity, ultimately, became the station's very downfall."

"Which means what, exactly?" Fenna asked.

"It means that whenever too many people become involved in a single plan, it begins to shift and buckle under the weight of their dithering motives." The old man brought up a holographic display of an ages-old orbital blueprint vaguely recognizable as the outer frame of the station.

"At first classified as an experimental development, project Pegasus was initially designed with the sole intention of determining the viability of a self-sufficient Deep Space vessel able to survive long periods of isolated flight. The problem with such an ambitiously complex venture was, of course, the difficulty and long amount of time that it would take to complete. So long, in fact, that during the length of the station's construction, the public became used to its presence in the sky.

"By the time of the Orbital Bloom, when the popularity of geosynchronous stations rose to an all-time high, the half-built TurTek vessel was so well-known it set the new precedent for semi-habitable, ongoing zero-gee constructions orbiting Earth. People began to set up permanent shop within its active multi-production sites, taking advantage of the flourishing resource market it brought and the ever-expanding orbital community it helped found.

"It was nearly half a century after the vessel began development that project Pegasus was chosen as the exclusive venue for the first ever zero-to-low-gee planetary Olympics. It was subsequently rebranded as the station Olympia, where it would serve as an example for the coming era of regularized orbital life."

Fenna cut in. "Ok, well, thanks again for another history lesson, gramps, but that says nothing as to why the station blew apart. What motive would anyone have for destroying it?"

"Yes, exactly," the caretaker agreed, nodding under his bulking top hat. "That's where things get complicated. You have to remember the original intent of project

Pegasus was to develop a Deep Space vessel, not an orbital station. The mere fact that it had become a publicized staple in the orbital community gave the goal of ever leaving Earth space much less a chance of coming to fruition. All of a sudden, the project development's own success had become its biggest crutch, restricting the very objective that had warranted its creation in the first place."

"Wait, wait, hold on!" Fenna objected. "So now you're saying that it *was* sabotaged from the inside? Quit jumping back and forth!"

"Very quick, my dear girl." The old man smiled emptily. "But, as I said, things were never that simple."

"So, why would anybody in their right minds wish to explode something that they spent so much effort building up, even if they thought its development was heading in the wrong direction?" Fenna asked, disbelieving.

"Oh, the disaster never truly exploded the station apart. That was a common misconception," the caretaker corrected. "Parts of the vessel split wide open, yes, and an entire habitation wing fatally decompressed, but the station Olympia—aka the combined efforts of project Pegasus— was never so badly damaged that it could not be fixed. We're talking about an enormous structure the size of a modern city, most of which barely felt the force of the shockwave rippling out from the tragic devastation."

"Huh!?" Fenna was shocked. "So why did I never find any news of the station undergoing reconstruction after the disaster? I had always thought that its wreckage had simply been cannibalized by the zero-gee community for parts."

"No, no, no, that would never happen!" the old man insisted. "The bad publicity surrounding the disaster made the space station instantly less profitable commercially, so it was put back into full development and rebranded yet again, changing its name to become the vessel Phoenix. Most of the people who had set up shop inside moved out as its public exposure cut to null... but the majority of the original helical vessel's structure remained, including most of its gravity-simulating mechanisms. Other than a much-needed comprehensive fix for the parts that were now broken, the only real difference between the station before and after the disaster was the fact that nobody was in any real rush to come visit anymore.

"And so, when the time from its initial projections came for it to distance its orbit further away from Earth, nobody much complained. Years from now, when it will be scheduled to be taken even further away and brought into orbit around the planet Mars, nobody will even notice. Thus, this end-result brings to light what could have been a possible, fathomable motive for the sabotage of the station in full bloom."

Fenna took a while to get her thoughts in order. "So you're saying it was all just a big shakedown?" she asked eventually. "You're saying the tragedy which killed my parents, along with thousands of others, was simply a tukking scheme to combat the Olympic station's popularity?"

"I agree with your disgust," the old man admitted, "but yes, that is a good summary. The Olympic station underwent a very public execution, tearing its success apart in the eyes of the world and irreversibly tainting its image."

"Son of a Taur!" Fenna yelled. She got up and kicked her floating chair away. "Who was the bastard who did this? I will rip him apart!"

"I'm afraid you are decades too late for that," the old man replied. "Or perhaps, decades too early."

"Don't you dare hold back on me!" Fenna demanded. "Who was it?"

"I honestly do not know," the caretaker declared, "but if my hypothesis is correct, it was most likely someone whose molecular data exists in the current TurTechnicks databanks and is awaiting a duplicated reconstruction at some future point in time. Only such a person would benefit from the faraway results of the project's scope."

"That coward!" Fenna raged. "Hiding in some future life!"

The elderly caretaker frowned, for once letting his emotions get the better of him. He heaved off his bulking top hat and placed down it on the ground, straining with every effort he took. "If you must, you may take out your anger on me," he said, sorrowfully looking Fenna in the eyes. "I am the closest one responsible for those let past my databank's gates." He stood up on two shaky legs, getting off his floating chair and stepping straight through the wavering hologram, which shut off behind him in the air.

"What are you doing?" Fenna asked, confused. "I'm not going to blame you for something you didn't even do!"

"Nevertheless, I realize now that I am done," the caretaker responded grimly. "I have served my role long enough."

"What are you talking about?" Fenna asked, feeling uneasy. "What role?"

"The role of TurTek, TurTechnicks, and everything in between," he answered with a dry chuckle. "I have been a caretaker for far, far too long—a cog in the entity of TurTek."

"Ok dude, that's fine. I'm not gonna keep you here," Fenna said. "But where would you go? Find some retirement community and take a nap?"

"No, I think I have napped quite long enough." He looked at Fenna. "You know, my dear, it would be rather nice to meet up with an old mutual friend one last time…"

"Wait, what?" Fenna looked back at him in disbelief,. "Where did that come from?"

"Come on, Ms. Caae, can you not perform this one final request from an old man seeking retirement?" The caretaker smiled innocently. "Don't you think that the time has come for me to shed the system which defines me and simply follow my own interests—for as short a while as I may have left."

"Fine," Fenna sighed. "You can come, but only until we find Jessie. And my ship is my ship. No trying to boss me around."

"Lovely!" the retiring caretaker approved. "Sounds like a journey well worth taking!"

"Oh wait. There's one more thing you have to do before I let you join me," Fenna insisted.

"Yes, what?" he asked.

"Your name. Tell me your real name."

"Hmm, I supposed you're right," the caretaker admitted. "Without my cloak of the company TurTek, I am left with nothing but my own true self…a man all but been erased by years of personal neglect."

"Ok, so what is it?" Fenna asked.

"My name was… is… William."


<><><>

For several days, the floating databank lab lay silent. Its lights remained off, its airlocks shut, and its life support system felt no imminent need to pump extra oxygen into its chambers. As the orbital station passed over the Great

Red Spot of Jupiter, an internal cycle-check triggered itself
to life, initializing a quick scan of the entire station. It
quickly noticed that it could no longer identify the DNA
of a TurTek representative within any of its rooms. In fact,
it found that it could no longer identify any living organic
material within its system whatsoever, just some residual
bacteria.

The TurTechnicks lab took a moment to review its
most recent official list of procedure protocols given a
situation such as this. It buzzed several of its systems back
to life and checked to make sure its land-pod exit system
was still in working order. Then, it pinged a wave down
towards Jupiter to determine the nearest densities of gas.
A surge of power sparkled across the station's pristine
white ceilings and floors, seeking out an individual
duplication unit ready and waiting for action.

Only once the TurTek station's computer was satisfied
that everything was in order and up to standard regulations
did it spark upon a decisive course of action, signaling its
inner processes to begin their irreversible preparation
sequences for sub-atomic duplication. A single pod out of
the many docked within the TurTek lab lit itself up,
registering an oncoming flood of information from the
databanks nearby. The lab loaded up all relevant processes
and began filtering through the incoming data, analyzing
the sub-atomic blueprints and verifying their stabilities
before signaling a final go-ahead and allowing the systems
within it to begin their preparatory cycles.

Inside the egg-shaped land-pod's circular chamber, a
crystalline duplication tank twirled down from the ceiling
and filled with translucent green liquid in preparation for
an upcoming volume of transmutational displacement.
Outside its curved outer surface, several exterior vents
opened to allow an influx of gaseous air. An external clip

holding the entire bulk of the land-pod in place separated from its hinges, and a hydraulic pump gently pushed the pod down towards Jupiter and out of the lab with the slightest momentum.

The egg-shaped land-pod floated out in space, stretching seconds into minutes into solid hours of silence. It continued to accelerate downwards and became ever more entrapped by the gigantic swirling planet's tremendously powerful gravitational force below. The further the pod flew, the faster it fell towards Jupiter, until eventually it busted straight through the planet's outer atmosphere and broke its long silence with a torrent of rushing noise.

The land-pod's open vents began to fill with the pounding of hydrogen, helium, and methane. Its inner "lungs" quickly expanded as far as they could go, savoring the wealthy intake of raw resources. Within the pod's "lungs," the molecules of gas began to break apart and separate into individual atoms. Those then split into individual protons, neutrons, electrons, and a powerful surge of nuclear energy. The system soaked up the energy, feeding the power of the land-pod's ongoing processes, and the elementary particles gathered up into the green liquid within the pod's duplication tank until they were thick enough in abundance to reconfigure, forming new atoms as the blueprints saw fit.

Within the flowing duplication tank, transmutation started up fast. Protons got mashed into neutrons as electrons were forced into artificial orbit, locking in place and solidifying into molecules. Water and carbon chained alongside nitrogen, calcium, phosphorous, and a host of newly created organic material, linking together and coagulating into strings of solid matter like magnetic dust.

Nucleic acids, proteins, lipids, and carbohydrates built up out of scratch, twisting and turning into existence within the translucent green liquid of the inner crystalline tank. Blood, tissue, stem cells, and cognitive neurons formed out of the ether as the blood vessels around them wove into a circulatory network, muscles stretched across solidifying bones, and a system of nerves assembled in a web of connectivity.

Bones clicked into place, organs slid into configuration, and layer-upon-layer of skin cells wrapped everything together and out of sight like duct tape around a tangle of wires. Hair materialized from out the skin, nails shaped around fingers and toes, ear drums wove themselves into existence, and gums hardened around the upper and lower jaw, pressing close into porcelain-white teeth.

Cells sparked to life, blood began to flow, and the subtle electrical currents in the ever-complicated brain began to react to each other's signals. Soon enough, the flurry of changes came to an end as the artificially constructed human body floating within the TurTek duplication tank matched the incarnation blueprints perfectly.

The falling land-pod shifted its exterior vents closed and ceased their roaring inward intake. Chemical particulates already within the pod's "lungs" pulled apart to provide the last bit of nuclear energy and blew outward with enough force to counter the planet's massive gravitational pull amid billowing hydrogen explosions. The pod arced upward in the air like a skyward rocket, shooting back out through the clouds several thousand miles past where it had entered, trailing long streams of nuclear energy that lessened as its target momentum came to be. It broke out into orbit and slowed itself down to an optimal trajectory as the last few bursts of extraneous material and radiation left its hull. The egg-shaped pod was then alone in a free-flying, orbital path outward.

The TurTek space-station lab still in orbit waited patiently during the day after it released its land-pod cargo. It began heating its interior chambers and re-filtering oxygen for maximum human comfort. Mission statements were summarized and several dozen data terminals preloaded with relevant information matching the probable needs of the oncoming occupant. Food, predicting his long and short term needs, was duplicated on the spot, placed into storage, and set to optimal temperatures. Nanorobots were pumped into the air set to update those already in the oncoming occupant's internal systems with the ideal bodily compensations for the local orbital environment and the radiation level constantly pounding the space-station from below.

A magnetic tether spread wide for its upcoming catch, syncing with the floating lab's external sensors to tell it exactly in which direction to stretch.

A full Jupiter rotational day later—about 10 hours Earth-time—the TurTek lab's external sensors sensed the incoming presence of its ejected land-pod coming back from the planet below. After repositioning its magnetic tether to align perfectly for the incoming strike, it waited.

Once the land-pod came back into view, it came fast and hard. Moving full speed, it slammed straight into the magnetic tether and latched on, utilizing the long umbilical to swing around the space station and allow itself time to slow down. The tether began to retract in concert, pulling the pod inward to greet the floating lab. By the time the land-pod reached the station dock, most of its momentum had already dissipated, leaving just enough for smooth entry into its normal parking spot. It hooked in, rotated into place, clasped onto the suction of an airlock, and soon came to a complete stop. But for the heat still resonating from its metal and the human being in its chamber, the land-pod had returned exactly as it had left, betraying no sign it had ever been gone.

The land-pod's airlock door snapped open inside the lab, and a man in a suit stepped out. He trod uncomfortably across the white-lit floor, scratching at his forehead as if he was forgetting something. The TurTek station lit a path of tiles on the floor before him—step by step by step—but it had yet to tell him where he was. So, when he reached sight of an outer window and gained his first view outside, he stood and gaped. The glorious view of the massive planet Jupiter was a lot to handle, even if he had seen it before. Then, however, he moved on, obediently following the lit tiles across the floor like a dog given the promise of a bone.

At the end of the man's path, an abandoned top hat sat waiting for him on the ground. He picked it up and heaved it onto his head, a porcelain smile spreading wide across his face. The man accepted a seat upon the hovering chair that came floating up from the ground. He rotated it to hide the view of Jupiter from his sight. *There are more important things to focus on.*

The newly duplicated man's bulking top hat started flashing images directly into his eyes, subliminally recapping the last 60 years of human development. Then the images slowed to display a direct visual feed while a stream of audio broadcast straight into his ears.

Within the feed were transcripts recorded by different versions of himself, some of which he remembered and some of which had led alternative lives than his scan blueprint. At the end of the transcripts, supplemented by a branded TurTek logo, was the bit of data he was waiting for: a single message designating his new identification and current situational orders.

**William VI 2128. Current given task: databank caretaker**.

The caretaker sighed, noticing all-too-well that this task had no designated timeline or schedule of events. Not only was there no knowing how long this assignment was meant to last, but there was also no sign of when he would have the chance to interact with another human being. He could be stuck here alone for just a day or for another 60 years. There was just no knowing.

# 14 : lift :

**"The final distinction between a plan of exemplary foresight and one of empty conjecture can only be found after retrospective analysis, when it is far too late to do any good."**
-Transcripts of William

### <8:36:45 a.s.t.><day 8><Anok>

"If you two continue to insist on ascending the lift, I am afraid this is where we must part ways," the TurTek representative decreed to the other members of his short-lived team. "I could no more betray my given mission than could a bird decide not to build a nest."

"The Hades are you talking about, *hat*?" Fenna asked, annoyed at the Rep's constant badgering. "There's nobody here but us four—who's to say what exactly your tukking mission is, anyway?"

"We have protocols in place to prevent straying too far from the overall plan. Otherwise, every little venture could lead to a wasteful dead end. Without such a system in place, none of us would have even made it onto this planet."

"Big woop, hat-head! Which one of us even wants be here, anyway? I mean, if we had awoken in orbit around

Earth, Mars, or the Greater Asteroid Belt, that'd be one thing, but here…" Fenna cast her voice down at him. "I really don't care. Go back to your little pod if you have to. I'm going up this lift with or without you."

"No! We can't split apart!" Enri insisted. "If you haven't forgotten, our terminals have yet to receive any long-range frequency waves. This means that if we stray too far from one another, we would be stranded without communication. Who knows if we could ever find each other again?"

"So what? What does it even matter?" Fenna asked. "We're all still stuck together on this godsdamn planet anyway. We're bound to run into each other again, whether we like it or not."

"There is no guarantee that getting back down the wave-spire will be such an easy thing alone. Split apart and there's no telling what could happen given an emergency."

"Yes, I agree," the Rep maintained, "and that is precisely why I cannot ascend this spire any further, regardless of what you two decide. The information we have yet to send TurTek is too significant to lose. Everything else has to wait until we find a way to compose a long-range signal and send our confirmations up to the station above. Otherwise, our entire mission will have been for waste. We might as well have never been created."

"Mission this, mission that!" Fenna yelled back. "Who gives a shit about the tukking mission!? We're here, we're stuck, so we might as well do whatever the tuk we want!"

"Pacem!" Fre'dd called out. "Please, everybody, lay your tongues still!"

"As I have already explained," the Rep repeated, "our mission parameters have been put in place for a very good reason. Following proper procedure benefits us all."

"Yeah, yeah, whatever you say," Fenna scoffed. "Go on ahead and follow your tucking mission already. Just leave us alone, why don't'chu?"

"Silentium!" Fre'dd urged. "Listen."

"Come on. both of you. Stop being ridiculous!" Enri insisted. "No matter what we choose to do, we should all stay together. That being said, I agree with Fenna that we should proceed onwards—now that we've finally found something of value. For all we know, there are accessible waves up there that we could use to contact the space station. *Not* going could actually cost us the mission!"

"Yes, perhaps that is true," the Rep agreed skeptically. "However, we cannot know anything for sure. Protocol dictates that situations like this proceed on the side of caution."

"For the love of Zeus, why does it matter?" Fenna asked. "Let him go already, Enri. Why do we even need him?"

"Stop! Quiet your words already." Fre'dd hushed. "Something's coming."

Enri finally took notice of his large companion's insistent urgency. He pulled up his wristband terminal and scanned for incoming vibrations. It beeped immediately and zoomed in on a point of visible movement within the pie-wedged room's network grid of metal, rock, and glass walkways. A large, glossy sphere with an ink-black whirlwind spiraled within. He gaped and stared, reversing the holographic recording and freeze-framing the image to interpret what he saw. He recognized its patterning.

"What is it?" Fenna asked, looking over his shoulder in genuine curiosity.

"The creaturas," Fre'dd whispered from down below. "They're coming."

Enri lowered his terminal-laden wrist, looking out into the brightly lit room and listening for whatever was coming. A scuttling noise intensified through the convoluted chamber, at first soft like a whispering breeze. Then it intensified in strength until it filled the whole room with a hailstorm of echoing sound.

"Get up here, now!" Enri commanded, tossing Fre'dd and the TurTek Rep the rope to climb.

"We have been over this already—I am not coming up with you," the TurTek representative replied flatly.

"Now is not the time to argue!" Enri yelled down. "Come up now!"

"Why would I..." the Rep began, but Fre'dd interrupted him as he picked him up like a small child and held him over his head high, bringing the Rep up directly below Enri and Fenna. "Now that was surely unnecessary!" he complained as Enri heaved him over the ledge.

"Herc', harness the rope through your belt," Fenna instructed Fre'dd below. "I'll gonna pull you up with my spinner." She took the turtle-shell pack off her back and clipped it through the rope, keeping an eye below to see that Fre'dd had followed her direction before proceeding onward.

Once satisfied, she signaled her device to start spinning him up, keeping it slow enough to prevent the large man from jolting into the wall. Within moments, the pack lifted him above the bottom of the golden doorframe, the height of which he feared almost as much as he feared the coming alien creature. He crouched down once he reached the top, hugging the golden metal tight.

"What's going on with you all!?" the TurTek Rep questioned in shock and anger at the turn of events. "Have you lost your minds?"

"Shh, keep quiet," Enri warned, pointing into the pie-wedged room. His wristband terminal projected a magnified image of what it saw before him, very clearly displaying a ten-foot Nokkian snake flickering in and out of view as it flipped end over end through the convoluted chamber. Like the walking trees of the blue forest outside the spire, the alien snake moved through stretching and swinging motions, grasping onto claw-holds in its path. It moved astoundingly fast for a creature its size, seemingly defying gravity as it swung.

"It's coming straight at us!" the TurTek Rep pitched aloud.

"SHH," both Enri and Fenna hissed. She slapped a hand over the representative's mouth to keep him quiet, inadvertently knocking the top-hat off his head in the process. It rolled down behind them, tumbling off the golden doorframe and falling into the tube-lift's interior chamber.

"I don't think the snake can see much out of its eyes as it swings. Its claws are moving so fast they scarcely leave the eyeball time to look around," Enri noted. "Fascinating!"

"Well then, we should get out of sight before it slows down," Fenna whispered back. "There's no way it would miss us sitting up here like landlubbing idiots!"

Across the room, the Nokkian snake came closer and closer upon every swing, pivoting and disappearing out of sight each time before it reemerged further down its complex path. It got louder and louder as it neared, striking claws against metal and echoing crisp, repeating clanks throughout the neighboring chambers.

Fenna tapped Fre'dd on the shoulder, feeling him shiver in fright. "Close your eyes. I'll lower you down into the lift. You'll be fine, I promise."

The large man nodded, gulping down his fears.

Fenna heaved the Rep off the ground and onto Fre'dd's shoulders, placing a finger over her lips to signal him to keep quiet. Fre'dd accepted the burden without complaint, closing his eyes and leaning back into the air, trusting Fenna's promise to bring him down safe.

"Move it, Earthboy!" Fenna grabbed Enri and jumped with him after Fre'dd and the Rep below. Catching their rope midair, she leveraged her weight against the golden doorframe's wall and ran straight down it. This let Enri drop down onto Fre'dd's shoulder opposite the Rep. Fenna landed graceful as a cat on the brass floor beside them. She signaled back up the smart-rope to her turtle-shell spinner. It detached from the golden doorframe and tumbled down at her.

"Oof!" Enri coughed out. "What was that for?"

The clanking grew louder and louder, until suddenly—**whizz**—the mysterious alien snake reached the golden vertical doors above and threw itself through their open frame without hesitation. It caught onto a marble pillar hanging inside and twisted upward around it like an anaconda engulfing its prey. Only then did it take notice of the humans below. The Nokkian snake reeled back in shock and slithered up the pillar into the shadows above, ending the sounds of its clanks and hiding its presence completely.

The four travelers stood frozen on the tube-lift's brass floor, staring up in nervous anticipation of what would come. Pointing his wristband terminal up and scanning for movement in the grid-work above, Enri did not take long to find it—but it took him a few extra moments to understand what exactly it was doing. The alien snake had stalled several dozen feet above the shivering humans and had stretched itself out between two marble pillars with both claws grasped.

"What in the hells?" Enri muttered. "Its eyes can't see anything like that!"

"Maybe it doesn't have to," Fenna replied under her breath. "Anyway, let's get out of its line of sight!" She grabbed him and pulled him across the brass floor, motioning Fre'dd and the Rep to follow along.

The Nokkian snake released hold of both clawed ends at once and dropped straight down, passing marble pillars left and right.

"Empress, protect us!" Fre'dd yelled out and covered his three companions under a massive protective embrace. However, no impact ever came. Instead, an awkward silence followed.

Moments before the Nokkian should have hit the humans straight-on, it spun in the air and caught upon a golden orb hanging beneath a marble pillar. Instead of spinning wildly under its shifting momentum, the alien snake used sheer muscular strength to bring itself under control and slow down to a wobble. It held itself strong like an athlete, extending down towards the humans with a claw open wide and a glossy, ink-black whirlwind of an eye gazing directly at them. The creature shifted sight from one human to another as it hung, staring quizzically at each and every one of them. They stood frozen as ice.

"Of what nature is this beast?" Fre'dd asked quietly. He mulled over the question in his head. "If it wished to strike us down, it should have acted already."

"Perhaps it's just sizing us up," Fenna speculated. "It's thinking of how to strike."

"It could have done that from up there," Fre'dd disagreed. "This is something different."

"We should incapacitate it now while it's indecisive!" the TurTek Rep demanded. "We cannot afford to undergo an attack!"

"No!" Fre'dd hollered back, uncharacteristically forceful. "To do so would be ungodly! Not even Ares would strike down those he is not yet at war with."

"Shh!" Enri whispered. "Pay attention—this is his turf, not ours—the least we could do is listen."

The Nokkian's galaxy-like eye dilated and opened up physically from the center out, like an ocean whirlpool. The eye blew out a gust of heavy citrus and made a loud, lasting yelping noise. The alien snake twisted back up the golden orb above and sprang sideways with enough energy to fling itself onto the golden lift's open doorframe, screeching all the while. It landed with a claw on gold and threw itself straight out of sight. For thirty agonizing seconds, everything was silent.

And then the clanking began, emanating from every direction at once. The many pie-wedged chambers in every direction around the lift tube began to resonate with the noise of countless echoing strikes, far more than one Nokkian snake, two, or even 50 could make. It built up into a hurricane of sound, hosting hundreds upon hundreds of cycling impacts on metal and stone. Eyeballed claws flung out from every shadows, grasping onto and clasping every conceivable surface they could find with the alarming speed of a well-oiled swarm, flooding together like sentient liquid.

"Shit, shit, shit, we shoulda hit it before it called for its friends!" Fenna yelled. She pulled out her twin pneumatic pickaxes, holding them out as a shield.

"We are done for!" the Rep yelled. "Our mission is done for!"

"Take guard, but do not provoke them any further!" Fre'dd urged. He pulled off his rumble belt—to which he had latched both Dirk's mobility belt and Enri's old terminal—and held it over him as shield in the air, leaving its rumbling turned off but its air thrusters turned on, blowing out a layer of wind above him.

"Hold on," Enri said. He held up his wristband terminal, recording everything he saw. "They're stopping out there."

Sure enough, each and every one of the Nokkian snakes stopped just outside the perimeter of the lift's open doorframes, clasping one eye-bearing claw tight on a wall as the other stared inwards at the humans. The last few Nokkian stragglers came in, scrambling over their brethren until they found their own uncovered branch to cling upon, and then the commotion died down completely. The alien snakes were surprisingly varied in physical characteristics and attire, some of which included glass-metal bracings, vivid colorings, hanging cloth, and some simply bare.

For several long minutes, alien snake and human being alike stood gut-wrenchingly silent, simply watching each other and waiting for the other side to act. None of the swarms came any further in, and none of the travelers moved an inch.

"They gonna rush us or not?" Fenna asked. "This is getting awkward."

"Non puto, I don't think so," Fre'dd replied. "Or they would have done so already. They are in dynamic formation, but not geared for battle."

"Then for what?"

"I do not know."

"Gods know they could sweep us away easily if they tried," Enri said. "But they're not doing anything, just looking. I cannot image what they are thinking."

"Who says they're planning for anything?" Fenna asked. "Maybe they're just curious."

The staring contest ended when the golden twin doors of the Nokkian lift clicked lightly and began to hiss closed with all of the alien snakes still safely outside. Beyond their sliding glass windows, a single Nokkian snake from the hundreds outside started to move, changing his positioning and straightening out to physically open its whirlpool eye deep. It began emitting a low, heavy grumble through the air. In direct response, the rest of the alien snakes began to click in rhythm, snapping their claws open and shut before their whirlwind eyes. The tube's twin golden doors clanked shut tight.

The golden frame of the lift-tube around the travelers began to reverberate and rattle. A buzzing shiver in the brass floor ran through their legs and the entire tram began to rise. The alien snakes outside dropped out of sight. Fenna and Fre'dd put down their weapons, loosening their defensive stances. Enri held down his ever-recording wristband terminal.

He looked over at the Rep beside him and gave a little chuckle. "Well, I guess we're all going up together."

"Yes, that appears to be correct," the TurTek representative agreed with a nod. He picked up his bulking top hat and heaved it atop his head.

"Up, up, up, up," Enri's old handheld terminal squawked out from off Fre'dd's multi-versatile belt. "Out of the darkness and into the light! Shiver and shiver until the sun come to sight."

"Oh shut up, you."

<12:03:31 a.s.t.><day 9>

The golden lift ascended for many silent hours, moving exceptionally fast despite its inner silence. Although the human travelers had no control over the alien technology, or any idea where it was going, their enthusiasm for exploring the upper levels of the wave-spire rose and rose as the increasingly diverse contents of the caves and chambers passed beneath them on their way up. The alien lift took many winding detours, stopping every so often and opening its four sets of vertical twin golden doors with a completely different environment than the last—most of which looked completely non-navigable to human beings.

One room was lined with white tiles and hung with sheets like spinning clay. Another looked surprisingly human-retro, lined with faded purple and neon green textured wallpaper with swiveling brass posts zigzagged throughout. A third room filled with waterfalls and vents of steam looked to have metal-glass rods hanging off rows of swinging chains moving up and down in an uneven, yet surprisingly graceful, motion. Not much of what the humans saw made sense, but that didn't stop them from feeling awe—especially Enri, who recorded everything.

Without even leaving the golden lift, Enri had been able to learn a lot about the variety of architectural styles this alien world possessed, and he wondered most of all why all the chambers were abandoned and empty. Since the group had been confronted by a tribe of Nokkian snakes a day before and miles below, only the occasional school of flying gekkons buzzed like bats in the caverns, and the rare occurrence of a room completely enveloped in a walking-tree jungle of cerulean blue, complete with wild beasts roaming about, crossed their paths. *Where are the sentient creatures who built these tunnels?* Enri wondered. *Such a prominent technological civilization should surely be thriving, not hiding in the shadows!*

Over the last day of ascent, he had seen more than a score of different regions with lift-stop transit rooms decorated in different Nokkian art styles, seemingly representative of several completely different societies that had existed in this wave-spire at one time or another. Enri was bombarded with so much visual information he could not make head or tails of anything, so he simply kept recording. The primary reason he and the rest of his group were even here was to act as mobile eyes and ears of the TurTek space-station orbiting far above, not necessarily to understand everything they found. As long as there was more to be seen and recorded into digital memory, Enri was more than content to keep moving onwards.

As it had done many times before this, the lift shuddered and began its arduous process of decelerating. The dark cavern outside several of its tall, narrow windows gave way to wide, open air and an expansive view of a vast wasteland outside as seen from miles above its surface.

Enri stood up from the brass dent in the circular floor on which he had been sitting. He walked over to the center of the chamber and peeked out the tall, thin windows high above him to see where it was they arrived this time around. However, other than a basic approximation of the height they had risen to, he could not yet determine a thing.

The golden lift's speed continued to decrease as its quivering increased to a rumbling shiver. Scattered across the circular floor and using brass dents as seats, Fenna, Fre'dd, and the Rep began, one by one, to get up and regroup alongside Enri. They stood silent as the capsule ground to a halt and its twin glass doors hissed open on both sides. The incoming rush of air forced the four companions to squint and shield their eyes. Their ears popped at the shift of pressure.

Fre'dd, Enri, and Fenna gasped at what they saw. The TurTek representative smiled.

# 15 :dreams and illusions:

**"Conscious decisions may far surpass those made in the backs of our minds, but their importance can make us blind to all else."**
–Transcripts of the Empress

### **<2108 C.E. - the age of finesse>**<Earth Orbit>

"Do you know what people used to call it, Jess?" the little girl asked whimsically, forgetting the turmoil unseen past the heavy illusions she had cast around them both. "When they saw a force they could simply not understand."

"Cyll, please. We don't have time," the worried zero-gee athlete replied. He was glad she was not panicking, but wary that she might not fully understand the true danger they were in.

"Magic, Jess, they called it magic," Cil'ette Viviane answered, ignoring his worries. She sat calmly in her virtual Zeun bio-dome garden among the child-sized, gold and green palm trees dipping down beside her. The rustling of a nearby stream and the breeze of wind in the air confused the senses when faced with the notion that their actual bodies were both still in outer space—and in danger. This serenity was but an illusion.

"Listen Cyll, if we don't leave right now, it will be too late." Jessie urged, hoping to push the girl out of her daze.

Although he had initially gotten quite a surprise at having his senses hijacked and his vision fed with false imagery, the shock had not been enough to completely dislodge reality. "We have to move now!"

"We don't call it magic anymore, Jessie, not like our ancestors did—we can't. Not unless we wish to look like fools. Now that our powers are real, we simply call them technology." She played with the grass under her fingertips and gathered up a flower to smell, then twirled it passively in her palm before looking back at him.

Jessie sighed and sat down on the ground across from the little girl. His virtual avatar disrupted the blue strip of grass beneath him, but he could not feel it on his legs as she seemed to—it was only an image in his eyes and a rustle in his ears. He could see the rotund flowers nearby, but he could not smell them as she appeared to do. He could splash the water and shake the palms leaves, but he could never feel the sensations that this little girl displayed with every touch.

"Cil'ette, I am so sorry this is all happening to us," he said as delicately as he could. "But it's not over yet. We are still at risk. The pod you are in could be about to crash into the broken station wing, and we wouldn't even see it coming!"

"Not right now, no," Cil'ette responded offhandedly. "Look, see?" She waved her hands in the air, and the virtual imagery of the bio-dome around her swapped its peaceful orbital view with chaotic live images of the Olympic station disaster going on outside, as seen from her own true eyes looking through the window. The figure of Jessie himself was seen staring forward blankly from outside the hatch, terminal-lensed eyes glazed over by the artificial imagery he was being fed.

"Gah!" Jessie sputtered upon seeing the magnified view of his own face.

"See?" Cil'ette repeated. As she had claimed, there appeared to be no imminent danger nearby, just rubble flying this way and that in the distance, smashing and breaking and falling towards Earth as it drifted in and out of view.

"That's good." Jessie nodded. "But we're still falling towards Earth along with the rest of the wreckage, so we still have to get out of here fast!"

"You'll have to go without me," she replied sadly. "I'm stuck where I am."

She turned her real body around and, with it, moved the landscape in the virtual dome around them. Strands of blonde hair wisped around the image as it rotated, floating around the little girl in zero-gee. The interior of the pod in which she was confined came into view. Smack dab in its center was a drifting dead body trailing globules of coagulated blood. Clouds of glass shards bounced off him as he intersected their floating paths, giving an eerie hint of how he had died in the first place.

"Listen, I will get you out of there. I promise!" Jessie swore to the little girl. "Can you find a suit in there that you can wear? Anything with an air supply?"

"No," Cil'ette responded glumly, trying hard not to cry. "There's nothing here…only my uncle… who was never really my uncle to begin with."

"I'm so sorry, Cyll."

She broke out in tears. "I just wanna go home!" The scenery of the virtual bio-dome reverted back to its initial view of serenity as Cil'ette Viviane hid herself deeper into her imaginary shell.

Jessie stepped his avatar forward and knelt down before the weeping Cyll. "We'll get you home, don't worry about that! I'll find you a way out of there before you know it."

"Okay, Jess." Cil'ette choked down her emotions.

"You're going to have to release me now." Jessie motioned across the virtual imagery all around them. "No more dreams, no more illusions. I have to go out there and try to find solutions."

"But without my dreams, I have no control! Anything could happen."

"Please, Cyll, just until we're safe, then you can come back to any illusion you'd like!" Jessie pleaded. "But for now, we need to see the truth just as it is."

"I'll only promise if you do!" the little girl insisted, huffing and puffing. "No more dreams and illusions until we are both safe! No more untruths."

"Yes, I promise," Jessie said, hoping he could redeem the situation yet.

"Are you just going to run away and leave me to die when I release you? It's ok if you do."

"What? No! Of course not, Cyll!"

"Remember, you promised to tell me the truth."

Jessie looked her in the eyes and held his avatar's hands up to brush her cheeks. "No, Cyll. I would never leave you behind. I have already lost far too many friends today."

"Ok. Then I promise as well. No more dreams." She gave Jessie back his vision and motor controls, casting away the virtual scenery around him. Out of his true eyes, he looked back through the murky pod window at her real face. It looked frozen passive with an opaque white murkiness glazed over her blue eyes. Through his suit's ear buds, he could still hear her breathing

*She is still in her dreams and illusions.*

"I'll be right back, Cyll. I have to scout the nearby area," he told the little girl.

"All right, Jessie."

He lifted the magnetic field off his hands—but not his feet—and pivoted himself up to stand. Then, walking step by step upon the pod's metal wall, his magnetized boots alternated strength and traction to help him move forward without flying off.

Jessie could see the calamities going on everywhere around him. The space station rubble, made of objects, structures, bodies, and junk, each with their own dynamic trajectories—spread like clouds in the wind. The rubble appeared deceptively calm from afar and, as a whole, moved in the same general direction towards Earth below. There, the bottom tip of the endless flotilla had already started to hit the upper ozone and burn on contact. A gigantic section of the station Olympia's single-helix wing far above the majority of rubble had completely broken off of the main craft and had started now to come down fast, smashing straight through everything else in its way— including the pod in which Cil'ette remained trapped. The entire disaster zone was going down, pulled gravitationally towards an imminent plunge into planet Earth.

Scanning his eyes across the orbital chaos, Jessie's terminal lenses ran an in-depth scenery-check of all plausible outcomes. The emergency wave channels broadcasting through his helmet speakers depicted pure chaos, intersecting a clustertuk of transmissions spamming alerts and requests from thousands upon thousands of people in need. Although service bots and rescue workers had already shown up on the scene to snatch bodies out of the air and liberate people from the throes of death, their numbers were far too few and scattered to do much good in the short time left.

"Jessie?" a young girl's voice rang through stronger than the rest. Jessie shut off all other feeds.

"Yes, Cyll?" he asked.

She paused. "Am I going to die? Will I fall down into the sky?"

"No, of course not!" Jessie answered in surprise. "Why would you say that?"

"I can see the images from your eyes," she replied forthright. "It won't be long now."

"Oh…" Jessie said awkwardly. He looked away from the imminent plummet, instead scanning the space around the debris field for a plausible path to safety. "Don't worry, Cyll, I'll find us a way! We're both going to make it out of this in one piece!"

"I don't want to die," she said, "but I don't want you to die either."

"Nobody's going to die!" he insisted. "We're going to find a way out of here!"

"People are dying all the time," Cil'ette Vivienne responded somberly. "What makes us any different?"

"Because we're going to find a way home!"

"No more dreams, Jessie, no more dreams or illusions!" Cyll squeaked out her words. "Remember? We promised. No more untruths!"

"You're right." Jessie looked down in brief shame. "The truth is I don't really know what's going to happen. But that won't stop me from planning for the best."

"Ok, Jess. I trust you."

Jessie looked away. Making another desperate scan to try and find a solution, his mind grasped onto an impossible play involving the falling station partition's solar sails and magnetic tethers. Although his chances of succeeding in this endeavor stood on close to nil, he knew that it was the best hope he had to save Cyll's life as well as his own. After a few moments, he realized that she was probably still streaming video feed from his terminal lenses and, as such, could see everything that he saw, chaos and all.

"Cil'ette," he said to the little girl, making a snap decision. "You're going to have to be brave for me. We can get out of here, I promise we can, but not if we give up before we even give a try."

"Alright," Cil'ette replied without further complaint. "What are we going to do?"

"We are going to improvise," he explained. "If we can't get you out of the pod you're in, the least we can do is get the pod itself out of danger!" Jessie released the magnetic field from his boots and separated himself from the pod in which Cyll was trapped. "Hold on tight," he said, "I'll be back soon with a tether."

"Dive tight, hero Jessie. May you have the grace of the gods."

# end

act I: Incarnation

# start
act II: Catalyst

# 16 : significance :

**"Every path embarked upon will have both downfalls and merits, unknown until found."**

-Transcripts of William

<11:32:17 a.s.t.><**day 14**><Anok>

Fenna was absorbed in her solitude, staring passively at a shimmering subterranean sea. Being alone can be either miserable or liberating, depending on circumstance and perception. But, feeling alone is a completely different beast—deeper, darker, and far more damaging to one's psyche. True loneliness comes from within, tugging at the heart in a relentless tirade of anguish, fueled by old feelings. Nostalgic memories become enemies, taunting the conscious mind with recollections of better days. Previous thoughts of comfort turn into bitter reminders of a life lost to the ages, never again to return. The blissful glee which had once accompanied them turns dark, holding naught but despair. The only respite to this pain is the hope that a heart torn asunder could one day be remade whole—for the very presence of happy memories proves that happiness is in fact possible, albeit fleeting.

Fenna Caae felt truly alone, both physically and emotionally. The first was intentional, as she had temporarily ditched her travel companions, trekking far ahead of their rambling pace as to ensure at least half an hour of solitude, but this was all but a defense mechanism for the second, for the emotional void left in the wake of being thrust into a whole new life. Her mind was a blur of conflict, tearing between memories of an old world left far behind and a new existence forced upon her, filled with wave-spires, aliens, and TurTek-duplicated bodies both of herself and her human companions. She didn't know whether to cry or rejoice, so she did neither. Her old troubles were long gone, there was no doubting that, but with them had gone everything else, including her former fiancé Enri Riatu's own set of memories, for he had indeed been duplicated alongside her on this strange Nokkian world, but from a previous version alive years he had ever met her. In his eyes, she was a stranger.

Fenna plopped down onto a metal-glass balcony, dangling her legs off its edge. As one of only four remaining explorers within this extraterrestrial land, she knew that hers were the first human eyes to ever lay witness to this particular scene. Every new landscape was a novel discovery, every finding an archeological landmark. She was used to it, by now relatively unimpressed by the majority of logic-defying sights she encountered. After weeks of hard travel upon the wondrously strange planet of Anok, Fenna felt like nothing could surprise her.

Two weeks into their journey, the TurTek-duplicated travelers had come upon the vast ruins of an ancient Nokkian metropolis, seemingly abandoned centuries before. Carved deep into a colossal wave-spire spanning the planet's land and sky, it appeared to have once been a hub of sentient life. Most of its facilities were still functional, containing every amenity from mass transportation to food and water on demand. The main difference between it and any city on Earth was that everything was vertical, from the walkways to the residential housing districts. The civilization that had once lived here had certainly been very different from humankind.

As she sat staring out into the sea which had at one time supplied an entire society with water, Fenna felt the weight of the Nokkian city looming behind her. A particularly eerie statue of a finned, waterborne creature hung in the air before her. She didn't mind its ghostly presence, as it helped remind her of her own faults. Once a hunter, always a hunter. She could tell its vicious nature by a single look, even frozen as a statue before her. This was a vast contrast to the intelligent species which had once inhabited this city—the Nokkian snakes. They were much harder to read.

Nokkian snakes were rather complex. Shaped like giant, two-headed caterpillars with taloned claws, the snakes were built to climb. They were muscular yet nimble, more at ease flipping across high ledges than travelling down on the ground. Under the claws on either end, the snakes protected glistening orbs the size of melons, both of which sported openings within their centers which seemed to simultaneously function as mouths and as eyes. This seemed like a rather imperfect way to see, as one of the two ends was more often than not obstructed by a claw or wall-hold as the snake held itself up in the air, and held to the theory that sight itself might not have been altogether important to the snakes, used mostly to gain momentary bearings as they swung across various surfaces high in the air. The Nokkian metropolis held many hints of such mobile behavior.

Instead of flat streets, the snakes had constructed high rising pillars, linked one to the other with branching connecters, and instead of cars they had lifts, travelling up and down at alarming speeds. Instead of public benches, the city had countless roosts, often dangling hundreds of feet in the air, and instead of town squares they had massive walls, usually decorated with an elaborate array of physical textures. The only aspect recognizably similar from an average human city was the skyscrapers, brilliant and tall as they bridged the subterranean caverns' ceilings and floors. The majority were shaped like miniature wave-spires, each a tiny representation of the majestic vertical world in which they were built.

Field after field of these mini-spires lined the metropolis' enormous chambers, branching out in every direction. Separate cavern-towns in the distance blended one into another with grace, each featuring varying styles of architecture and degrees of structural decay. There were residential suburbs filled with bright, glistening artwork, cistern caverns holding wide, shimmering lakes, open-air chambers, deep dark pits, and far-winding caves bridging together distant segments of the gargantuan wave-spire.

The Nokkian city bristled with video displays made of woven fiber-optic and real-matter holograms powered by floating magnets. There were walls like gears, made of blue wood crafted into mysterious three-dimensional forms that spun in and around each other in complex intersecting patterns, and ceilings like pinwheels, weaving colors through the air. Perhaps most intriguing of all were the mystical, life-like statues of various alien creatures placed throughout the city's caverns and chambers. These exquisitely crafted pieces of work affected the human travelers most, mesmerizing them with life-like realism, and, more often than not, giving them quite a fright at first glance. Among them were creatures they remembered from their travels up the wave-spire, like the Nokkian snakes themselves, the flying buggers, the blue flipping trees, and many of the creatures from the walking forests far below. Beyond that, there were far more species that Fenna and the others had yet to encounter. Some looked less like animals than random formations of organic material, some hosted appendages with no conceivable function, and some depicted creatures reminiscent of ones that existed on Earth, give or take a few limbs and joints. The waterborne creature hanging before Fenna represented the latter category, as it vaguely resembled a prehistoric beast of the deep blue sea. Its presence somehow calmed her, reminding her that there were monsters out there greater than she.

<11:49:15 a.s.t.>

"Zeus Fenna, you're godsdamn hard to reach!" Enri Riatu approached in huffs and puffs from behind. He sat down beside her, allowing himself to catch his breath. "There's no way Fre'dd or the Rep can climb this."

Fenna made no sign that she had noticed Enri's presence. The terminal lenses in her eyes flickered with video overlay, so he could tell she was watching a recording of some sort, but he could not tell what. He wondered whether it was video-feed from their own travels on Anok, or something from her previous life.

Personally, Enri could not imagine anything more interesting than their discoveries on Anok. The last few days alone had presented them with so much variety that it boggled his mind. As the adventurers had come across and begun to explore the Nokkian metropolis, many mysterious questions began to pop forth—not the least of which was the reason for its abandoned state. Scraps of paper and cloth strewn around the major hubs provided hints about the population's absence, as did giant illuminated posters lining its buildings, often ripped but still lit under lasting technology. Cobblestone paths covering ceilings, floors, and walls were slowly being torn apart by blue plant life overgrowing its bounds.

How old are these ruins? Enri wondered. How long ago had they been vacated? Had their former population simply evolved beyond their need for the city, or had they fallen victim to some sort of world-breaking catastrophe? And, if some plague or natural disaster had been responsible for wiping out such an advanced civilization, who was to say it would not happen again? Would all attempts at human colonization result in sure failure?

According to their companion, the TurTek representative, this question needed answering before the next phase of their mission plan could go forth. Whether or not this wave-spire could support continual residence would determine whether or not TurTek would initiate full-scale colonization efforts. If not, they would have to pack up their bags and leave, departing out towards the stars on the space station currently orbiting the planet. They would live and die on the station, crossing a fraction of the light years needed to reach anything nearly as interesting as Anok.

Enri sat down beside Fenna. "Hey Spacer, how's it going?" he asked. She didn't answer. He frowned and looked away, staring instead at the horrifying sculpture suspended over the shimmering water before them. A distant light from far across the subterranean sea provided the only illumination in sight.

Several minutes passed before Fenna noticed Enri sitting beside her. As soon as she did, she muted her music. "What up, Earthboy?"

"What is this thing?" Enri nodded towards the scaled statue before them. "You think there are any real ones swimming down there?"

"Let's hope not," Fenna replied, wiping the flickering imagery away from her terminal lenses. "The less giant freakin' sharks out there, the better."

"What if they're peaceful, like whales or something?"

"Na, believe me Enri. A hunter knows a hunter."

Enri glanced at her with a frown. "Alright Fi, if you say so."

Fenna's stiffened. "That name is not for you," she whispered. "Where did you even hear it?"

"From you, whenever you talk about your brother. It's the happiest I ever see you."

She looked away. "Yeah well, I'm not a child anymore. It's a mistake to reminisce."

"Fenna, are you okay? What's going on?"

"It's... nothing, just old memories. There's no use in talking about them. I am not—and never will be—that person anymore. There's no point thinking otherwise."

Enri patted her on the shoulder awkwardly. "You don't have to do that—disconnect entirely from your former self. Just be ok with where you are today, not where you used to be."

"You're right, I know you are. But sometimes it feels like forgetting everything and starting fresh would make life so much easier."

"Sure, if you can do that, go for it!" Enri chuckled. "But without our memories we are shells, mere impressions left behind of someone else who came before us. Just like this empty city, left without any of its inhabitants."

"Tuk, Enri!" Fenna brushed his hand off her shoulder. "What am I supposed to do with that? This planet, this tukking alien world, and all the shit that happened after we landed—how do I fit in with all this taurshit? What am I supposed to think about myself now? I'm basically just a copy of some long-dead spacer woman, remade with no chance of returning to anything resembling normality." She wiped a tear from her cheek. "You get what I'm saying? What am I? What is this life I have found myself within? What's the point of following Representative Hat-head's tukking mission up the spire? What's the point of even doing anything at all?"

Enri gazed into Fenna's hazel-green eyes. Her terminal lenses had shut off, leaving only her natural colors. "The point is whatever we choose it to be," he said. "Our meanings in life are exactly what we make of them. Take the Rep, for instance—he has no qualms about his duties, no matter where or when he finds himself reborn. Regardless of his many duplicated pasts and scattered gaps of memory, his role remains the same…"

"A puppet on strings," Fenna interjected.

"Yeah, no argument here." Enri nodded. "He is 100% TurTek's puppet on strings. But that's beside the point. The company of TurTek isn't down here on Anok with us—but the Rep sure is. He's been with us the whole time, going through the same taurshit as us, just as human as the rest of us. There is no oversight here forcing him to follow TurTek procedure, so technically he can do whatever he wants, and yet, he still follows their agenda to the dot. Why? Because he believes in it? No, not necessarily. I mean yeah, he probably believes in it, but that is not the ultimate reason driving him."

"Yeah? So what is?"

"He's driving himself, Fenna, that's what I mean. He is who he is, so he does what he does. It never even occurred to him to stray from TurTek's path. In his mind, he is TurTek."

"Okay, so he's a puppet without strings. So what? What does that have to do with me?" Fenna asked. "Back home, my purpose was always known, every day pointed towards the same singular goal. But here, that purpose is nontransferable. Here, on this random tukking planet, I have absolutely no connection to the goal we are following and no real reason to get up in the morning and keep moving. I mean, what the tuk do I care if TurTechnicks decides to colonize this planet or not? The truth is, I don't give a shit."

"Well then, make new goals, make new plans—whatever you want them to be! You don't have to follow the rep's motivations, make your own! Colonization effort or not, Anok is pretty remarkable, no? Given the wealth of discoveries we have already made here, it shouldn't be too hard to find a worthwhile path."

"Not everyone is as godsdamn curious as you, Earthboy," Fenna replied, exasperated with an argument she felt she had heard many times before, although in another world, another life, and from a man who had a completely different set of memories than the one sitting beside her. The echoes of her past never seemed to leave her alone, even in a world so far from her own.

"Hold that thought," Enri said as a message flashed on his terminal. "Fre'dd and the Rep just sent us updated coordinates. They must have found a viable campsite!"

Enri's wristband terminal projected a three-dimensional map of the Nokkian metropolis into the air displaying a location within a nearby residential cavern-town.

"Hey look, it has running water and reflected sunlight!" He stood up, excited. "Maybe we can finally replenish our supplies."

"Great," Fenna sighed. No matter what set of memories, Enri was still Enri, unnecessarily enthusiastic as ever. She knew from experience that this goofy attitude would soon grow on her, which was part of the problem. Would getting too close to this particular Enri pay disservice to the one she had known long ago? There was little respite from the turmoil in her mind.

"Hey wait, the Rep sent us a written note as well. Hmm, let's see. 'Phase I complete: Anok colonization potential confirmed. Phase II initiation authorized.' Oh damn, must be quite a campsite! Fenna, come on, let's go."

Enri held out his hand to help Fenna up. She slapped it away and stood up on her own.

Fenna turned her terminal lenses back on, receiving the same updated map coordinates as had Enri. She nodded at him, and then jumped off the ledge, trailing a smart rope harnessed to the spinner on her back.

: to be continued :

www.ingramcontent.com/pod-product-compliance
Lightning Source LLC
Chambersburg PA
CBHW062134170626
46813CB00002B/692